CHUM

A Novel

JEFF SOMERS

TYRUS
BOOKS

F+W Media, Inc.

Published by
TYRUS BOOKS
an imprint of F+W Media, Inc.
10151 Carver Road, Suite 200
Blue Ash, OH 45242. U.S.A.
www.tyrusbooks.com

ISBN 10: 1-4405-7004-3
ISBN 13: 978-1-4405-7004-9
eISBN 10: 1-4405-7005-1
eISBN 13: 978-1-4405-7005-6

Printed in the United States of America.

10 9 8 7 6 5 4 3 2 1

Cover image © Frank Rivera.

This book is available at quantity discounts for bulk purchases.
For information, please call 1-800-289-0963.

CONTENTS

I.

MARY'S WEDDING

Tom and I were standing on the church steps, smoking cigarettes and enjoying the ozone smell of a late October storm coming. I was freezing, but was manfully pretending otherwise. We leaned over the wrought-iron railing, blowing smoke into the wind and tossing sentences back and forth.

"Bick cleaned up pretty good," Tom said.

"That's the consensus."

It was the kind of day that let loose a little patter of rain every time you ventured out to do something, and then produced a thin, watery ray of sunshine the moment you retreated under cover. We were each wearing black suits, white shirts, shined shoes. We were each smoking cigarettes from the same communal pack. We were each about the same height and weight. Standing elbow to elbow, leaning over the railing in the same postures, we were each slightly aware of being twins.

Suddenly, Mike skidded out onto the steps, his breath puffing into steam. His tuxedo was askew.

"You see Bick out here?"

"They've lost the groom," Tom said to me, quietly.

"Again."

"Haven't seen him, Mikey," Tom said over his shoulder.

"I hear he cleans up nice, though," I added. "Mare still in hiding?"

"Who knows—no one can get into the women's room to check."

We heard Mike's shoes skid back into the church, the sound of panic, and resumed our weather watching. It was peaceful.

The bride was, at last report, weeping in the bathroom, having a vague sort of commitment crisis. The door was guarded by bridesmaids Flo and Kelly, in pink dresses that sounded like paper tearing whenever they moved—and resembled marshmallows from some breakfast cereal. Mary was attended only by the maid of honor, so no one was getting inside for a first-hand report.

"Hope someone secured the Communion wine," I said.

"Bick, I'm sure. We should be checking the closets and other hiding places," Tom replied.

Clicking heels, and we both turned in time to see Denise sweep outside in her little black dress and the cape she used to great dramatic effect.

"There you are," she said, putting her hands on her hips. "You could be lending a hand, you know. It's chaos in there."

"Hey, hon," I said, turning to lean my back against the railing. "That's why we're out here. The chaos."

"We could only increase the chaos," Tom added, flicking away his cigarette. "We're chaos instigators."

"You look gorgeous, you know," I said.

She snorted in the way I knew meant she was pleased. "Well, I guess it's best that you two stay out of trouble. Have you—"

"Bickerman hasn't been out here," Tom said.

She snorted again, somehow communicating her low opinion of Tommy.

"Has the bride reappeared?" I asked.

She shook her head. "The official cover story is that she's heaving her guts up from nerves."

Tom barked out a laugh. "That's fan-tastic. The bride is puking her guts out. Thanks so much for your concern."

I smiled. "You gals were out pretty late last night, rumor has it."

She eyed us coolly. "Didn't I forbid you to play with Tom anymore?"

I nodded. Somber. "You did."

She turned to go back inside, and Tom and I turned to lean against the railing again.

"Do you suppose the reception's on no matter what?"

"What, open bar, free food, blitzed bridesmaids and all?"

"Sure."

I sighed. "Tom, I don't think so."

"We've got to set this right, then. I didn't wear my school clothes just to admire the goddamn parking lot."

"A noble suggestion."

A moment of silence, then, between us.

More high heels, and we turned in time for the breathtaking view of Miriam, Maid of Honor. The younger of the Harrows sisters, just eighteen and painfully gorgeous. Tom and I held ourselves upright through practice and determination, and I made a conscious effort to keep my mouth closed.

"Guys, crisis passed. We're on in ten minutes."

I nodded feebly. "Thanks, Mir."

We didn't dare watch her ass as she walked back into the church. It would've burst us into flames.

Tom and I turned to lean against the railing again, and lit up our final cigarettes.

"Crisis averted," he said.

"Still a bad omen."

More shoes on the floorboards. Tom and I passed a tired glance between us before we turned around to find Luis beaming at us.

"What are you *doing* out here?" he said in his heavy Spanish accent. "The wedding is going to happen soon."

"We're waiting for a cable from the governor," Tom said.

"A stay of execution."

Luis, as was common, had no idea what we were talking about. His English, while excellent, was not subtle. His common reaction was to smile broadly, which he did.

"Come inside. You should not wish for bad things to happen to Bick and Marie." He nodded sadly. Their names came out *beek* and *maree*. "Life is very hard."

I put a hand on his shoulder. "We'll meet you in there."

Luis seemed to be struggling for something more to say when Mike, bald head shining in the weak sun, a perfect shade of rich brown, skidded back onto the porch, almost tumbling down the stairs. The three of us just looked at him.

"Conference," he panted. "Bick's in the bathroom, now."

We walked through the corridor toward the basement bathroom like Important Men, in nice suits, with grim demeanors. We walked in step. Next to me, I could feel the Glee, dark and tense, rising up in Tom like wings spreading. I was wary of the Glee. The Glee had done Bad Things before. Although usually amusing things, I had to admit.

The bathroom was at the end of the dim corridor. We stopped outside of it. Tom tried the handle, shook his head at us, and we both pounded on the door.

"Bick!" Tom shouted. "Bick, you punk-ass motherfucker I'm fucking wearing *dark socks* for you so this had better involve bloody puke!"

"Go away!"

The voice of Bickerman. Nasal but always at top volume, it took a moment before I could put my finger on what was subtly different about it: an almost complete lack of sarcasm.

Tom looked at each of us in turn. "I'll need five minutes."

"The door," Luis said somberly, "it is locked."

Tom shrugged, and with a sudden jerk banged his shoulder against the door. It gave with a small cracking sound, and Tom slipped inside, slamming the door shut behind him.

We took up our positions: Mike and Luis standing together in front of the door, me leaning against the wall across from them, smoking a cigarette. On the wall directly across from me was a stark white and red sign: NO SMOKING. As usual, I ignored it. We all did, always. It had become a silent game without rules that we played, smoking where we weren't supposed to.

There was no sound from within that we could detect. There was a vague smell of licorice, which was maddening, as it had no obvious source.

"Do we have a backup plan in case he goes out the window?" I asked.

Mike looked stricken. "Why do *we* need a plan?"

"Because the girls will need someone to tear apart if he bolts, and he won't be here."

Luis nodded gravely. "It will be horrible."

On cue, the sound of high heels and the temporarily twin forms of Kelly and Florence appeared in their pink bridesmaid uniforms. Mary's best friends, Kelly dating back to their paste-eating heydays in Mrs. Fox's kindergarten class, and Florence credited with teaching Mary how to roll joints in college. Between paste-eating and joint-rolling, they had rounded Mary's education off nicely, and were rewarded now with the most ridiculous outfits ever fever-dreamed by a designer. Humiliated, they had each been terrors from the moment of the first fitting. We'd spent the intervening weeks hiding from them.

"Is he in there?" Kelly demanded as they drew up before us. Kelly had a sharply turned up nose and dark brown hair, giving her an automatically snobbish appearance. She always appeared to be looking down her nose at you. She was curvy, and sometimes seemed to like it, and sometimes seemed to think she was hideous.

I exhaled smoke and tried to stay calm. "We're not at liberty to say."

"Oh, for God's sake, Henry," Flo snapped.

Flo was a tall girl, so tall she'd obviously been made fun of during her formative years by cooler, shorter classmates. Dark red hair, gone to gray but carefully dyed. She still walked bent over, trained through the years to hide her height. She wasn't exactly pretty, but her sheer length of leg was enough to make her attractive, as was the fact that she could (and often did) drink any one of us under whatever table happened to be available.

"We had time for Mare's bullshit," I offered reasonably. "Why not Bick's?"

Luis, not quite grasping the exchange, smiled broadly, as if enjoying the show.

Flo and Kelly each stiffened, regarding me with dangerous expressions. "Mary," Kelly said through clenched teeth, "experienced a momentary existential moment of doubt that had to be worked through. Her fiancé is simply being an ass."

The women were always so sure of themselves. It was intimidating. I woke up uncertain. I didn't know how to function, how to dress. You fought back when you could.

"How about: They're both asses, as we're all standing outside the john like idiots."

"Henry—" Flo managed, and just then the door opened. Tom stepped back into the corridor, shutting the door behind him and taking the scene in. He was flushed.

"Ladies," he said with a slight nod of his head. Then he looked around at all of us. "He'll be out in a minute."

I grinned at Flo. "He'll be out in a minute."

Denise was already seated as Tom, Luis, and I gently pushed and shoved our way into the pew. She smelled heavenly, and I placed a lingering peck on her bare shoulder.

"Everything back on track?" she asked.

"No," I sighed, "but I think they're getting married."

"It is very beautiful," Luis sighed. "So wonderful that Bick and Marie have found each other. I had my doubts, you know, about them, but today has shown me that they are right for each other."

"How's that?" Denise asked brightly.

Luis was in Serious Philosopher mode, which usually only showed up at parties and other alcoholically fueled occasions. "Look at how they react today, to the doubt. They react the same way. Each of them, locked in the bathroom, with a single advisor. They are so similar." He nodded wisely. "They will be very happy."

Denise nodded. "I like that. Luis, you're a gem."

He smiled slyly. "Yes."

I made a show of looking around the church. "This crowd feels angry."

"*Hmmph. You* smell like old cigarette butts, mister," she said primly. I pinched her on the thigh, making her giggle, so she hit me lightly on the shoulder.

"Mike looks like he is going to piss himself," Luis observed.

Denise and I looked up the aisle, to where Mike stood in his tux, nervously pacing in front of the crowd. Bick and Mike had been friends since high school—a dull, boring kind of friendship made up of football games, drinking binges, and occasional phone calls. We all hated him instinctively. He was like talking to wallpaper.

"Combust spontaneously, more like it," Tom said, pushing his head between Denise and me from behind us. "That would be great! With all that holy oil and those diaphanous priestly gowns, this whole place would be in flames in moments."

"Why would that be great?" Denise asked seriously.

Tom looked at her. "You're right. Substitute 'exciting' for 'great.' God! Smart women are so threatening. It's quite a turn-on, actually."

"It's true, I fear Denise," Luis added helpfully.

"Shut up, all of you," she hissed, looking at me for some reason. "They're beginning."

Bick had joined Mike up at the front of the church. They stood tugging at their cufflinks pathetically.

"It's obvious: tranquilizers," Tom said happily.

"You would know. You were the one in the bathroom for those intimate moments," Luis pointed out, an expression of innocence on his face.

"I will never betray that tender young man's trust," Tom said immediately. "Here we go!"

Denise took my hand and held it in her lap gently, which made me nervous, of course. Weddings and women are nerve-wracking, I'd always thought. So many bad examples wuffling about, looking grand in their finery, their gold bands on their fingers. I slid a finger inside my collar and pulled on it.

Tom began a low-volume color commentary on the whole show.

"To those of you joining us mid-program today, welcome to the romantic event of the season, the Bick-Mare wedding. Bick, all-star skirt-chaser and recent Boozehound Hall of Fame inductee has been off his game thus far, with a barely raised eyebrow at the sight of so much bared female flesh—weddings having become fashion shows for the less pious among us. Mare seemed to be in better shape for this bout early in the running—marching about as if she owned the church and ordering her minions about with thunderous confidence, but recent gastrointestinal-cum-existential crises have weakened her position with the crowd."

Luis made a vain attempt to listen in and then sat back, his smile in place, Spanish thoughts comforting him.

"Now we see Bick and his main defenseman, the defenseless Mike Billings getting into position to receive the kickoff . . . and there it is! Stunning little sister Miriam leads the offense here, and what moves she has! *Ouch!* Jesus, Hank, control the woman, will you?"

"She's stronger than she looks," I said.

"Miriam in fine form today, a future Hall of Famer I'm sure. Flo and Kelly both look like they've been eating lemons back in the ready room. Likely pondering their own unmarriedness in the harsh light of Mary bagging the lame—but serviceable!—Bick out of the thinning ranks of unmarried men *sans* social diseases or criminal records.

"And there—a perfect formation! Huzzah! I've never seen three chicks in such ugly dresses move so gracefully despite the binding nature of their skirts!

"Ah, now, the moment we've all been waiting for, the bride! Moving with the slow care of the drugged, she seems to glide, most probably on wheels and just pushed gently down the aisle by her father."

I looked at Denise, and she rolled her eyes.

"I have no influence," I admitted. They blamed me for Tom. I knew that. And it was true. Tom was my fault.

"Obviously."

Tom sat back. "I'll be appreciated by the French after I'm dead. Heathens."

"We're lost."

I refused to look at Denise. I kept my eyes straight ahead. The rain was coming down hard enough to make visibility low, and I wasn't sure I'd see a sign if one actually loomed out of the storm at us. The reception was in thirteen minutes; we'd been driving for an hour and a half.

"Who in hell sets up the reception so goddamn far away?" Tom groused. "These people are idiots."

"They will be drunk," Luis said from the back seat. "They will not miss us. It will be days before the police are contacted."

"I need a drink," Tom said quietly. "Badly."

"There won't be any drinks left by the time we arrive," Denise added.

I glanced at her and said nothing.

"Pull over at that gas station. Let's ask them."

"Where?" I asked her.

"Sweet lord," Tom said, "who let the blind one behind the wheel? No wonder we're lost. Right over there!"

I lit cigarettes for Tom and me. Luis settled back with his eyes closed. Denise had scampered into the little grocery store all the gas stations had now. The rental car was off, clicking contently, and the radio was on very low. The rain hitting the car was soothing.

"How long you give them?" I asked.

Tom sat forward immediately, as if he'd been thinking about the very subject. "Well, let's be logical. Bick drinks, and Mary doesn't like it when he does. Mary drinks, but doesn't think she has a problem, when she very obviously *does*. Mary is jealous and controlling. On the other hand, Bick is snide and weak, while Mare is easily annoyed and shallow."

"Be fair," I admonished, "they're both shallow."

"Fine. Put all that together, and I don't give them a day over seventy years. Eighty years, tops."

"What?" Even Luis popped open an eye.

"Sure—think about it this way: Bick and Mare are already expressing their troubles to each other. No hiding, no bullshit. If they're pissed off, they let each other know it. *That's* the secret to success, dammit. No bull. You're pissed? Be pissed. Then you deal with it." He held up his hands. "It's the pussyfooting around that makes trouble."

I digested that amidst smoke. "My God—that's depressing, man."

"Sure is. That's why I can't wait another second for a free cocktail. Ever notice the similarities between weddings and funerals? People get dressed up. There are religious ceremonies with bizarre, unexplained pagan overtones. People weep. People get up and make speeches about the principles. Ceremonies are held in places designed specifically for that purpose." He sighed out smoke. "Man, it's *creepy*. Marriage equals death."

"So the secret of a successful marriage is psychotically spitting anger at each other at the slightest irritation, and marriage equals death. Thanks."

He shrugged amiably. "Hence: cocktails."

The passenger door tore open, and Denise threw herself into the car. She held up a scrap of paper triumphantly. "Details!" she announced. "We'll get there yet!"

I smiled. "I don't know. Tom has been informing me how depressing weddings are. I'm not sure I want to go anymore."

She continued to settle herself damply. "I'm sick to death of this poison-pal relationship you and Tommy have. Shut up and drive."

Tom hit me lightly on the back of my head. "Cocktails, dummy!" he hissed jocularly. "To stave off ennui!"

"You just shut up," she snapped.

I was trying, unsuccessfully, to identify the vegetable on my plate when Flo crept up to our table with a handful of skirt. She leaned in to whisper in Denise's ear, and then Denise wiped her mouth and stood.

"Be back," she said in my general direction. "Girl business."

Instantly, Tom was sitting in her vacated seat. "My God, man, look at the people at this table! It's Gabba-Gabba-Hey time here. It's the *Freaks and Geeks* table. How'd this happen to you? You used to be cool."

"I'm obviously being punished."

"Maybe Denise is being punished. Let's have a shot of something horrible."

I stood up and we made our way to the nearest open bar, where a perky brunette kid smiled wickedly at us as we approached, dollar signs in her mercenary eyes.

"Hi!" she chirped. "What can I get you handsome men?"

Tom pretended to peruse the bottle lineup behind her, then slapped a fiver on the bar dramatically. "Three Kings, baby. We need inebriation."

She lined six shot glasses—plastic medicine cups—on the bar and began pouring whiskey. "One of you guys mourning the bride here?"

Tom shook his head. "We can't dance unless we're drunk."

She paused to study us carefully. "Are you guys related?"

I blinked. "No. Why?"

She shrugged. "You should be."

Tom and I each took a shot glass and turned to regard the reception hall. I raised my shot into the air. "To Mare and Bick! Let this not be the happiest night of their lives."

We drank, winced, coughed.

Tom nudged my elbow, handed me the second shot glass. "Is it me," he asked wetly, "or is Kelly like the *über*-Kelly tonight?"

I followed his small eyes to the dance floor, where our favorite friend-of-a-friend was kicking up her heels in a group of debauching girls, laying the boogie down. I gave her my professional lecher's eye, which didn't creep out often with Denise around.

"It's a Wedding Glow," I decided.

"A what?" he asked, and we tossed back our second shot, which was infinitely worse than the first. I gagged and struggled to breathe.

"A Wedding Glow," I croaked. "The smell of sex is in the air, eh? The whole place here is just filled with pheromones. Fertility. Family. Marriage. Formalwear. It's like the prom, but we're adults now. The whole ceremony, you know, designed around reproduction. Girls start breathing the air in this tight, confined space, and they just get hot and bothered. Hence, the Glow. That's why so many unhappy affairs begin at weddings, you know."

Tom absorbed this manfully. "I've never had an affair at a wedding," he said sadly. "You'd think, what with all the booze and the dancing and the reluctance to tell the truth and the available rooms that it would happen, once. But no dice."

"No dice on what?"

I blinked in the face of Miriam's sudden arrival at the bar. I opened my mouth, but nothing came to mind.

"Consummating my unrequited love for you, Mare's little sister," Tom supplied. "Shot?"

Miriam nodded. "God, yes. You have no idea the stress on the unmarried sister at these things. No one does. I didn't, until today."

I nodded and kept a careful smile on my face. Tom handed me my third shot, and I held it politely until he'd procured one for Mir.

"Uh," I said, sensing the need to say something. "Uh, having fun?"

Mir dazzled me with a smile. In one sense, Mir was like her sister: blond, with big brown eyes that did most of her communicating, and perfect posture—the Harrows sisters walked ramrod straight wherever they went, the lasting gift of their largely unamused mother. But where

Mary was angular, the fine lines of her face clear-cut and stark, Miriam was blurrier, softer, rounder.

Tom handed her a little plastic glass with overdone ceremony, to which she offered a half-assed curtsy. Then she brought the shot up to her nose and sniffed it.

"What is this?"

"Take a chance. Chin-chin!"

We drank. Mir coughed, once, ladylike, and laughed.

"That was good, actually," she announced. "Tommy, you're my mixologist. I'm appointing you right now. I'm in your hands."

Tom leered in a friendly way. "How old are you again?"

She ignored him professionally. "Henry, you're quiet."

I was, in all honesty, suddenly and forcibly drunk.

"I propose a pact," Tom announced. "Throughout the evening, on the hour, we three will gather here and have a drink in honor of the Bick-Mare union and all the joy we intend to get from it via merciless and often vulgar jokes at their expense."

"You're on," I agreed immediately.

"Agreed," Miriam giggled.

"What are we agreeing on?"

I felt Denise before I saw her and was seized by a spasm of inexplicable guilt. To cover I put my arm around her and said loudly: "Tom is causing trouble and I'm supervising."

"Don't listen to him, Neesie. We're forming a drinking club here at the reception, invitation only. Care to join?"

Denise made a face, her arms sliding around my waist. "Lord, I can't drink like that. I'd be in a hospital."

"I'll see you guys back here later," Mir announced. "I've got maid of honor duties, you know."

I studiously did not watch her walk away. "So, how was the girl business?"

Denise shrugged. "Buy me a drink, sailor. You don't want to hear about all that stuff."

"Sure we do," Tom protested. "Hot chicks in formal wear—lacey underthings, all that jazz. Pillow fights, I'm guessing, and lesbian experimentation. We want to hear it!"

Neesie rolled her eyes at me. I ordered her a white wine, and we went back to our table of freaks and losers, very obviously the people that Mary wanted nothing to do with.

"What do they do? It is so mysterious," Luis asked me with inebriated solemnity. The girls had once again abandoned us for unknown reasons—cavorting, fights, desperate boyfriend-and-husband swapping arrangements—none of us knew. Luis had joined me at my Loser Table with heavy effort, sitting down and sighing. He was drinking martinis.

"I look around, and all of the hot women have gone away," he observed mournfully. "If we knew where they went, we could go there too."

This I could not argue with. "It's obviously me," I said with equal gravitas, leaning over drunkenly to speak into his ear. "Every time I show up, the women run for cover. Even Neesie."

Luis nodded gravely. "Yes, this is true."

"Thanks." I looked around. "I'm going to have a cigarette. Want to join me?"

He shook his head. "I will wait here and see if the women return when you are gone."

I slapped him on the back as I stood up. "I knew I could count on you."

I wandered out into the lobby, shaking out a cigarette. Outside the hall, it was a muted hurly-burly, a sealed-off noise with a thick maroon carpet and vague strangers walking on their own. I stood and lit a cigarette in clear violation of the law and the rules of polite society and watched other overdressed people walk around and ponder their place in a world where you end up at a ridiculous affair like this.

"Got another one of those?"

I turned and coughed a little in the face of Miriam. She was a little flushed, her cleavage heaving fresh from the dance floor. I once again felt my voice leaving me and stood for a moment making "ums" while patting myself down for cigarettes.

"God, it's good to get out of there," she breezed, accepting one from me and lighting it from mine. "Family family everywhere and not a place to hide, you know? Jesus! Not to mention the marriage thing. Mom just staring at me the whole day, mentally matching me up with every guy. I've been introduced to more goddamn men tonight than through an entire year of college." She sucked in a deep drag. "And that's a *lot*."

I stared dumbly until it dawned on me that a response was expected. I struggled to formulate one. Finally, I said "Yeah." She smelled like salt water.

"You know, it's true what they say about brides. They're nightmares. Mare's always been a bitch of an older sister, but these past few months . . ." she snorted.

"Hard, huh?" I managed.

"You have *no* idea," she laughed. "All I can say is I feel a little sorry for David. He's soft, you know? And I swear if I have to hear my mom refer to me as 'the single one' one more time . . . I'm eighteen! I'm supposed to be out at bars, doing shots, having sex, not getting married!"

I perked up a little.

"I mean, I think Mare's nuts for getting married this young. Twenty-eight! I say, wait until your thirties, you know? Enjoy yourself a little and *then* get married."

I nodded. "Are you enjoying yourself tonight?"

She snuffed out her cigarette on her shoe. "A few more drinks and I will be." She paused and put a hand on my shoulder. "Henry, you're sweet, you know that? Thanks for letting me prattle on like this." She leaned up on her toes and kissed me lightly on the cheek, and I had a heady rush of images: cheerleaders, Catholic schoolgirls, Girl Scouts selling cookies. It was one second of pedophilic euphoria that reminded me forcefully that Miriam was eighteen, firm, and illegally drunk.

Then she was twisting back toward the ballroom, and I needed another cigarette.

I sat down and felt the cool breeze immediately. When Denise looked over at me sweetly and said, "Have a nice chat?" I stood up again. "Tom needs me at the bar," I croaked.

"You have fun over there," she chirped.

I staggered over to where Tom and Mike were more or less holding each other up near the bar. I took Tom's shoulder and leaned in close.

"Emergency. Come on."

Once in the bathroom, Mike and Tom weaved by the sinks and I paced before them.

"So what's the emergency?" Mike asked. Tom seemed beyond speech, peering owlishly at me as if I were some wondrous hallucination come to deliver the word of God to him personally.

I stopped. "All right. You know how Neesie . . . and Miriam . . ."

"Oh, shit," Mike wailed, looking down at the damp floor. "Henry, what did you *do*?"

I threw my arms out helplessly. "I talked to her! I had a cigarette with her! It wasn't anything . . . it wasn't my fault!"

"She's eighteen, man." Mike shook his head at me. "You're twelve years older than her. When you were twelve, she was just born."

I just stared at him in amazed shock.

"When you were eighteen, she was *six*," Mike added.

"I didn't *molest* her, you ass," I said pleadingly. "I talked with her. She pecked me on the cheek."

"Saint Pats," Tom gurgled. We looked at him. He was goggling at us in an amused way that implied a lot more than those two words seemed likely to convey.

I nodded. "Saint Pats."

Mike sighed. "Right. Well, you didn't do anything, right?"

"Fuck you."

"Fuck it," Tom suddenly slurred. "Let her fume. You're innocent. Go back to that table like a man and tell the woman to shut the fuck up."

There was a moment of unbelievably awkward silence. I felt it on my skin like something sticky.

The door burst open, and Bick marched in, his almost-white hair standing up in a gummed mess of hair spray and sweat. He stopped before us in his half-undone tuxedo, panting, his usually pale face red.

"That's it," he said thunderously, "I'm getting a divorce."

"Jesus Christ," Tom hissed. "Have a cigarette."

"Who knew what a wedding could do to a woman?" Bick continued, snatching the lit cigarette from Tom's palsied hand and taking over my pacing. "I have witnessed a slow descent into monster by Mary Harrows. She is now a monster. She isn't human anymore. I have just married a monster."

"Better send out for supplies," Mike said tiredly. "Looks like we'll be in here for a while."

"How did this happen?" Bick went on. "Why didn't one of you stop me? Why am I just now finding out she's a monster?"

"What happened?"

Bick rounded on me. "What *happened*? My God, haven't you been listening? She's become a monster! She put on a white dress and became a monster!"

"I think we all need to calm down," Mike announced, putting his hands up in the air as if a crowd of people were threatening him.

"Oh, try to expel that pole from your ass, Mike." I scowled. "I'm going to be punished by Denise simply for being stupefied in the face of stunning gorgeousness, and Bick has legally committed himself to a Pod Person with a striking resemblance to Mary. We're also fabulously drunk. Anything I missed?"

"I'm nauseous," Tom offered with a grunt.

"And Tom's nauseous, dammit. So Mike, can the happy bullshit, and let's crack open the fucking suicide pills, okay?"

Bick sat down on one of the sinks and smoked. "You don't get it, Hank. We'll never get out of here alive. There's a monster out there, and she's in charge."

"What happened?"

Tom held up a hand. "Excuse me."

He slumped into one of the stalls and began retching.

"Well," Bick continued, "screw it. I'm married to her now. So what if she's a little controlling, right?"

I slapped him on the back. "Absolutely, my pasty friend. Certainly none of us care."

"It's settled then," Mike sighed, "we'll never know what she did."

The door cracked open, and Luis poked his head in. "I have been sent to retrieve the men. The women are quite unhappy with the lack of men on the dance floor." He pushed his way in and leaned against the door. "What is that terrible noise?" He paused and smiled slightly, nodding. "Ah: Tom."

"I don't know," Bick said. "I guess I'm happy to be married, you know? But she was such a pain in the ass this morning, moaning about having doubts, being unsure. And now that we actually said the words, she's been acting like I'm a moron she's saving from himself." He snuffed out his cigarette. "Granted, it's only been a few hours."

"Hey, Luis," I called out. "Did Denise say anything?"

"No. She is apparently no longer speaking to men."

Mike looked at his watch. "Guys, I hate to be the voice of reason, but we can't stay in here forever. We have to leave the bathroom."

"Shit," Bick groaned. "He's right."

A gloom descended on us all. Tom flushed the toilet but remained on his knees in the stall, moaning. Mike rubbed his bald head nervously. Bick sat staring down at his shiny black shoes. Luis seemed casual and at ease, hands thrust into pockets. I ran a hand through my hair over and over again.

When Tom joined us silently, straightening his tie, we all pretended not to notice.

"Well," Luis announced, opening the door and backing out of the bathroom. "I am going to dance with your women."

"Hell, let's get a drink," Tom added, proving once again that he was a remarkable organism.

Bick slid off the bathroom sink. "Come on, let's face it like men, then, eh?" He pointed at Tom. "Don't let him have another drop. That's an order."

I glanced at Luis. "An order. Thank goodness for the suicide pills."

Luis paused in the doorway and placed a hand on my shoulder. "What is wrong? Tell Luis what troubles you."

Exasperated, I shrugged him off. "Come on, men. Time to face the Troubles with dignity."

"And cocktails," Tom breathed heavily.

I marveled at Bick as he swept Mary across the dance floor. Sweating like a pig, cigarette dangling from his lip, he was red-faced and grinning, a charmless man who nonetheless got by on sheer self-confidence, a man who convinced you to like him simply because he liked himself so damned much.

I sat alone at my table, all the other guests somewhere else, and Denise also missing, possibly even driving home without me, for all I knew. I sat at ease, legs crossed, burning cigarettes and drinking steadily, trying to project a nice Hemingwayesque aura of rugged ennui.

"My, we're grumpy."

I froze and looked up from the floor. Shiny black shoes. Perfect, hose-clad calves. Ridiculous maid of honor dress. Miriam, grinning at me, listing slightly as she attempted to remain standing under her own power. Her eyes were squinty, her cheeks bright red.

I opened my mouth in terror. She was gorgeous, and I couldn't remember my own name. She took this as a sign, stepped forward, and sat down in my lap, her arms around my neck.

"Henry," she breathed, "you're *so* nice."

"Oh, Lord," I exclaimed. "I'm really not." She felt delightful, a wonderful weight. Dread seeped through me.

"Yes, you are. You are!" She gazed down at me with a serious expression, intently drunk. "You are, Henry. You're so nice. You're the nicest guy I know."

Improbably, I could sense an erection on the horizon and hastily, blurrily, considered my options. I could: a. dump her unceremoniously on the floor and flee; b. try to talk some sense into her; or c. feign unconsciousness.

All three options had dire drawbacks. The first could result in injury and humiliation. The second would get nowhere, I could sense, and would only prolong the time during which she was pressing her supple body against mine in full view of everyone Denise and I counted as mutual friends. The third possibility would probably only result in Miriam unconscious on top of me, which would be worse, somehow, than option b.

I was paralyzed. Mir was studying my face with an intent look I recognized as "going to kiss." It was a sort of thousand-yard stare women got when they'd decided to throw caution to the wind and just plant one on you. Somewhere, in the portion of my brain that was still functioning, I knew I had seconds before I was ruined.

I was saved, then, by Tom, who appeared from the surrounding blur with a cigarette burning between clenched teeth to bend and pluck Mir from my lap with a manly grunt, hefting her in his arms as she squealed attractively.

"Put me down!"

"No way, lass," he panted, turning away. "We're going to dance."

I slumped in my chair and considered Doom, its feel and smell. Tom looked back once and winked. I offered him my middle finger, limply.

"You're popular tonight."

I glanced up as Kelly sat down in the seat next to me and put her feet up on the next chair. I gritted my teeth, awaiting the sharp comment, the taunt. She just looked at me for a few seconds and then shook her head.

"What?" I asked.

"Nothing. I was coming over to save you, but Tommy got here first. We're watching out for you, is all."

I raised an eyebrow. "Really?"

"Denise is upset enough."

I nodded. "I see. Thanks."

She looked me over again. "Listen, I sympathize. You didn't ask for some drunk coed to throw herself all over you in front of your girlfriend."

"The implication being," I slurred slightly, "that I wouldn't mind it if Neesie weren't here."

She shrugged. "You didn't exactly run away from her."

I snuffed out my cigarette. "Fuck you, Kelly."

"Hey!" she laughed. "Jesus, Hank, pay attention: We like you. The women are looking out for you. You can't get a better deal than the women looking out for you, dummy."

"Where's Denise?"

She sighed. "Bitching about you to Flo. Don't worry, nothing unusual."

I looked away. Kelly stood up and clucked her tongue at me.

"Listen, don't worry about Miriam. She's . . . friendly. She's thrown herself at just about every older guy who crosses her path. She's kind of wild. Mary thinks letting her go away to college was the worst possible thing; apparently, she barely escaped high school without serious trouble, and now the general Harrows' fear is that she'll show up pregnant and in rehab someday."

I blinked. "That's supposed to make me feel *better*?"

"Poor baby! Come on, dance with me."

I looked up at her distrustfully.

"Don't worry: I'm approved company. It's safe."

Kelly proved to be a better dancer than I would have expected, moving gracefully and with an enthusiasm that proved to be infectious. I'd never interacted much with her; out with her and Flo and Mary and Denise and Bick and the whole lot of them, Kelly and I had barely managed to get past the awkward initial meeting. Intimacy wasn't easy, under those crowded circumstances. As I faked my dancing skills, hamming it up a bit, I felt an onrush of affection for her and ogled her silently.

After a few sweaty moments, Luis appeared at my elbow.

"May I cut in?" he asked in his courtly manner. It didn't mean anything. Luis had a courtly manner almost genetically.

I pounded him on the shoulder. "Be my guest, *mi amigo*," I panted. "I'm about to have a heart attack."

He squinted at me. "Do you require medical attention?"

I found Tom at the bar, drunkenly hitting on the brunette bartender, who regarded him with something like amusement.

"How's it going, Tom-O?"

He sighed, turning his back on her. "She isn't allowed to drink on duty. My powers of seduction are greatly hampered by sobriety."

"Plus his breath smells like puke," she added, smiling.

"Where's our favorite underage drinker?" I asked, winking at her.

"The wild child Harrows? I dunno. The moment I put her down she stalked—or rather weaved—off to scam more booze from unsuspecting suitors."

I sighed. We leaned, elbow to elbow, against the bar. "Women that beautiful should not drink so much," I said.

I could feel Tom eyeing me. "You feeling okay?"

I ignored that. "Where's Bick?"

We scanned the dance floor and saw no sign of his tall, charmless body. The table of honor gave us Mary, a white blur surrounded by well-wishers.

"Dunno."

"Let's go find him, then."

"Do we have to?"

I shrugged. "Beats waiting for Neesie to find *me*."

He snorted. "*Hmmph. Says you.*"

Out in the lobby, sunk into one of the soft leather couches, Mike was entertaining a group of people with stories about David Bickerman, who was, Tom and I agreed, unusually entertaining for such a classless bastard.

"So there's Bick, after hours, out in the cold, still standing there when we get out. Christ, we all just assumed the bastard'd gone home. He's like, blue. So he's waiting there for us and he gestures us over and says, 'This is the guy's car, the Beemer'—the guy who had him thrown out you see. 'We're gonna slash his tires.' We laughed, but he was serious."

The pop-eyed disbelief on Mike's face was more amusing than the story.

"I remember that," Tom offered, horning in on Mike's audience. "Every time the goddamn bar door opened, he was gone like the fucking wind, into the shadows. I'd glance over to say, 'Watch yourself, someone's coming,' and there'd be nothing but a ghostly outline of where Bick had been, like in cartoons."

Everyone laughed. Mike looked a little sour.

"Speaking of Bick," I said, "anyone seen him?"

Someone offered: "I think we just saw him go by a few minutes ago with someone, toward the elevators."

I nodded and dragged Tom off. Mike looked relieved.

Tom wasn't done. As we moved toward the elevators, he was still griping. "S'true. He got us all to hunker down to slash that asshole's tires, and every time a cricket fucking rubbed its legs together, he was gone."

I rubbed his arm soothingly. "Water under the bridge." I pulled out my best Luis impersonation. "Tonight is a night for celebration."

Tom doubled over, red-faced, laughing. I pushed my hands into my pockets while he gasped, and looked around, innocently.

"Oh, man, that's fucking funny." He looked up from his squatting position. "Holy shit, is that Bick?"

I looked up in time to see an elevator closing. Bick was obvious in his tall graceless tuxedo. Then a glimpse of fabric, a high heel, a unique pink dress, and the elevator closed.

I stood staring, for some time.

Tom started laughing again. I kicked him, lightly.

"Sorry," he gasped. "Sorry, man, but that is goddamn hilarious."

I grabbed him by the arm and pulled him erect. "All right," I said seriously. "Is this a male bonding moment or do we have to convene the Women's Council?"

That sobered Tom. "You think it's that bad?"

"Don't you—if it's what it looked like?"

He scratched the back of his head. "That's a terrible seal to break, Hank. The girls. Christ, they'll tear him apart."

"Yep. And it looks like he'll deserve it."

He closed his mouth with a click, then shook his head. "We have to at least make an effort to confirm or deny before we throw him to the girls. There ought to be a presumption of innocence before we go tell everyone that Bick is humping bridesmaids somewhere."

"All right," I said, striding purposefully toward the elevators and exhaling smoke. "Let's see if there's any reason to cut his balls off, and if there is, we're going to feed the fucker to the girls."

"Yeah!" Tom enthused. "This is fucking *fantastic*!"

In the elevator, smothered behind two immense old dowagers in fur coats and sheets of pan-fried makeup:

"Where are we going?"

I didn't look at Tom. "I'm guessing the tenth floor. That's where Bick's room is, anyway."

"He'd do it in his own room? My God." He sounded excited.

A moment of silence, between floors four and five.

"If he's not in his room," I added, "what then?"

"Miriam's room, of course. Her and some cousin are sharing one."

I blinked. "We know it's Miriam?"

Tom squeezed my shoulder. "Man, get a hold of yourself, okay? It was Miriam. Which doesn't necessarily mean anything."

Six, seven, eight.

"Should we get physical?" Tom wondered. "You know, violent?"

"Why, for God's sake?"

"Well, the whole moral thing, you know, defending Mare's honor."

"Dammit, Tom, take a swing if you feel morally compelled to. But don't expect me to wade in."

The doors opened on the tenth floor, serene and empty.

"Then why are we up here?"

I didn't have an answer to that one. I stepped out of the elevator, counting off rooms. The floor was all in blue, various micromanaged shades of it in a powdery, dry-feeling configuration that urged me to hold my breath as I walked the hall. I wondered if hotels bought carpet and wallpaper and paint in bulk and then just used it until they ran out, entire floors spray-painted a certain color for no better reason.

I paused. "Ten-fifteen, that's it, the Groom's ready-room." I fussed with my tie. "What should we do?"

Tom shrugged his jacket onto his shoulders, winked at me, and made purposefully for the doors, two wooden doors with the number in gold, each with big, ornate handles. I watched Tom dumbly for a moment, and didn't step forward and reach for him until he'd actually paused before the doors and taken the preparatory step backward, a little wobbly because the man was, I realized suddenly, fantastically drunk.

"Tom!"

He rocked back, weaved, and kicked the doors open with a loud whoop and a crack of broken wood.

"Bickerman!" he shouted, red-faced and grinning. "Send the girl out with her underwear still in place, and no one gets hurt!"

It was the Glee. I let my arms fall to my sides and looked down at the dark blue of the carpet, defeated. The Glee had done Bad Things before, and it had done it again. The fucking Glee.

Bick's face, ruddy and amazed, appeared around one corner of the door. "Jesus fucking Christ, are you two fucking crazy?"

I gestured at Tom. "He is. I'm just stupid."

"They're gonna bill me for this goddamned door, you know."

"We're here," Tom announced happily, "to defend Mary's honor."

Bick stared at Tom for a few seconds, then looked back at me. "Hank, maybe you could step in for a moment?"

I nodded, still looking down at my feet.

"Tom," Bick asked reasonably, "can you give us a few minutes?"

Tom nodded, all solemn dignity. "I will smoke a cigarette."

As I passed Tom, I squeezed his shoulder. I stepped through the remnants of the door and into the room. I paused then, because on the oversized bed lay Miriam, snoring loudly, her mouth open, her dress still on, albeit with both straps off her shoulders.

"Hank," Bick announced, "I have a problem."

I nodded. I sat down in one of the big stuffed chairs and put my head in my hands, eyes just over my fingers so I could see.

"Jesus, Bick, you're a fucking asshole," I said reasonably. "She's your goddamn sister-in-law."

He held up his hands. "Whoa! Whoa!"

I hid my eyes again. "Fuck, man: your *underage* sister-in-law."

Bick was shaking his head. "Whoa! Okay? First off, she's eighteen. She's not underage."

I shook my head in my hands. "Oh, Christ, that's the wrong tack to take."

"Okay, okay. Sorry. The point is, nothing was going on. You're right: She's my sister-in-law. We were just talking. We're family, for God's sake."

I nodded, my head still in my hands. "Okay. Okay, fine. So let's get her out of here then, okay? Unless you're so innocent and sure of yourself you don't mind if Mary comes up here and sees her hot little number of a sister passed out on your bed."

Silence, and when I looked up, Bick was deep in thought, his smooth little forehead wrinkled and tortured. Finally, he looked up at me. "Okay. But I can't exactly be seen carrying her snoring through the halls, huh? I mean, Mare's a monster now. The Monster will not be amused."

I nodded. "Right. Hey, Tom!"

Tom popped into the room in fine fettle, red-faced and happy to help. "You rang?"

I sighed. "Go get Luis."

Luis swept his gaze across the room, and then looked me in the eye. "It is not right to mock marriage like this," he declared.

I clapped him on the shoulder. "We know, Luis, really. Now listen up, you're needed."

He shrugged his jacket on and cocked his head. "What do you need? Luis is here to help."

"Luis," I said, taking a deep breath because I felt shitty and was beginning to approach sober, "you are rumor control. You are in charge of disinformation. It's your job to keep the women downstairs and unsuspicious until Tom, Bick, and I rejoin you."

Luis blinked. "The women? You want me to lie to the women? Oh, Henry, that is dangerous."

Tom clapped a hand on Luis's other shoulder. "No more dangerous than not helping us, my Latin friend."

Luis glanced at the hand and then back to me. "I am rumor control," he said.

"Yes!"

"What," he asked, "does that mean?"

"Good Lord," Tom exclaimed, leaning in to examine Luis carefully. "He's drunker than I am!"

Luis appeared offended. "We have all been drinking heavily."

"Luis!"

He focused on me again.

"Rumor control means you must guide the conversation down there away from topics such as: *Where is Bick?* Or *Where is Miriam?* Or *What in hell are Tom, Henry, and Bick up to now?* Okay?"

"Guide conversations," Luis confirmed. "*Si*, I understand."

"Being in charge of disinformation," I continued, "means making sure that none of them come up here. Especially Mare, but none of them."

"Use force if necessary," Tom advised.

"Force," Luis repeated seriously.

"Okay, go. Luis, you are the man."

He nodded. "Yes." He turned and made his way out of the room, careful to not stagger.

I turned to Tom. "All right. Where's Bick?"

Tom shrugged. "Dunno. I think he slipped away."

"Fucker." I pushed my hair out of my face. "All right, you get her feet, I'll get her shoulders."

"Where are we going?"

"Her room."

"How will we get in?"

I swore. "Check her bag for a key. Otherwise, we always have you and your subtle way of entering a room."

He rummaged a bit, eventually dumping the contents of her bag on the bed. "Check!"

"Thank God for small blessings. Let's go."

I slid my hands under her armpits, Tom gripped an ankle in each hand, and we lifted her off the mattress. She sagged for a moment, but Tom made no move to exit the room.

"Henry," he said.

"Yeah?"

"We're bad guys, aren't we?"

I looked down at Miriam's peaceful, upside-down face. "Yeah. We might be."

II.

SAINT PATRICK'S DAY

The sheer motherfuckery on display was stunning, just stunning. Instant motherfuckers, just add alcohol—and none of the morons were even Irish, as far as I knew anyway. And Tom wasn't even around, which made the levels of motherfuckery absolutely stunning, since Tommy usually supplied all the motherfuckery in any situation.

Mary was being a saint, as always, displaying an unwise amount of tolerance for Bick's amateur-status doofusness. I tried to catch Florence's eye, but she was talking to Mike pretty seriously, so I just finished my drink, reached out, and grabbed the Sub-Doofus, Henry.

"Get me another beer!" I shouted over the tinny, disturbing noise of the Clancy Brothers.

Henry blinked dimly at me and then took the glass and fought his way to the bar. I turned to Denise for moral support and leaned in to her ear. She and Henry were fighting.

"Why do we keep coming out on this fucking holiday?"

Denise shrugged. "We're optimists, I guess."

She so didn't want to be there, especially when Henry had walked in with Bick and Mary and Miriam, who had of late become quite a little slut; seasoned, no doubt, by a half year of debauchery away at school. I wasn't sure what the whole story was because Denise's withering glance told of more than just a dislike. I was keeping my eye on the Sub-Doofus, seeking clues: Had he boffed the little tart? Then again, the way she came in hanging off him—not that she didn't hang off every guy she saw— maybe that was all it was. Maybe Denise just saw through her gosh-shucks kid routine and saw the inner slut coming out.

Insult to injury: The bar was some faux Scottish monstrosity, which everyone seemed to have mentally agreed was *close enough*. It was unbearable, and the dick-to-me ratio an unsatisfactory ten-to-one at least. I glanced at Denise and gave up because she was just standing there with her arms wrapped around herself, pissed off and trying very hard to make Sub-Doofus Henry burst into flame by sheer force of will.

Bick and Mary were all of a sudden doing shots at the bar. Fucking happily engaged people, I hated them. Well, I loved Mary, but I hated Bickerman. He was a fungus growing on all of us, although she seemed very fond of him. Wedding just a few months away, and she had us in those horrifying dresses.

A quick series of grim psychic visions of the rest of my life, watching them drink themselves into a *Who's Afraid of Virginia Woolf*-daze in a sad succession of divey bars.

With Denise hating the world, Flo somehow making do with Mikey, the Bicks halfway to passed out, and Miriam chatting up the bartender with her wide-eyed, tits-out enthusiasm, that left me with . . .

"Here you go."

The Sub-Doofus bearing a foamy beer for me and a bourbon for himself.

I sipped beer to help swallow down my growing ball of dismay at the evening's prospects and smiled wanly at him. "Thanks, Henry."

He smiled back, a bit of foppish charm, I thought. "You're speaking to me?" He glanced at Denise. "I thought I was on the blacklist tonight."

It wasn't so much the motherfuckery, I reflected, it was the gleeful unconcern with which the motherfuckery was bandied about that irritated me, mostly. I decided to be cautiously snotty, with an option for increased snottiness depending on what level of insincere BS the Sub-Doofus handed me.

"Well," I said sweetly, "what did you do to her?"

He laughed and shook his head, stealing a glance at Denise. "Ah, Kel, we don't have time for that list." He winked. "Drink and be merry, for tomorrow we shall die, eh?"

There was a lot of genuine sadness there, I thought, so I lowered the attitude provisionally. "I'm sorry. I didn't mean to make fun of you."

He winked again. "Sure you did. But that's all right. It's the Female Problem."

"Excuse me?"

I shifted my beer, ready to hurl it in his face. I'd done it before. Not to the Sub-Doofus specifically, but at other men.

He didn't seem concerned. "How long have Neesie and I been dating? Five months. She hasn't decided where I fit in yet, so all she does with you and Flo and Mare is study me carefully, right? She's rubbing me hard, searching for problems, for imperfections, for reasons to give up on me."

For motherfuckery, I thought.

He shrugged. "It's okay, it's natural. Why commit until you've kicked the tires and put it through its paces, right? But the Female Problem is that during this trial period, all her friends only hear the bad stuff about me. She's daring you to tell her that I'm not worth it, to point out the fatal flaw."

I blinked. It almost made sense.

He coughed a little around his drink. "Then, if I survive, and she embraces me as her boyfriend, her friends are amazed: They can't believe that she's settling in with this guy about whom they've heard nothing good for months. That's the Female Problem."

"That's," I struggled, "that's interesting."

He winked again, a gesture I was beginning to find really annoying. "Of course, a certain percentage of men deserve it."

I couldn't help it. I was amused and hid a smile in my foam.

"Careful," he admonished, "or I'll rub off on you, Kel."

I spared a guilty glance at Denise.

"She's in a mood to suspect infidelity with anyone," he went on with an air of injured innocence.

I picked Miriam out from the crowd, entertaining two blotto men wearing ridiculous green sweaters. One of them seemed to have found something fascinating in the offered cleavage of her white blouse. I nodded in her direction. "Coming in with her spread over you like butter didn't have anything to do with it, right?"

He nodded. "Sure it did."

I squinted distrustfully at this display of honesty. "So why set her off like that?"

The Sub-Doofus looked at me for a long moment, considering, I thought. "Kel," he said seriously, "she's my friend's fiancée's little sister. I am not going to treat her like a leper just because Denise hates her perky tits. And second, you can't always control what other people do."

"What does that mean?" I was sniffing the air for motherfuckery.

"It means, what was I supposed to do? Shove her to the floor and denounce her as a whore?"

I considered that, and realized my beer was miraculously gone. This was the power that men had, I knew. They talk and talk and before we know it we're blitzed and have our shirts open.

I sent the Sub-Doofus to the bar for another drink and thought about what he'd said. Maybe the Sub-Doofus was right in a sense: We hadn't given him much of a chance. But then, he was right: Denise hadn't let us know it was okay to. You couldn't start liking the boy toy until she did. It was unseemly, otherwise. He returned and slipped a better-poured beer into my hand, with a confident smile that told me he thought he was pretty fucking charming. Well, I could see why Neesie liked him—most of the time, anyway.

"Where's Luis?" I asked.

He shrugged. "The Spaniard? Not his sort of holiday, or so he says. I say to him, 'What about drinking, drunk women in bars, and fake Irish accents? They're not up your alley?' He looks at me and says . . ." here the Sub-Doofus launched into a passable Luis imitation. We all had a Luis shtick. "He says, 'The Irish are as dogs to my people.'"

I caught myself giggling and hid behind my beer. The Sub-Doofus was smiling. "At any rate, he may yet show up when he realizes everyone he knows is out at some bar." He blinked, innocently, I'd swear. "Christ, that's kind of sad, actually, now that I think about it. I'm going to go give him a call, see if he wants to join us now that he's had some time to reconsider his Aryan ways."

"Sure," I said, a sinking feeling telling me I was going to have to force myself on someone before one of the strange men, their bellies looking like they had a fucking Blarney Stone stuffed down their shirts, took note of me.

I don't ever need to go to the gym because hovering over the most disgusting toilets in the world, urinating without making skin-on-funk contact in the wonderful places my friends bring me to, keeps my leg muscles strong. In this paradise the women's bathroom was right next to the men's room, which was unfortunate. I stood with Flo and tried to keep still despite the ongoing biological processes inside me. That was okay. The place was hot and smoky, and I felt lightheaded, but not in a bad way. There were still three girls ahead of me. The men's room line cha-cha'd past at lightning speed.

"I don't think they even drop their drawers," I said to Flo. "I think they just wet themselves in private and come right back out."

"Trough," Flo slurred.

I looked at her. Flo was tall and dark-haired, and I'd always been jealous of how skinny she was. She was fussing with her hair, which was tied back in a complex series of clips. As the night wore on and she drank more, the clips miraculously loosened. "What?"

"Haven't you ever been into a men's bathroom? It's just one big trough. They stand around it and piss into it. That's why there's never a line. They just squeeze in between two other guys and let loose."

"Yuck." I considered this piece of intelligence. "When were you in a boy's room?"

She rolled her eyes. "At a ball game once. I was dating Phil at the time, remember him? Phil Dublen? I really had to go, so he ushered me into the men's room, stood guard outside a stall."

Dublen . . . Dublen . . . "Oh, *him*; I remember him. Always wore that sports jacket, looked like he slept in it. Wasn't he rich?"

She shook her head. "No, he just inherited some nice sum once, that's all. He was pretty poor, actually. Nice kisser, though."

"Why'd you break up with him again?"

She scowled. "He mooned about this other girl, this waitress he knew. Never shut up about her. So finally I was like, Hello! Here I am, in the flesh. She's not!" Her face darkened. "Let's just say his response was not the right one."

The line moved up one person, as Miriam emerged from the bathroom, almost falling into us.

"Hi, guys!" she said, hugging us and pulling herself out of a fall at the same time. "This is so much fun! We all ought to go out more often! You guys are so great!"

She was drunk as a sailor. I smiled and helped steady her. "Mir, baby, go find your sister. Have a Coke or something."

She giggled. "Okay!"

When I turned back to the Pee Situation, which was getting desperate, I noted two guys now waiting in line for the men's room. They were doing the typical motherfucker move, which is glancing at Flo and I about chest-high and then talking to each other.

"Hi," I called over to them.

The dark-haired one looked embarrassed. The less dark-haired one smiled his way-cool smile at me. "Hey."

"Are you going to say hello, or what?"

He blinked. "Hello?"

"You were staring at our tits. I figured you'd at least say hello."

He laughed and pushed his way into the bathroom. His dark-haired friend looked ready to burst into flame.

"Sorry," he said.

I shrugged. Only one away from the bathroom, I was in a generous mood. "Buy me a drink, you're forgiven."

Back at the bar, Bick had managed to worm us some bar space and two precious chairs, claimed by Denise and Mary. Denise appeared to be unclenching a little. She sipped a fruity-looking drink and had allowed the Sub-Doofus to stand next to her. Progress, of a sort.

"What're you drinking, sweetheart?"

This from Bick, the Chief Doofus, who knew that I hated it when he called me sweetheart. I smiled sweetly. "A red, sweetcheeks."

"I like her," he said to Mare. "She's sassy. And you, Florence?"

"Same," Flo said cheerily, joining us. "My God, that bathroom is just *gross*."

"We'll sneak you into the men's room next time," Mike offered. "It's gross too, though."

"But gross with *an element of danger!*" Henry added dramatically.

Denise rolled her eyes at me, and I pretended I was laughing at her. Girls had to stick together and all that, no matter how deviously charming their boyfriends tended to be at the most inopportune moments.

"Anyone seen Mir?" Mary asked, looking around. "She's been gone a long time."

"Just saw her by the bathrooms, actually," Flo offered. "Thought she was coming back this way."

Everyone had to scream to be heard. Bickerman disengaged from Mary and settled his jacket onto his shoulders squarely. "I'll take a look around, make sure she's okay."

Mary bussed him affectionately on the cheek, and he was off, the Brave Avenging Fiancé. The Sub-Doofus handed his glass to Denise gently and turned to address us. "And I have to go to the bathroom like nobody's business, so Mike, I leave you with four damned attractive ladies. Hope you're up to it, buddy."

Mike let him shoulder past and leaned in toward the rest of us. "I didn't hear a word he said," he bellowed.

A moment of quiet enveloped us; no one knew exactly what to say to Mike, who was nice but uninspiring.

Mary, a saint as always, engaged her fiancé's best friend in a conversation, and I let my mind wander, relieved. Mike was nice enough, but his conversation tended to make me sleepy, and I felt for Mare, who was burdened with him at all times through Bick. I was beginning to wonder if marrying the Doofus was going to end up more trouble than it was worth. I was starting to feel a little hot and dizzy, anyway, and my underwear suddenly seemed too tight. I couldn't have managed small talk with Mikey if my life had depended on it.

"Is it just me," I asked Flo, "or is Henry growing on you, too?"

She shrugged. "He is sweet, mostly."

"Yeah," I mused. "I think Neesie's doing well, with this one."

Another shrug, her eyes dancing around the crowd of red-cheeked men pushing each other out of the way for beer. "The way she isn't speaking to him, I'm not too surprised if they don't make it much further."

I squinted my disapproval at her. "Nah, I think he's doing well. Normally, I don't think she'd let him stand near her if she was really mad."

I glanced over to where Denise was making a half-hearted but well-intentioned effort to join Mary and Mike's conversation. She kept scanning the crowd, looking for the Sub-Doofus. It was wall-to-wall drunkards, all of them vaguely resembling her boyfriend in at least the basic details: height, weight, complexion, sarcasm, pudginess. It was kind of depressing, sometimes, to have the commonness of the available men thrust under your nose.

We ordered another round and summoned more small talk to cover the growing obviousness that three of our party were missing. Denise gave up the pretense that she was engaged in conversation, knocking back her drink in a huge, ominous gulp.

"Oh, for God's sake," I muttered, taking her by the arm. "Let's go find him, then."

"And the fiancé too, while you're at it," Mary slurred after us. "If the little Rotter's been chatting up the chicks, kick him in the nuts for me!"

Mary drunk was not a pleasant sight, and the one good thing to come from her perplexing infatuation with the soft white form of Bickerman was his assumption of the Mare-Wrangling duties out at bars. It was a demanding job, and the Doofus got some amount of credit simply for tackling it in good cheer.

"I'm sorry," Denise whispered in my ear, her cheek hot against mine, her breath sweet with Schnapps. "It's just that—"

"You don't trust him," I finished. "I know."

"I'm terrible. He's been good. I should give him credit."

"Fuck him. If he's been good, he doesn't need credit."

Pushing your way through crowded bars, crowded dick-heavy bars, was an Olympic-level sport, really. It was strenuous work requiring dexterity. Darting for openings, keeping your eyes everywhere to defend against gropers, sliding past defensive blocks in the form of pie-eyed pickup lines—it was exhausting. By the time we found the bathrooms, I was out of breath. Two Harry Reems look-alikes in muttonchops and denim jackets parted before us, and I was breathless, because there they were.

By the pay phones, with the phone numbers from a thousand wasted evenings printed on the pasteboard walls in blue and black ink, and the cigarette machine, where the yellow plastic knobs had been rubbed shiny by a thousand desperate hands tugging them for nicotine fixes.

First, his back, the gray jacket he was wearing, the back of his head distinguished by the ballooning of those ears, great flaps of pink spreading out proudly. His posture was relaxed, careless, one elbow on the cigarette machine, leaning in toward the wall.

Then, in slow motion, he shifted his weight, and there she was, against the wall, hands locked behind her back, her face flushed, her eyes shining, her fucking eighteen-year-old nipples poking at her blouse as if they already had his fingerprints on them. One hand reached up and pulled at his lapel, pulling him back toward her playfully.

He turned, and his expression was ghastly. Horror.

"I'm going to throw up," Denise said. "I've got to get out of here."

She pulled me back the way we came. I turned one last time, and my eyes locked with the Sub-Doofus's, and there it was: horror, amazement, terror, and something else. Before I could put a name to it, the crowd moved between us, and then it was just people, and Denise pulling me.

"Calm down, sweetie."

Denise kept walking briskly. "We've got to keep drinking," she announced. "There's got to be a bar around here somewhere."

I glanced at Flo, walking with her arms crossed across her chest, weaving just slightly, the International Pissed-Off Drunk Girl Signal. Flo looked away. She'd been having a good time.

"Okay, sweetie," I said to Denise. "Let's have a drink, talk about this."

"No talk. Just drink."

"Calm down. We didn't see anything. Calm down."

She snorted. "He was practically making out with the little cunt right there!"

I caught up and matched her stride, which was fast and angry. "But he wasn't, and we didn't really see anything. All I'm saying is, let's calm down and think about this."

"Fine. First a few drinks, okay? If you want, go back in there and talk to Little Lord Fuckpants about it."

I swallowed my sarcasm and let us walk five steps before jumping back in with the brat. I opened my mouth, and she stopped to whirl on me.

"You were getting mighty chummy with him back there, but I thought my *friends* would be on my side."

My mouth fell open. "Chummy?"

"You and Little Lord Fuckpants chatting up a storm. Having a grand old time, huh?" she spat. "Anyone else, okay, you expect that sort of shit. But not *you*, Kel. Not you."

A stabbing pain through my gut, knee-jerk guilt. Never ever, ever flirt with other girls' boyfriends; it was an obvious rule; it was what allowed society to exist. But fuck that, all I'd been was *polite* to the poor guy, dragging along her sullen little ass and trying to make the best of it. I felt righteous indignation was probably my best course of action.

"Fuck *that*, Denise. I was just being *polite*."

She stopped suddenly, whirled to face me and Flo, who was sullenly trailing us, dragging her purse like a fucking dead poodle, which is probably what she felt the evening was beginning to resemble.

"I just want someone to be on my side, damn it," Denise hissed fiercely. "That dumbfuck is so goddamn charming everyone's always *defending* him."

Which wasn't true. Flo and I had been running him down for no good reason ever since she unveiled him, as girlfriends were supposed to do. I let that pass, though, seeing in a quivering lip and shining eyes a flash of daylight in the mess the evening was becoming.

"We *are* on your side, sweetie," I cooed, with a half-hearted "yeah" from Flo somewhere in the background. "We're here, aren't we?"

She nodded, smiling a little wanly. "C'mon," she sniffled. "We've got to keep drinking."

I could almost hear Flo brighten behind us. I squeezed Denise's hand in a sisterly way and we moved on.

Motherfuckery was universal. A natural resource. We were running out of oil and air and comfortable shoes, but fucking *motherfuckery* was being brewed up constantly.

"Jesus," Flo whined, spinning her phone on the table. "Can we *go*?"

"*Jesus*," I spat back at her. "Shut. Up. Florence."

I loved Flo. I loved her so much it made me angry, but she'd been whining nonstop for two hours and I wanted to pinch her tongue between my fingers until her eyes popped out of her head. I wanted her to leave if she wanted to leave. She wanted permission.

I also wanted to pinch dear Denise. I wanted to pinch her head until it exploded.

She was dancing. On the jukebox, an endless parade of terrible music; old, boring songs featuring saxophone solos and synthesizer riffs. Currently dancing with Combover and Gut, one man with two outstanding physical attributes. Who thought he'd hit some sort of pornographic lottery this evening, because he hadn't yet met *me*. And my foot had an appointment with his balls.

Somehow, Denise had absorbed six or possibly seven shots of tequila. Somehow two of the buttons on her shirt had come undone. Somehow she'd started dancing in the middle of the goddamn bar, and somehow when Combover and Gut had boogied up to her, she had not run screaming. She just continued dancing, floating on a thick wave of feminine motherfuckery.

Combover and Gut spun her and pulled her close to him, wrapping one arm around her waist as she giggled. Stupid Denise letting this fucking nightmare grind his dumbfounded erection into her ass. Stupid Denise smiling stupidly.

Combover and Gut thought he was taking Denise home. Or, more accurately, Combover and Gut thought he was taking Denise out to his rusted-out Chevy Nova. Where she was most likely to vomit into his lap with his big, calloused hand on the back of her neck applying friendly encouragement, a move perfected back at the prom and never improved upon. I watched Denise jiggling as he hugged her to him, her boobs dancing ecstatically.

I wanted to kick them *both* in the balls.

When she fell, sliding from his grasp and bouncing once on the sticky floor, there was a weak round of applause from the other men. I stood up.

"Thank *God*," Flo muttered, following suit.

Motherfuckery. Denise sat on the sticky floor, laughing, face red, boobs jiggling. We were twelve. We were sneaking booze from our parents' cabinet, cutting our arms, calling each other fat whores and crying, crying, crying. Over boys. Over motherfuckery. Somehow it had all turned into Motherfuckery. Motherfuckery for motherfuckery, and I was sick of it.

"C'mon, sweetie," I said, taking hold of one arm and pulling. Flo was there, hauling on the other one, and I forgave her a small percentage of her sins.

"Aw, man," Combover and Gut wheezed, slicking back his single long lock, like the swipe of a black marker on his head. He was smiling. "C'mon, the night's young. Drinks . . . a round on me!"

I ignored him. We had Denise up on her wobbly legs. She didn't look so good. I imagined her vomiting into Flo's lap in about ten minutes, and felt better.

"Wanna stay," she slurred. Then threw her arms around me and squeezed. "Stay with me!"

She didn't offer any resistance as we walked her toward the exit. Combover and Gut followed at a safe distance, protesting. Flo backed into the doors, pushing them open, and we wrangled her out into the parking lot. I lost my balance for a moment and we spun around, and then she was standing in front of me, her face suddenly bloated, her eyes big.

"Uh-oh," Flo muttered.

Denise bent at the waist like a gymnast and vomited. Directly onto my shoes.

"Mother-*fucker*."

I stared at the back of her head for a moment, and thought: They deserve each other.

III.

THE FOURTH OF JULY

If I were telling the story, I'd start it off with: *I'm perverse, and I know it, and that's fine.*

Other people know it too, or sense it, and for some of them it isn't fine, but hey—what can you do. I can help being perverse the same way the sky can help being blue. Fuck 'em if they don't care for it: I am a celebration of life's perversity, all rolled up into one attractive fucking package.

I looked around. I'd known them all. Many times. There were only about four different types of people, after all, and their patterns and behaviors were obvious and painful to watch as they scratched it all out in slow motion. I knew them all so well I could predict the future. For example, the second Mike the Stupid Fuck said something about fireworks, I knew the day would end with one less hand. I couldn't wait.

The Bickermans were throwing a shindig because that's what pleasantly engaged couples living in sin do—they rush toward the yawning chasm of boredom and murderous familiarity breeding babies and contempt in equal amounts. They throw barbecues on the Fourth and invite everyone over and stand there smiling until their lips bleed. Bickerman Alpha, the male of the species, is a nasty little ass, but so far the little cow Mary—Bickerman Beta—hasn't figured that part out because she's not the type to let her man run amok diddling everything in a skirt and still stand by him, twanging the sad banjo and wearing the dunce cap on her head. Bickerman Alpha looks good. He's a deceptive bit of produce, though: firm and delightfully scented on the outside, rotten and mulchy on the inside. I know. I'd whored around with him enough.

The Bickermans' place was standard, filled with furniture from a catalog and a mash of colors and textures that set my teeth on edge. Five minutes in the Bickermans' place made me want to burn it down. The yard was nice, though. Shared with everyone else in the complex, but nicely tended. I preferred Hank's squalid apartment, four rooms, all earth tones and dust. When Hank threw a party in the winter he hung coolers of beer off of his fire escape. You crawled through his bedroom window and looked down, all you could see was the sturdy knot and a quick flash of rope. It was so wild and overgrown back there, like a fucking jungle. You couldn't see anything, and the beer just got swallowed up. Henry said he'd tossed plenty of debris back there. He called it the Black Hole. You tossed it in the night, a high arc in the air; the mini jungle swallowed it, and it was like it had never happened.

Everything at the Bickermans' place was right out in the open where you could see it, and that was the goddamn *problem*.

I patted my stomach. I'd eaten four hamburgers, drunk six beers; I lit a cigarette out by the rose bush and let out a magnificent belch, a classic, and thought again that I should carry a goddamn tape recorder with me because there's one more thing lost to my descendants forever.

It was a bright sunshiny sort of day, eh, and warm and logy and stuffed like a bratwurst was I. I turned and held my beer by the neck, letting my cigarette dangle from my mouth and casting an eye over the herd. What was great about knowing everything about everyone—really, what was great about being a tiny god in someone's backyard—is that you can just wind them up and enjoy the fun.

Henry raised his beer toward me and I nodded, hipper than him. Henry I'd never be free of. I suspected we'd been twins in the womb, torn apart when I started to eat him, dished off to separate foster families. I liked Henry; he was an unimaginative drone sometimes, but there were flashes, brief and exciting, of a true libertine lurking somewhere inside his pleasantly handsome face. He had a good sense of humor, too, and if I had no better places to be than where the Great and Powerful Bickerman lured me with his best meats and brews, I might as well hang out with Henry. Except, I wasn't hanging out with Henry because Henry was still under house arrest from the Miriam Molestation Incident back in March. I spurn the Irish holiday because it brings out every heavy-breasted panter within range, but I wish I'd made an appearance at that one. Just to see everyone's faces.

Denise was holding Henry's hand as if she might turn at any moment and find Miriam attached to him by the penis. She turned and followed Henry's gaze to me and offered me a wan, disapproving smile. Denise doesn't like me, or, as I suspected, she secretly lusts after me (as most women do), and in her fierce determination to repress the feeling she is cramped up painfully, lashing out at everyone around her. Poor thing. For Henry's sake, I'd avoided really turning the full force of my charm on her, but maybe it would be better to give her a taste. Might calm her down a little.

As for the Molestation Incident, Henry had told me she'd just about accepted his insistence that nothing had happened between him and the Sorority Slut. These are the lies couples tell each other—about 50 or 60 percent of all romantic conversation is lies for the Greater Good. She might have decided that nothing had *actually* happened, but watching her tight grip on the poor sod, I knew that she suspected she'd merely witnessed a busted seduction, and regarded little Miriam's ass as her number-one enemy. Having conducted an exhaustive comparison of the two women's asses, I had to agree with her: Miriam's was fantastic.

"Why are you standing here alone, Thomas?"

The dulcet non-English tones of Luis; wandering, as usual, oblivious to the usual rules of polite society. I could not say with authority whether Luis was bizarre because of the cultural gulf between him and the people he'd chosen to live with, or if he was simply a bizarre person—if Spaniards also gave him steady looks and long pauses when he spoke with them.

"I am here alone, my Romantic friend, because I suffer from a fear of crowds, sometimes, and needed some air."

Luis responded to every statement with squint-eyed incredulity, wisely assuming that all Americans would lie to him first and only tell the truth when pressed. I wasn't sure if this meant that Luis was intelligent or incredibly paranoid. It was hard to tell with someone who spoke English like he had marbles in his mouth, and when I knew about three words in Spanish, all expletives.

Luis was, I admit, beyond my powers. This was unprecedented, but I'd learned to accept it. Luis was therefore unpredictable, despite doing pretty much exactly the same thing in every situation. Luis was chaos.

"If you fear crowds, Thomas," he said, charmingly pronouncing my name *Tohm-Mas*, "why do you spend so much of your time in bars?"

I returned his squinty stare. "Booze lowers inhibitions, allows me to mix. Why do you want to know?"

He shrugged. "No reason."

I nodded and proceeded to ignore Luis, which he always took well. Luis enjoyed supreme confidence and assumed that unless you actively drove him away, he was wanted. I envied that, sometimes, that myopic, borderline-insipid peacefulness. I killed off my beer and let another enormous belch escape me. "Well, let's rejoin the crowd."

"Okay."

I made for Henry, who was really one of the few people I could stand on a regular basis. Denise saw me coming and whispered in his ear, swirling off in a cloud of sundress. Denise quite rightly attributed some of Henry's bad behavior to me. I admired flashes of her legs as she twisted away and clinked Henry's glass as I arrived on the scene. Denise had wonderfully long, tan legs you couldn't help but imagine wrapped around your waist, urging you on with little digs of those exquisite ankles. Henry, by comparison, had the blurry red look of the halfway drunk.

"I've always known," he said happily, "that you liked Luis better than me."

"The correct phrasing," Luis said in his slow, careful second language, "is 'better than I.'" As usual, he said this with dire seriousness.

Henry clinked his beer against Luis's in good cheer. "I'm sure you're right."

I oriented myself on the Future Bickermans of America. Bick was making a show of flipping burgers, and his luscious fiancée was giggling airheadedly. She wasn't stupid, but she liked playing it for Bick, who liked his women to be silent cows who sighed and giggled and came just from looking at him, a difficult combination to come by. Mary Harrows was one fine piece of ass. She was wearing short shorts, tennis shoes you just had to imagine placed delicately on your shoulders, and a sheer white T-shirt that revealed nothing but a bikini top beneath. Wonderful breasts. Not especially large, but wonderfully shaped. I stopped staring at her by closing my eyes and imagining her ripening sister, who was less well shaped (flatter, somewhat) but prettier in the face, in her old cheerleading outfit from high school.

"Tom?"

I opened my eyes to the disappointing sight of Henry and Luis. I smiled. "Sorry. Enjoying a little group sex fantasy with the sisters Harrows. What were you saying?"

"Nothing," Luis offered. Painfully honest at all times, he was constantly entertaining.

I looked around to re-orient myself and caught Mary giving me a few moments of her attention. I winked, and she looked away. I chucked my empty beer bottle into a convenient barrel and went in search of another. Henry and Luis followed lazily, and we moved across the warm, damp grass.

"What's the countdown now?" I asked. I dreaded the Bickerman wedding. I think we all did. There was much to dread.

"About four months, give or take a few hours," Henry replied immediately, a loyal and useful lieutenant to the end.

"It's going to be a disaster," I proclaimed, pausing at the cooler to fish around ice water for a beer. No one argued. They all knew it. I think even Bick and Mare knew it, on some level. They had the wide-eyed stares of people who have seen the burning bush and know the end is nigh. So did everyone else, for that matter. I'd had it myself since high school. Luis maybe didn't have it, but his higher brain functions had yet to be confirmed via independent research.

Then again, I made everything up, on the fly, all the time. I just entertained myself.

"Not the wedding," Henry finally offered, trying to find the fire in his belly. "The marriage, yes. The wedding, though, I think will be sedate. They're both too image-conscious."

I gave Henry a steady look. "Henry, I sometimes can't decide if you're really that dense or if you use it, cunningly, as protective coloring." He blinked in his lovably dimwitted way. "Image-conscious? These people don't have that level of awareness, Hank. Look at them."

We all glanced over at the Future Bickermans of America just as Bick leered reptilianly at Kelly's passing form, while Mare studiously chatted up his odious work friends.

I put my hand on Henry's shoulder. "They're fucking animals."

I suddenly became aware of Luis.

"Bick, for example," he said in his direly serious tone, "is actually a panda."

Henry burst into the slightly unbalanced laughter I found so endearing about him. It was brain damaged, completely innocent. You heard Henry laugh, and you knew you could trust him.

"Tom-O," he sputtered, "two weeks ago you told me they'd last forever, two weeks from now it'll be exactly one month. You make everything up, all the time."

I scowled. I hated it when the monkeys saw the pattern. "I do not."

"You do! You speak with complete confidence, all the time, but Christ if you don't just make it up, from the air, every time."

I looked at Luis. He nodded. "It is true, Tom," he said, pronouncing my name *Tohm*. "You lie as you breathe. It is okay. We know, and adjust accordingly."

Before I could respond to this, which was not information I wanted freely distributed, Mike bounced up, short and bald and black and wearing ridiculous tan shorts that went almost all the way to his ankles, which meant they were really just short pants and that just made me angry for reasons I couldn't quite put my finger on.

"Come on guys, we're going to shoot off some fireworks," he announced with adolescent glee.

A psychic vision of Mike bleeding from the stump of his arm flashed before me. Henry and I exchanged a dubious glance. I fixed my gaze just above Mike's left shoulder and studied an interesting-looking tree in the backyard while Henry said something to placate the idiot. Luis just stared off into the distance, thinking things in Spanish.

"Ah," I said. "Fireworks." Then I turned and walked off. It was more effective than one might imagine.

I had a fresh beer, so I was free to wander the crowd and sow dissent. I didn't know many people at the party; I was the black sheep friend that Bick sometimes denied, and Mare . . . well, Mare usually preferred to have nonverbal communication with me.

And like a movie script, there she was, alone, futzing with the potato salad, fighting a losing war with the flies and vermin. I studied her pert little rump in those shorts for a few moments as I approached.

"They get us in the end, you know."

She whirled, startled, and then fixed me with her "withering" stare: narrowed eyes, pursed lips. All in all, her best attempt at "withering" came out looking more like "constipated." All women, it had been my experience, thought of themselves as real ball-breakers. Very few of them were.

"What?" she snapped.

"The flies. You can shoo them now. They'll have the last laugh."

For Mare, I knew, I was just some unwanted baggage on the Bick side of the family, though she couldn't seem to shake a certain drunken attraction for me. Henry, I thought, she liked. Mike, well, you could ignore Mikey pretty easily. Luis was so bizarre most people put him in the same category as furniture: It wasn't the accent, it was the serpentine and creepy proclamations that escaped him, like gas.

"I get it," she snapped. "Death."

I eyed her breasts appreciatively. I wondered if she'd complained about me to Bick, and if he'd promised anything to her by way of punishing me. Or if he'd just laughed. Depending on what mood you caught Bick in, either was possible. Her eyes narrowed further, and she put her hands on her hips, which was Mare's main way of telling you to back off (whoa), so I dragged my eyes up to hers.

"Thomas," she said crisply, making an obvious effort, "can I help you?"

"You're gorgeous."

She stared at me for some seconds, just a blank, empty stare I gave her a lot of credit for, then she let out a frustrated little yelp and marched past me, probably to complain again to her fiancé that I was a miserable jerk. Problem was, Bick knew I was a miserable jerk. Nothing she could tell him about me would be much of a surprise to him.

I smelled her perfume and savored it. Then, I piled salad, flies and all, onto a plate and dug in, washing it down with cold beer. I was alive and happy as hell, and I doubted if there was another living thing vibrating with such enjoyment as I was right then and there.

Off in the distance on the other side of the yard, in a place hidden by the house, I heard a loud explosion and some screaming. I grinned and began to saunter.

The emergency room was white, white everywhere, and was giving me a sun glare headache or something. Or perhaps it was beers in the sunlight and then a few hours of breathing, or again perhaps bad potato salad covered in gross fly-borne germs. At any rate my head hurt and all the white in the emergency room was killing me.

I glanced in Henry's direction. "I'm going to grab a smoke. Tell the herd."

"Fuck that," he groused. "I'll join you."

"Where are you going?"

The shrewish snap of Denise, who was apparently convinced that Henry was somehow more involved in Mike's injuries than was being let on. No doubt she thought I'd puppet-mastered the whole thing, and she feared that letting Hank have a smoke with me would result in more injuries, possibly death.

Henry ricked his head a little as if swallowing bile but turned with a placating smile. "Just going to have a cigarette, honey. Be right back."

She nodded. I noted the absence of Miriam, probably giving the girl a sense of security regarding Henry's prick.

Outside it was blissfully gray now, dusk everywhere, and my head felt immediately better with some fresh air and some low light. I shook out a pair of cigarettes and lit them, handing one to Henry. He smoked it with his hand curled around it in a peculiar way I assumed he'd once seen in a prison movie.

"She still giving you hell about Miriam?" I said.

He nodded. "She's convinced I was inches from cheating on her."

"What do you want? Mir's eighteen, gorgeous, and a flirt. All women hate her. I'm surprised she doesn't burst into flame from their combined hatred."

He smoked. "Looks like Mike's gonna be okay."

"Fucking pussy. A little second-degree burn. You'd think he'd had his thumbs blown off the way he was screaming. And why do we have to sit out here staring at the floor waiting for them to send him out with his bandaged thumbs? What purpose does it serve?"

"To show Mike that we care, I guess. Support."

"But I *don't* care about Mike."

Henry laughed. "Then I guess you're free to go."

"I guess I am."

We stood and stared in different directions. Four burgers and eight beers were worming their way through my system, and I tossed my cigarette to the floor.

"I gotta go take a dump," I said. Henry stared into the dusk. I went back inside and avoided looking at anyone.

The bathroom was one of those oft-soiled places that looked infectious no matter how clean it actually was. The grime was so beaten into the porcelain and metal there was no such thing as really removing it; you could just scrub away that day's growth and hope for the best. I paused for a moment upon entry, reviewing my options. Depressed, I selected a stall with the minimal amount of obvious defecatory mishaps, checked the lock, and went to work.

I sat there and stared thoughtlessly at the stall door before me. I had a meditative approach to lavatory visits. You got few enough chances to just sit and enjoy some industrial-strength silence. The bathroom was a perfect place to do it.

The outer door opened and I closed my eyes against the invasion: a perfectly squalid lavatory, ruined. When I heard Bickerman's voice, I shuddered.

"Monster!" he hissed. Then, running water. "Goddamn monster!"

I waited a moment to see where he was going with that, eavesdropping being one of my more favorite activities. All that followed was some moaning, so I cleared my throat.

"Christ, Bickerman, you ain't married yet."

Nothing for a moment. I sat and listened to my guts gurgling within me, begging for some sort of action on my part. It was the proximity of Bickerman. He always stirred up my digestive system. It was the simultaneous disgust and leering hope for fun. He was the most entertaining monkey I'd ever had.

"Tommy," he finally said, sounding winded. "You doing anything deviant in there?"

"Yes. But it's all scatological."

"Can you believe That Stupid Fuck?"

That was Mikey. Bickerman always referred to Mike as "That Stupid Fuck" in private.

"Some huge number of idiots in this grand country blow their hands off every summer playing with fireworks. That's why they're illegal. The Stupid Fuck had it coming. Besides," I added as a sop to their inexplicable friendship, "he got off lucky with some burns. He won't even be a visual liability at your wedding, much is the pity."

"Christ, don't bring up the nuptials. I'm considering fleeing the country."

"Don't be such a cunt, Bickerman. Besides, she'd find you. And sic her faithful minions Kelly and Florence on you. You'd be lucky to be brought back without significant facial reconstructive surgery required."

"I swear, Tommy, sometimes that bitch just crawls under my skin and does a little tap dance. Sometimes I just want to belt her one to just shut her the fuck up. The Bitch is out there now, telling me, over and over again, that this is the quality of friend I hang out with. Guys who get poor Mike to almost burn his face off."

The Bitch, of course, was Bickerman's inscrutable secret code for Mary. She was convinced that Mikey was an innocent, and Henry and I were evil bastards. She was pretty much right, but the contest of wills was getting messy.

"Ah, the quality of friends. We're terrible. Say the word, *mi amigo*, and we'll fade away. Promise. No hard feelings."

"Fuck that. Without you and Hank, all I'd have is That Stupid Fuck to keep me sane in this goddamn world of women I've fallen into. At least you and Hank know how to have a good time, and keep your mouths shut. Mike wouldn't know what to do with himself."

I had nothing more to say on the subject. I sat and stared. After a moment, I heard the door open and shut, and I was alone in the bathroom again. The bastard hadn't bothered to say anything, just left. I was irritated for a moment, but Bickerman was far too entertaining to stay mad at. I wondered, with breathless awe, what wonders he'd get up to once he was *married*.

IV.

CHRISTMAS

I ran a shaky hand over my face and picked up the glass, held it up before me. I drank it fast, didn't even taste it. Nothing affected me anymore. I put it down on the bar hard and winked at the bartender. She nodded and held up a finger. I'd been drinking here all day. We had a system worked out.

I closed my eyes and there it was: huge, invisible, coming closer. A million trees shivering in terror, me kneeling in the damp grass, arms out, waiting.

A group of really drunk guys were singing carols near the juke, where some evil person, long since fled, had plunked down six dollars' worth of John Denver and the Muppets. Everyone thought this was hilarious. I tried to ignore it. The bar was decked out in blinking lights and tinsel, and the bartenders were all wearing Santa hats. I opened my eyes and looked at myself in the mirror behind the bar, which was obscured by bottles and tinsel and disgusting fake snow-in-a-can spelling out holiday wishes. I noticed I was wearing a Santa hat, too. I didn't remember owning a Santa hat.

Hands on my shoulders, aftershave, and a heartily bullshitted "Ho-ho-ho" and Mike had found me. I raised an empty glass at him. He was blurry, and I felt nauseous.

"What are you doing here, Hank?" Mike wanted to know. "Is anyone else here? I'm here with some work buds. I think everyone else is over at Ray's."

"I'm hiding from Bickerman and Tom," I said truthfully. "I don't want to get ratted out, okay? So if you see them, you didn't see me."

Mike smiled his clueless grin. Kind of sweet, actually. "Hiding, huh? Owe some money?" he cackled. "Here, I'll buy you a drink."

The bartender slopped a shot glass and a beer in front of me, extracting a damp fiver from my pile and walking away without a word.

Mike chuckled. "Not kidding around, huh?"

Another cackle. I held up the shot glass to him and smiled a good imitation of a smile.

"All right," he laughed. "Buy *me* a drink."

I shook my head. I needed every dime for myself.

Finally, a flicker in his wall of insincerity. "O-kay. Guess I'll just get back to my work buds. See you around, Hank. Hope you feel better."

I just about let him go and then caught him by the arm. I didn't look up at him and had to swallow back vomit before I could talk. "I mean it, Mike. Don't tell Bickerman and Tommy where I am. They'll ask."

"Okay, Hank, okay."

I let him go. I sat there and swallowed reflexively for a while, trying to keep a lid on whatever shameful expulsion was coming up, and finally stood up and weaved my dramatic way to the bathroom.

Kneeling in the crud that coated every disgusting tavern restroom everywhere in the world, I heaved into the toilet and tried not to notice anything or smell anything or, indeed, have any of my five senses functioning at all. When I was reasonably sure I'd hit empty, I sat down on the damp floor and leaned against the stall wall and lit a cigarette. The busy traffic of the bathroom ignored me, for a while. There were plenty of places to piss, and no one wanted to know about the guy sitting in pisswater, until one of them knocked on the stall door.

I closed my eyes again.

It was dark and windy; the wind was epic. Booming, hissing wind. Moving through the tall grass and the trees. I was tiny and forgotten. Insignificant.

Something was coming.

It was huge. Its footfalls made the ground tremble. There was the crack of trees tearing loose as it came. I stared into the gloom and all I could see was purple sky and black trees. All I could feel was the wind. I was so tiny, I would be stepped on and flattened into the soft loam and never noticed.

"Buddy, you okay?"

I shook my head. Kept my eyes closed. "Sure."

"Some of us gotta take a dump, you know?"

Christmas Eve, party time, and some have yet to master their bowels. I opened my eyes again and waved my cigarette around. "All right. Don't blame me for what's in here. It's only half my fault."

Feeling less wobbly, I stood up, damp with pisswater and wondering what I was going to smell like to other people. I pushed open the stall door. A beefy guy in a suit greeted me.

"Jesus," is all he said.

I decided to go get some air. I left my coat on the chair. I left my money on the bar. I pretended I couldn't see Mike on the way out. I walked outside into the snow and the wind and just kept walking. It was about two miles to my apartment, and I figured I might die on the way.

Numb and persistently nauseous despite my best efforts, I stopped across the street from my building to stare.

"Fuck me." I repeated it in my head: *Fuck me.*

Tom and Bickerman both grinned at me. They were warm and plump with coats and scarves, looking hale and hearty. Bickerman, with a flask in one hand, spread his arms.

"Henry!" he bellowed. "Thank God you're alive!"

I wasn't, really, but why bother telling them that? They were blocking the front door anyway. I hung my head and stumbled toward them.

"Christ," I heard Tom say, "you look like fucking terrible. Maybe you need to see a doctor."

"How far did you walk like that?" Bickerman demanded.

I shrugged. My feet were completely numb. I imagined them as black blocks of ice. "How long have you guys been here?"

"A while," Tom groused, snatching the flask from Bickerman. "We heard you were all by yourself somewhere, drinking. We were a little worried. We tried a few of your usual haunts but didn't find you, so we came here to wait."

He offered the flask to me. I took it gratefully and sniffed it. Brandy. I took a swallow and felt worse. "Very kind of you."

Bickerman slapped me on the back and pushed me gently toward the door. "Let's get inside."

Doom. I felt it nibbling at me. I'd been fleeing the Doom, but the Doom had found me. Such is the doom of men, that they forget. The temple of doom. My apartment. I was finding it difficult to stand upright. "Anything to get you guys out of sight. I don't want my neighbors getting a good look at you."

We took the stairs in single file: Tom, me, the Bick. Bickerman kept his hand on my back, as if he was pushing me up before him. There was some confusion at the door as we sorted ourselves out so I could open things up. Then we stepped inside. It felt oppressively hot, as if my skin were burning.

"Man, Henry, this place is a fucking sty," Tom complained. He spun around. "Where do you keep your liquor?"

I nodded at the upper cabinet over the stove. He glanced at it, then looked back at me. He sat down at the kitchen table and took his gloves off. I looked them both over while Tom rubbed the cold from his hands and Bickerman made a show of walking around the kitchen, looking the place over. They were both wasted. Tom had the sharp-eyed look he gets when he's loaded, and Bickerman never can sit still when he's fucked up. I concentrated on breathing. I kept my eyes on Tom because he was sitting still. He stared back at me. He appeared to be vibrating.

"Got any coffee?" Bickerman suddenly demanded, turning to face me.

"Instant. Maybe," I said.

He nodded, but didn't actually ask for any. I was suddenly exhausted. Keeping my eyes on both of them, I pulled out one of my chairs and sat down. I felt like I could've fallen asleep sitting right there across from Tommy.

Bickerman sat down too, next to Tommy. His so-blond hair was almost white and was standing up in a weird way. His stubble was dark, though, and against his pale skin it made him look sick.

"We're just making sure you're okay, buddy," Bickerman suddenly said. "It's been a tough time for all of us."

"You most of all, I'm sure," Tommy added. Bickerman took the lead as if it were manna from heaven.

"You most of all. All three of us. It's a terrible situation, and we're all having trouble handling it. All of us."

Tommy nodded slowly. "The point is, we stick together. Support each other."

I nodded, because they wanted me to acknowledge this bullshit. "I'm depressed. So what? I was having a few drinks. So what? You don't have to worry about me."

Their pretended indignation was amusing. They threw up their hands, and Bickerman stood up again.

"What! Listen to this guy!" he exclaimed.

"Hell, Hank, we know that!" Tommy said heartily. "No one's worried about you. Well, we're *worried* about you, about your health. Your well being. But not about anything else."

Tommy smiled at me. Tom's smiles are hideous, and he uses them only when really trying to get by.

"I'm fine," I lied. I felt like I was stuffed with poison and bleeding antifreeze all over myself. I felt like the kitchen table was my new best friend, that without it I'd fall over, that it was the most comfortable place in the universe.

"Hell, Hank. It's Christmas Eve. We're all out with friends, Luis is dressed up as the thinnest fucking Santa Claus in the world, and you're at some strange bar where That Stupid Fuck goes with his *work buds* drinking yourself into an early grave," Tom laid it out for me. "Denise asked about you. Kelly and Flo wondered."

"Miriam was really hoping you'd show up," Bickerman added, giving my refrigerator a thorough inspection.

And I was suddenly glad for the booze and the nausea, because I could let that pass over me without a flinch, staring Tommy in the face.

"I'll see everyone tomorrow at Flo's party," I offered. I couldn't keep this up much longer, I knew. "I'll be in a better mood. I just get depressed around the holidays . . . drank too much . . . need sleep." I was struggling to give them enough. Feeding them is exhausting. Had been for weeks, ever since Thanksgiving.

"Jesus, listen to the living corpse here," Bickerman said good-humoredly. "My fucking wife's dead, and I've got more cheer and holiday spirit."

I forced a grin onto my face, my skin cracking and my teeth bleeding. "Jesus, it's three in the morning, and I just walked two miles in the fucking snow with bad shoes and no coat. I'm already hung over and you idiots are sitting in my kitchen. You'd be fucking depressed, too."

Tom laughed, glancing at Bickerman. "Henry's a bit cranky, huh? C'mon Henry. It's fucking Christmas. Spare us some good cheer!"

Bickerman pulled the flask from Tom's hand and toasted us.

I looked at them from under my eyebrows. They were pale, the cold itself, the winter, manifested in my kitchen in the forms of old friends. Old acquaintances. Old young men. Tom's hair was getting long, curling everywhere, a vital head of hair. He was wearing a vest and a tie, undone, perfectly rakish, calculated. Bickerman's hair stuck up from his head like a wig, like brush bristles. His face was pale and red at the same time, a flush. Thin but jowly. He was wearing a long, beat-up old overcoat he'd had for years. Mary had forbidden him to wear it in public during her Remaking Bickerman campaign early in their relationship. He'd obeyed but had worn it all the time since she'd died.

Suddenly, he thrust the flask at me, shining with Bickerman saliva. "Come on, Henry, have a fucking Christmas drink with us, you god-damn pussy."

"Bick," Tom said calmly, "let him alone."

"Fuck you," I muttered.

Bickerman stared at me. "What did you say, you little cocksucker?"

"Bick!" Tom snapped.

"I said fuck you." My voice was level. Quiet. I lacked the energy for more volume. "I said get the fuck out of my apartment. I said I was drinking alone because I didn't want to see either of you. That's what I said."

For a moment, nothing but the sound of breathing in my small place.

Bickerman stared at me with his half-smile, his pre-fight face, like he was still in high school. Tom stood up and stepped between him and me, and I was grateful, because I felt like all my bodily fluids had pooled in my feet, and I doubt I could've raised my arms to fight. I was sweating.

"All right, Henry," Tom said quietly. "We've obviously imposed on you. Let's go, Bicky."

Tom, contemptuous of Bickerman as always. I listened to them shuffle out, eyes closed and head down. The click of the door shutting behind them followed me down into sleep.

The next morning: Christmas Day. Children and religious types wetting themselves in excitement, the rest of us greeting it as the overgrown commercial hell it really was, wandering through the day in wide-eyed despair for the whole race. Or at least the Christians. My head came up off the table and out of the little lake of drool I'd created. I winced, collapsing into a stiff-shouldered scream of cramped muscles, my entire body demanding that I return to my original position and soak in the drool for a bit longer. I resisted and was punished by the cascading misery of headache, nausea, and numb legs. I knew that if I stood up, I'd have to throw up, and if I didn't stand up, my head would explode. And I wasn't sure I'd be able to stand up anyway. And I wasn't even sure my head wouldn't explode in any event, no matter what I did.

Twisting minimally and straining my eyes, I turned to see the clock on the wall behind me. It was one in the afternoon, and I was late for so many things that the only reasonable response was to put my head back down and close my eyes.

Then the phone rang, and I once again popped up into sudden, horrifying pain. I jumped up, fell over my own feet, and landed ass-first on the kitchen floor.

"My God," I muttered from somewhere above myself, "is this the end of Henry?"

With no better options, I began to crawl to the phone, dragging my useless body behind me like a shell. It was freezing, though I remembered feeling burnt by blasting heat the night before. I pulled myself across ice, across Freon, across internal weather I hadn't suspected existed in my small apartment. Four seasons in one apartment—maybe there was a Sahara in the bathroom.

At my desk, I pulled myself up into my chair with amazing reserves of desperation, thinking to myself that I didn't want to be an invalid, that I had to figure out ingenious ways of living without the use of my legs, which had obviously withered away while the circulation was cut off overnight. I lifted the receiver and put it gently against my ear, thinking that this would be how I ended my days, dragging my useless husk of a body behind me, clumping along the floor, hung over forever.

"Hello?"

The number six was blinking red on my answering machine.

"Henry? Are you okay?"

It was Denise. I hadn't spoken to her in a long time.

"Fine." Aside from having lost my legs, which will likely have to be cut off and my torso glued to some sort of wheeled dolly so I can pull myself along. "Why?"

"It's the afternoon, everyone's wondering when you're coming? And—" I could hear her clicking her teeth together, which was what she did when she was unsure. "And Bick and Tom said they saw you last night and you weren't looking too good."

"I'm fine." I will be begging for dimes from the good people who will look down on my truncated form with pity. "I wasn't feeling well. They were very drunk. You know how that story ends."

Another moment of teeth clicking. "Well, are you coming? Flo's got quite a spread here. It's really impressive."

The number six again, blinking. "Well, as I've already missed most of the family events scheduled for today, I guess I've got nothing cluttering up my schedule." Except possibly filling out loan applications for the shockingly expensive surgery to remove my blackening, rotted legs and purchasing their plastic replacements.

"Okay. I'll tell everyone you're still coming." More teeth clicking. "Hank? I'm glad you're coming."

Will she still find me charming when I'm a horrible cyborg with mechanical legs? "See you there, Neesie."

I hung up and regarded my stiff, numb limbs. Pins and needles had begun to torture me.

Flo, we'd all discovered shortly after acquiring her as a friend through Mary, threw a huge, no-holds-barred party every Christmas Day. It goes on all night and is designed for people to come to after they've been driven crazy by their families. It was the sort of party that can potentially break leases.

Already a few brain cells lighter from the night before, I considered, briefly, teetotaling. As the afternoon progressed and the blood returned to my legs, the poison seeping out of my stomach, and my own family berating me telephonically for what seemed like days for missing all the important family events, I changed my strategy and decided that having a few less brain cells was exactly what I needed. I showered, neglected the shave, and dressed up in nice pants, a crisp white shirt, and a natty old sport coat. I was an unshaven mess, but managed, I thought, to look halfway disreputable, instead of just seedy.

I flipped my wine bottle in the air and rang the bell. Flo lived in a cheap, one-story house that she loved, she said, precisely because she could beat the shit out of it and not lose much on the investment.

The door tore open. Flo, wearing tight black jeans and a flimsy white blouse, pulled me in for a wet kiss on the lips and a fierce hug. Her red hair was slicked back and pulled into a ponytail. She felt wonderful. She smelled better.

"Henry!" she breathed in my ear. "I was worried you weren't coming!"

To avoid having her sense my sudden and improbable erection, I pushed away and struck a pose.

"Dahling!" I shouted joyously. "I wouldn't miss it! Now," I continued in a more businesslike tone, "where is the liquor?"

"In me, mostly," she giggled, putting her arms around my neck and leaning forward, looking up at me. "I'm wasted." She pulled me inside. "Come on in! I gotta go hostess. By the way, Bick was looking for you before."

I held onto her arm tightly. "You don't go anywhere until you show me where the goddamn liquor is."

She laughed and pulled me into a warm, damp sea of people until we stood before a card table piled high with bottles, damp and cool, an oasis. "Here you are. Poor Henry. Mix whatever you like. There's food around here, too. Somewhere."

I shook my head. Even though she had gone, I muttered. "No food, thanks. Food just makes me sick."

I examined the bottles with delight. Not top-shelf stuff, but adequate. I poured three fingers of bourbon into a plastic cup and then a finger or so of soda. I drank it fast, coughed, almost died from blood rushing into my spongy brain, bursting vessels, and then stood there gasping, warm again, burning. I poured four more fingers of bourbon into the cup, and another finger of soda. Armed, I turned to face the crowd, and found Tom grinning at me, not a foot away.

"You're looking better," he said around a stubby cigarette.

"Working on it, trust me," I said as brightly as I could, holding up my cup. "Merry Christmas."

"Yeah, yeah, merry fucking corporate holiday," he replied. "Neesie's been asking for you."

I stared at him, conscious of having nothing to say. Tom and I used to chat amiably for hours, saying nothing but not feeling it. Just making noises at each other. Waiting for newbies to walk by so we could skewer them. I stared at him, then knocked back the rest of my drink.

"Make you one?"

I was already drunk, five minutes in. As I waited for Tom to reply, seeing him devise some sort of witty response to a simple question, I knew I'd need every drop.

"Sure, though I could just stand near you and breathe the fumes," he finally said, eyes twinkling.

I nodded desperately, slopping booze into plastic cups. Christmas carols in the air.

"Cheers!" I shouted and sipped my drink for a change, feeling a little flushed and woozy.

"Listen, didn't mean to impose on you last night, buddy," he said with what passed, for Tommy, for sincerity. "Bick had a load on, and he got an idea in his head. Shit, we stood freezing our asses off on your stoop for a fucking hour. The drink is good, but the drink makes you fucking stupid."

I knocked my cup against his. "Amen, brother. Now, if you'll excuse me, I have to mingle with my people, before they grow wroth that I have ignored them." I winked, sucking more life-giving booze. "My fans, you know."

"Sure," he winked back obscenely. "The women have been asking after you. You know their judgment has been clouded by the drink, too."

I forced a smile. "I'm popular, huh?"

He nodded. "Don't let it go to your head."

I moved through people I knew, people I'd known for years. Some of them made faces at me, as if they wanted to say hello, touch base, get caught up. I hadn't spoken to many of them in quite a while. I gave them all my best polite smile and kept moving. I had no time. I had no energy. And I was not nearly drunk enough.

I didn't know where I was going, but what I found there was Miriam.

She was standing almost directly in my way, as if she'd plotted my physics, and, knowing my speed and my direction, knew where I would end up. She stood looking in the other direction, wearing a pair of low-riding faded jeans apparently painted onto her hips, and a halter top that reminded you that she had nothing on beneath it. Her hair was loose and long. She was standing with a wine glass in one hand, the other hand on her hip, lazy, just a girl who knew she was gorgeous. You hated it about her, but you couldn't help yourself. It terrified me.

I stopped and stared at her, too long, mouth open, hands forgotten, locked up; she turned, saw me, and smiled. It looked like any other smile a pretty girl gives to a guy she doesn't dislike, or maybe even likes. Wide eyes, goofy grin. Nipples and no make-up. I broke out into a sweat of terror, took an involuntary step back.

"Well?" she said over the noise. "Come here and give me a hug, dammit!"

I made my legs work and she enveloped me in an embrace, pressing herself against me fiercely. She surprised me with a kiss on the lips, a quick peck of wine.

I pushed her away as gently as I could. She went partway, keeping her hand on my elbow. I felt like a jackass: We'd just been at the funeral not two months ago, crying, drunk as lords and not a sinful thought in our heads.

We stood that way for what seemed like a very long time.

"So, how are you?" I asked, making noise. I wished I'd taken more booze with me.

"Okay," she said somberly. Then she brightened. "Tonight is the first night I've really been out somewhere, and I decided it was going to be the beginning of a new leaf for me. I'm going to get drunk and dance and relax."

I licked my lips. She was looking for a response from me, but I felt made of tinder, dry and spidery. I opened my mouth and small, white spiders came out.

"Me, I'm just looking to pass out soon."

I followed this with a smile, or what I imagined was a smile; it may have been a gash in my face or a deepening chasm of darkness welling up to swallow me, the party, the whole world. Based on Miriam's expression, the latter seemed most likely.

And then there was Luis.

He came to us in slow, silent motion, a drunken smile on his face, a hand on my shoulder, then an arm around my shoulders. He stood there a moment nodding and looking from me to Miriam.

"You are," he said slowly, his English particularly elastic, "beautiful."

"Me? Or her?"

Miriam giggled. Luis collapsed in what looked to me to be faked laughter. When he came up for air, I realized he wasn't faking.

Suddenly, he grew mock-serious. "Naturally, I cannot mean you, Henry, for you are not beautiful. I referred to the lady."

Miriam offered a half-assed curtsy. "Thank you, sir."

"Henry, where have you been? I was making myself ridiculous last night and you were not there to enjoy it."

I shrugged. "I was hiding from mine enemies, Luis. But I'm here now. Do something ridiculous, and I'll enjoy it."

He smiled craftily. "That will require more drinking, as it did last night. I will come find you when I am sufficiently ridiculous." He turned away. Miriam giggled again.

"I miss you guys," she said, looking me in the eye. I looked away.

"Uh, I need a drink," I said, meaning it. I turned and walked away from her, sweating, desperate. But the room was seeded with mines, and Denise caught me by the jacket before I'd made it halfway to the bar. In self-defense I finished the watery remains of my cocktail in one gulp and split my face into the biggest grin I could manage.

"Neesie!" I enthused. "You look great!"

I quivered with the effort.

"So do you," she replied without conviction. I appreciated the lie. I knew how I'd woken up in the morning; I knew it was stamped on my face, the latticework of the scratches in my kitchen table imprinted on my papery drunkard's skin.

I wasn't lying, though; she looked fantastic, the usual post-breakup glow that made all your ex-lovers briefly burn brighter than ever before. Maybe it was the sudden weight loss associated with grief, maybe it was the decision to start actively attracting men again. Maybe it was just the way they were suddenly free of you, the dead weight that had been clawing at their feet all this time, making them tired.

"Tommy said—"

I held up my hand. "Don't ever believe Tom. I sure don't. I categorically deny anything he said."

"You used to like each other's dark sides. You were even beginning to look alike."

I squinted at her as I practiced my one-handed cigarette light. I puffed smoke. "I didn't believe a word he said then, either."

She seemed at a loss for words for a moment. "How are things? How's work?"

I looked at her sadly. Work. We'd never had to talk about bullshit polite crap like that before. How's work, the weather's been, at least you have your health . . .

"Work's good."

. . . not the heat the humidity another day another dollar you've lost weight . . .

"What else have you been up to?"

I opened my mouth. Then shrugged. "Drinking, mostly."

She smiled at first, a familiar and heart-wrenching there-you-go-again smile. Then she lost it. I thought, where the hell is Luis when you need him?

"Why don't you and Tommy hang out anymore?" she asked.

"To hell with that. He was sitting at my kitchen table last night. Him and Bickerman. Bickerman and him. We were all drunk as lords."

She nodded, still looking at me with intolerable sadness. "They were looking for you last night."

"They found me." I glanced at my empty glass as if just noticing that it was empty. "You want a drink? I'm heading to the bar."

"What? No—Henry, wait."

I paused and kept my eyes away from hers.

"Why do you have to hate me?"

How could I answer that? She had broken up with me, but that wasn't it. I didn't blame her. I didn't want to be with me, either, but I couldn't explain, especially not then. Maybe there had been a slight window of opportunity for honesty. If so, it had been very brief, and in my booze-logged condition back in November I'd had zero chance of noticing it.

I gave her the only truth I could.

"I don't hate you," I said, turning away. I almost made it to the bar, when I saw that Tom and Bick had made themselves at home there, mixing their own brands of drinks. I spun on my heels and froze, unsure until I spied the bathroom, marked with both a male and female reindeer, invitingly open, unoccupied. I pushed for it and kicked as hard as I could, drifting into it, shutting the door slowly, inconspicuously, eyes shut against the jinx, wishing myself temporarily invisible. Almost making it, until someone pushed gently against the other side.

"Henry, what in hell are you doing?"

Good Christ, I thought, it's Miriam; where does she find the energy?

I sank back onto the toilet and slumped there, and she pushed her way in carefully, shutting the door behind her and leaning against it. She smelled wonderful and listed slightly until she located her balance, buried somewhere under the gallon or so of wine she'd taken on. A full glass, dark red, was in one hand. When had that happened? Time was getting away from me. I considered reaching out and taking the glass.

"You're hiding," she accused.

I nodded, staring at the floor. "I'm trying to."

When I glanced back up, half the wine was gone. I blinked in amazement. She looked to weigh about ten pounds; I had no idea how it was possible for her to drink like that.

"What's wrong? Henry, I wish you would tell me."

I wanted to. Suddenly, sitting on the toilet in Flo's house with the surviving Harrows sister, I wanted to tell everything and be absolved, or damned, but rid of it just the same. I looked up at her beautiful face and might have opened my mouth to tell it all. I think I even opened my mouth, but it just hung there, useless. As I watched, she drained her glass and set it with drunken care on the sink.

She was on me. She was soft hair and diffused perfume and heat and soft, yielding skin. I was frozen, I was stone, I was hard and useless, and my mouth hung there as she kissed it.

My whole body was in slow motion.

First there was the return kiss, ancient instinct, genes struggling and informing my involuntary muscles that there was a good genetic chance, decent hips, good long-term child survival. Just the minute and graceful movement of a few muscles, in perfect sync, meeting her and leading her and following her. This seemed to go on for an hour, and that low, rising volume roar in the back of my head was—

I closed my eyes in dumb autopilot. Opened them. Blinked, and I wasn't kissing Miriam, I was making out with Mary. She was staring at me as we kissed, and winked.

I convulsed. Reached out. Stiffened, half stood, and shoved her away, and she stumbled back and hit her head on the medicine cabinet.

"Fuck!" she hissed. "Henry!"

I held out one hand, palm out. Warding her off. I was panting. "Don't. Don't."

For a moment we were suspended there. Panting, staring. My hand out, my one thin defense. Mary's ghost in the room with us, snarling, broken. Miriam tore the door open, stepping out of the bathroom with an almost calm, businesslike manner. I shut the door after her and splashed water on my face for what seemed like a day, then opened the door myself. Tom and Bickerman were standing there.

Tom opened his mouth to say something, so I shouted "Boys! To the bar, where you will do shots with me!"

They exchanged a look as I threw my arms out. "Uh, Hank," Tom started, but I cut him off.

"Nonsense! We're all friends here. Have a fucking drink with me, you cocksuckers."

My face was cheerful. I trapped them both in an embrace and began gently pushing them along with me. At the bar, heart pounding, I did a little jig to extricate myself from them, grabbed a bottle, tossed it into the air with drunken exuberance and caught it, leering at them.

"Tequila!" I barked. They both grinned, smiles blooming on their faces, surprised out of hiding.

I gathered up three half-assed shot glasses and poured a dollop of tequila into each, passed them out, and held mine aloft.

"To friendship!" I announced. This amused them, the bastards, and we clinked glasses and swallowed liquor. I broke out into a sweat. It was cheap stuff. Bick broke down into coughs.

"Flo . . . not sparing . . . any fucking . . . expense," Tom managed, grinning.

"Again!" I shouted and brought the bottle up.

They acquiesced amiably enough, holding out their glasses (Bick holding his up from his position nearer the floor) and I filled them both almost halfway. Tom eyed me as if watching for sudden moves. Hanging onto the bottle, I held up my glass again, but this time Tom, with the Glee dancing around him like a cloud, beat me to the toast.

"To Mary!"

This caused Bick to choke again, and Tom and I locked stares as we drank.

Bick came up for air, and as I brought the bottle up, Tom grabbed Bick's glass and held both out for me. I grinned.

"No mas," Bick coughed weakly. *"No mas, por favor!"*

"Yes, *mas*, goddammit," I said mildly. "Don't be a party pooper, Bicky."

"He means don't be a pussy," Tom offered, winking at me.

Bick came up red-faced and gasping. "Fuck you both," he growled, grabbing the glass from Tom and slopping tequila everywhere. He held it up and waited.

"Well, bright boys? What are we toasting this time?"

"Nothing," I said quickly, before Tom could get smart. I was sweating freely and feeling woozy. "Just fucking drink."

I swallowed liquid nausea and nodded. The world was coming at me in waves, gently lapping at the edges of my sight.

I realized with a slow drooling embarrassment that I was clutching Tom's lapels in an effort to keep from sliding to the floor. He was stumbling, trying to support my sudden weight, and looking down at me with Glee-filled amusement. It was infectious, and I felt laughter fighting with my rising gorge.

"Is this," I panted with suppressed giggles, "the end of Henry?"

Tom's laughter followed me down.

"You awake, dummy?"

Denise resolved into clarity, and I instantly wished she hadn't. I felt digested.

"Christ," I moaned thickly, "they took the legs, didn't they?"

"What?'

I moaned. I looked around. "Where the hell am I?"

"Flo's spare bedroom."

"How long have I been out?"

"About three hours. The party's still going on."

"I feel terrible."

"No, you feel *terribly*."

"Not one of your more endearing features," I groused, "correcting people's grammar, and being wrong about it."

She shrugged. "At least I have endearing features."

"Ouch." I stretched experimentally. "Tom and Bick still here?"

She nodded. "Terribly drunk. They keep trying to come up here to bother you, but we won't let them."

"We being—"

"The Ladies Auxiliary."

We existed in companionable silence then. I closed my eyes and felt a small portion of myself for damage. There appeared to be nothing permanent. The idea of sitting up worried me, so I tabled it for later discussion and just lay there, swallowing the urge to tell her everything, to go back to the days when she was the first person I told anything to. I'd resented it and hated her for it, the gentle probing, the constant attention and interest. I'd hated it. I'd hated her. Finally, I'd had a secret too big for Denise and had to let her go. I swallowed it back.

"You don't have to sit there," I said, kindly, I thought. "Go back downstairs, have fun. Find out what jokes they're making about me."

"I don't mind."

She said this simple thing so nobly, so goddamn-awfully full of wonderfulness, that I couldn't wait to kick her in the ass when she left the room. Wonderfulness just irritated me. Through superhuman effort I swallowed back something horrible and just lay there experimenting with my nerves. I hated wonderfulness, I realized with a start, because I have none of it. It's just horribleness in me, a seething ocean of horribleness. I just ride the waves.

I didn't want to, but I had to keep talking to her. "Denise?"

"Yes?"

"Don't let Tom or Bick up here. Okay?"

"Too late, asshole."

Bick was at the door, and a hand snaked around from behind him and pushed the door open completely. Like bright, pale, softly glowing ghosts, it was Bickerman and Tom, Tom and Bickerman. They both weaved with a drunkard's lucky uprightness.

"Denise," Tom said carefully, working hard, I could tell, to not slur his words. "May we please have a moment with Henry alone?"

"No," she snapped. "Why don't you two leave him alone? Get your nasty little kicks elsewhere."

The two men started giggling, hanging onto each other. Tom turned to Bick and said in a stage whisper: "I think she's angry with us."

Bick made a shushing gesture, as if it were a big secret, and Tom composed himself with great effort.

"Ma'am, you have mistaken us," he said carefully. "We merely—"

"I know what you two idiots merely want to do. Now just leave him the fuck alone, okay?"

They both giggled uncontrollably.

"Out!" she shouted, shocking them both. She stood up and pushed Tom, hard, making him stumble back. "Out!"

Bick fell back under her glare, and she shut the door with an authoritative click of the latch. "goddamn assholes."

"Thanks," I said.

"Tell me what's going on with you three." It was more a demand than anything else. Then she laughed. "I feel like I'm always asking that about you and goddamn Tommy. I always want to know what you're up to."

I closed my eyes, and I was sitting in a dark wooded area. It was just before a serious storm. It was dark, *dark* dark because the moon had been hidden by the unseen clouds, and I was sitting in a clearing with the acidic smell of oncoming rain in the air and constant, invisible motion around me. I was sitting in the clearing because my legs had been previously removed, cleanly, surgically. When lightning flashed in the sky, the treetops were outlined against it, jagged. When the thunder had passed, the only sound was the restless shuffling of the leaves. It was like a constant tide, never receding, always covering half the distance and thus never wetting you.

When I opened my eyes again, Denise was staring at me with an intense wrinkle above her nose. "Are you going to tell me?"

"Oh, Christ, no."

Then I had Disapproving Denise, which had been my constant companion when we'd dated. So familiar. I had a fleeting stab of affection for Disapproving Denise.

I closed my eyes again. The feeling was enormous, an enormity somewhere just beyond the trees, stirring them with its gentle weight, unnoticed. The wind trickled over me, a faint touch, and the tall grass stirred in sympathy with my hair, and the leaves. I could sense, somewhere beyond the trees, a massive wave, a wall of water, heading toward me. The wind was just the air being pushed ahead of it. It was peaceful, waiting in the dark, listening closely for the first signs that it had finally arrived. The sudden vacuum. The roar so loud it was silence.

I opened my eyes. Denise had left.

V.

MARY'S WEDDING

I was trying unsuccessfully to identify the vegetable on my plate when there was a tickle and a whisper in my ear.

"Mare wants a divorce. Know any lawyers here tonight?"

I glanced up at Flo, who was smiling just slightly, a sad smile, a totally appropriate smile. Sadness at the situation but humored resignation because we all knew the marriage was doomed, and none of us would be much beyond slightly surprised if it really did end the same night as it began. I stood up, glad to leave the dinner behind. Henry looked up at me with those annoyingly puppyish eyes, terrified of being left alone. Sometimes Henry was a little annoying.

"Be back," I said, stroking his hair. "Girl business."

I fell into step with Flo, her holding up the skirts of her ridiculous dress to help her avoid falling on her face in front of everyone she knew.

"She's in the bathroom again," Flo said heavily.

I shook my head. "We shouldn't have let her drink. We all know it's a disaster when Mary drinks. She's a problem drinker."

"What were we supposed to do, sit on her?"

"For fuck's sake, she's been married for five minutes!"

"Are you yelling at me?"

"No." I took a deep breath as we left the room and turned toward the restrooms. "I'm just mad. I can't believe she's being so childish."

The women's room was bright white and smelled like ammonia. This was never an encouraging sign because the power of the chemical smell in a bathroom was, I thought, a good gauge of the mess it was masking. I hated mess. I hated things that smelled bad, too. The bathroom was blindingly white, but put me in mind of both.

Kelly was teasing her hair in the mirror. She glanced at us in reverse. "Third stall from the end," she said. She sounded tired.

Flo and I approached the only stall in use and knocked lightly. Mary's weeping was theatrical, and I felt better. Mary didn't ham it up when she was really upset. This was just another drama moment. I felt a strong urge to ignore it, let her soak in her own bullshit, but we had a wedding reception to get through. I decided I would sweet-talk her back out there and then tomorrow I could write her off.

I knocked again, louder. Snuffling noises, and then "Denise?"

"You okay, sweetie?"

A click and the stall door opened a little. I stepped inside and closed it behind me. Mary was sitting on the toilet, her dress rumpled, her makeup running. A big glass of Scotch in one hand and a cigarette in another. I had never seen someone unravel as quickly or as thoroughly as Mary did when bombed. It was breathtaking to watch.

"He's a cheating cocksucker. Already. *Already*, Neesie!"

Mary began to sob again. Everyone called me Neesie. I didn't know why. I hated it. "What happened?"

"He's a fucking prick, is what happened. I married a man and he turned into a fucking prick."

This brought up more tears, and I cooed and stroked her hair, trying to calm her down. I was uncomfortable leaning over her, but there was no way in hell I was going to make contact with the floor of this bathroom. The smell of ammonia was dizzying.

"But what *happened*?" I asked. I'd heard enough of Mary's drunken ramblings to know you had to guide the conversation firmly. It was either a firm hand and the patience of a nun, or slapping her across the face. Since it was her wedding day, I knew the latter wouldn't be acceptable.

"All day, at our *wedding*, he's eyeing every piece of ass that crosses his path. My own sister!"

At mention of Miriam, the whole bathroom seemed to fill with jelly. We all hated Ms. Hot Pants. Even Kelly, who loved everyone, eventually.

"My own sister!" Mary wailed. "It's like his eyes are glued to her ass!"

I took a deep, calming breath. "But what *happened*?"

"Nothing, yet. I haven't let the bastard out of my sight." I ignored this obvious bullshit and stood up.

"Jesus, Mare, nothing's *happened*?" Mr. Bickerman certainly was an ass, and I wouldn't be surprised if he was banging half the women attending the reception within a year, if he hadn't already, but I was damned if I was going to spend the party trapped in this skanky bathroom because of Mary's DTs or whatever. "Get out there and dance with your husband. He hasn't done anything. Tomorrow give him the cold shoulder about his roving eyes, make him suffer. But don't fuck up your own wedding over it."

Mary stared up at me with teary awe. "You really think so?"

I was beyond caring. I opened the door to the stall and nodded cheerfully. I took Flo's cigarette, took a puff, didn't inhale, and felt energized. I was going to get this bitch out of the bathroom by sheer force of will. "Come on, Mare, he's probably out there wondering where in hell you are. Let Flo fix your makeup, and then get out there before people start to talk."

She stood up. "You're right! I guess I am being silly."

There was more as she emerged, but I was already walking to the exit with lots of hip, feeling cocky. Kelly held out a hand as I approached, and I slapped it playfully. Denise the Great, kicking ass and taking names. And saving weddings. I made a mental note to stop hanging out with the Bickermans. They both sucked.

Smiling, I scanned the reception hall for Henry, who was dopey and who hung out with Tom too much, but was basically a nice guy. I found him, as usual, with Tommy. There was also Miriam, Ms. Hot Pants herself, giggling at something Henry said. Henry with what could only be described as a look of stunned disbelief on his face. Disbelief at what was a mystery, although "at being spoken to by Ms. Hot Pants" ranked high on my suspicions.

My Henry: lovable in many ways. Surprisingly thoughtful in many ways. An incredible ass, of course, but all men were. Henry was plagued with having been a quiet, ignored kid in high school and college. He never got laid, that much I can tell you. Now that he'd joined a more mature relationship with the rest of us through simple age, he was doing all right. But the ghosts of his lame past still haunted him, I thought; a girl like Ms. Hot Pants would never have paid him any attention in school. Now here she was, and merely by virtue of being ten years older, Henry looked good to her. Part of me didn't blame Henry for being flattered. Part of me wanted to knee Henry in the balls.

With Mary's smeared makeup fresh in my mind, however, I decided to be happy. I could knee Henry in the balls any time. They were my balls to knee. Tonight was for dancing and drinking and showing Ms. Hot Pants that she was a skank. I smiled and walked over to them with even more hips. Tom ran his reptilian eyes over me, as usual, and I had a brief flash of New Year's and his hands on my breasts in the den. I shrugged that off, too, because I was badass.

Miriam threw out her tits and laughed, holding onto Henry's arm. "Agreed!" she said in her stupid little-girly voice that all the pedophiles I found myself with on a daily basis loved.

"What are we agreeing on?" I said.

Henry and Ms. Hot Pants looked like guilty children, but Henry recovered nicely by pulling me toward him. Tommy looked as oily as always. The pert brunette at the bar shook her head and smiled slightly, as if it were all a big joke.

"Tom is causing trouble, and I'm supervising," Henry said.

I smiled at Tom, who shook his head. Tom could be a dark sort of charming sometimes. "Don't listen to him, Neesie; we're forming a drinking club here at the reception, invitation only. Care to join?"

He leered at me. Prior to New Year's, I'd been able to shoot him down when he leered at me, for Tom was one of those guys who didn't think it was a bad thing if he ogled your chest in front of everyone, and who didn't think you ought to be put out by it. I looked into his eyes and knew he had secret knowledge of me, though. It soured my mood a little. Thirty seconds—just half a minute. No time at all. But it meant everything, between Tommy and me.

I covered by laughing at him, which felt good even if it was forced. "Lord, I can't drink like that. I'd be in a hospital."

He winked at me, the bastard, and I could feel shadows of his hands on my breasts again, ten months ago now.

Ms. Hot Pants coughed lightly. "I'll see you guys back here later. I've got maid of honor duties, you know."

Yeah, I thought, like doing the groom and half the room. Whore.

"So," Henry asked stupidly. My Henry; it cheered me up, seeing him so stupid. "How was the girl business?"

"Buy me a drink, sailor. You don't want to hear about all that stuff."

"Sure we do!" Tommy said, leaning against the bar. "Hot chicks in formal wear, lacy underthings, all that jazz." He winked at me again, and an unbidden blush came upon me. "We want to hear it!"

Bastard. I hated Tommy.

Henry turned and ordered a white wine for me, and I stared at Tommy, who grinned back and winked again.

"Let's go sit down, want to?" I asked Henry.

He handed me a glass and nodded. "Yes. My head's spinning."

We were three steps when Kelly appeared in front of me. I blinked and pushed my eyebrows up as high as they would go.

"Oh, Lord, are you kidding? *It's been five fucking minutes.*"

Kelly smiled and shook her head. "Afraid not. Henry, sorry but I have to steal her again."

He sighed, releasing me. "As long as you're not just huddling to talk about me and my faults."

Kelly grinned wickedly and pulled me away before I could set his poor mind at ease. I turned and waved as I was dragged off.

"Now what?"

"Mare took your advice as far as leaving the bathroom. Unfortunately, we forgot to tell her to stop drinking. She's physically attacked Bick."

"Excuse me?"

"No harm done, because the Doofus just grabbed her wrists and laughed a little, handed her off to Flo and me, and then stumbled off. He seems to find it all quite amusing. The motherfuckery is just stunning."

A red coal of pissed-off anger settled into my stomach. "Jesus, is she twenty-eight or just eight?"

"Less," Kelly snapped. "We should never have let her drink."

I quoted Flo. "What were we supposed to do? Sit on her?"

Kelly broke into guffaws, the loud, sloppy laughs she was well known for. "Oh, shit, what an image. Thanks. I needed that."

"We're not heading back to the bathroom, are we?"

Kelly nodded. "You're damn right we are! 'Cause that's where I would want to spend the balance of my wedding day. In the bathroom."

We pushed the door in, and Flo just rolled her eyes at us, smoking a cigarette in a tense pose. "The honeymoon stall," she said tiredly. "You're on your own now. I need a drink badly."

I stomped to the end of the bathroom and pushed the stall door in roughly. I paused in surprise. Mary was sitting calmly, looking pensive.

I tried to recover my anger. "What now?"

She shrugged. "Nothing. I was being silly. I see that now. I'm just embarrassed."

"Oh." I glanced over my shoulder at Kelly, who shook her head and walked away, hands in the air in exasperation. "Don't worry. There's nothing to be embarrassed about."

"You all think I'm a drama queen or something."

"Yes," I admitted. "But we're all in here thinking that. There's nothing to be lost by going back out there. Besides, you have to dance with your husband."

She looked at me with glassy calm. I didn't like it and wanted to be out of there, wanted to be with Henry, who for all his goofiness is real and warm and sincere. Not crazy and weird like Mary.

"I do?"

"Yes, honey, you do. Everyone out there paid for the ticket. You have to give them the show."

"Okay."

She stood up and pushed past me, slumped and seemingly exhausted.

I stood staring at the toilet for a moment. The ammonia smell was strong, and I sucked air in through my mouth, carefully. When the door to the bathroom opened and closed, I slumped against the stall and sighed. Kelly appeared.

"Come on, Hard Luck Woman," she said. "Let's get the hell out of here before she comes back."

I needed new friends. I'd known Mary for years—though I'd never ascend to Kelly-dom, would I, no matter how long—and my reward for all those nights in the dorm hugging out her crying jags, all those nervous breakdowns, all those creepy double-dates with low-quality suitors—my reward was this hideous dress, half the fucking reception in the bathroom, and having to dance with fucking Mikey. My reward was spending more time with all of the assholes Mary'd inherited via David, these boys who thought I was stupid, who thought I was plain. Fuck them.

It was fascinating. Weddings were fascinating—the things you saw, and quite often—but then they were always the same things, because people are all the same. I knew, somehow, that there was another me, or several mes, wandering the earth. Having the same thoughts, working the same jobs. All of us, seeing the same things at weddings. It was depressing, and a little boring.

Take Henry, there. Looked philosophical enough, wandering out from the hubbub with his drink, smoking a cigarette, might be contemplating his mortality and the small part in the universe he plays. Struck a vaguely interesting pose. Then Little Sister Barbie found him, swaying over and scaring him half to death, and he just looked like a little boy, terrified but fascinated by a girl and not sure why. Or maybe *quite* sure, but it doesn't matter: Scared men are just not attractive.

Henry giving Miriam a cigarette and managing to make some desperate conversation with her. She had her tits in his face; she's enjoying it. Toying with him. Mary and I had a roommate like her in college. Used to walk around in her underwear, but, strangely enough, only when we had boyfriends around. Little Sister Barbie was like that: She didn't want to actually fuck anyone, just enjoyed being ogled.

Now here was an interesting twist: where Denise appears, all smiles, and then stops with a look like she'd just stepped on a bug in bare feet. Denise had about as much tolerance of Little Sister Barbie as she had cleavage in that horror show of a dress, which is to say none.

It's strange but compelling, watching the whole scene without dialogue, but I could make up the words:

HENRY: Gosh, you're so cute I can't remember my own name.

MIRIAM: Here, let me put my hand on your arm affectionately. Now I'll tell you that you're sweet. That ought to have you wanking off in the bathroom to me for months!

HENRY: Boy-howdy. I'm so oversteamed with lust I can't even see my stern girlfriend over there trying to set us on fire with the power of her mind.

DENISE: You're gonna have to wank off, buster, because even though you haven't done anything I can point to definitely, you won't be having sex with me any time soon.

Denise marching off without saying anything was a surprise; I thought she'd attack them. Violence was in the air, thanks to Mary. I was waiting for a big scene, a brouhaha, something exciting. She just turned and marched off, and Henry and Miriam didn't even see her.

I'm not sure what it is about weddings that brings out the ridiculous in people, though I'd guess it was the booze.

Henry watched Miriam strut off with his tongue lolling out, then collected himself and returned to the party.

Now the groom appeared, sans blushing bride, who should never be allowed to consume alcoholic beverages unless a sloppy witch is what you were hoping for. My best friend, Mary the Sloppy Witch. The groom, however, is one of those dry fellows who never appears drunk. It just fills up his hollow leg and he gets redder in the face, until you could read by the dying-sun light of his cheeks.

And behind him, miraculously, is Little Sister Barbie—Little Sister-*In-Law* Barbie—resurrected and undaunted, laughing and chasing after the groom as if she hadn't just been out here teasing Henry. He turned and she jumped onto him, laughing, and then hung on for dear life.

And Christ, get me some popcorn because here comes the bride, and the bride does not look happy. Round Three.

And *pow!*, the bride leaped into action with a loud slap across the groom's face. Little Sister Barbie got a sharp word out of the corner of her eye and slinked away, shaking her head but not looking too upset—strumpets never are because there's always another sucker willing to protect them.

And suddenly I was loving this wedding.

This is how I saw it: Buried under drama queens, I decided someone ought to be keeping the Sub-Doofus out of trouble. So I hunted for Henry because he obviously needed supervision.

I liked Henry. Pervading opinion was, actually, that he was a decent sort, if none too bright, and the only black mark against him was his toadying of the Loathsome Tom. This could be overlooked because we all knew that men stopped developing in their teenaged years, and relationships like that hardened into emotional concrete. Henry was a good enough guy. Neesie was needlessly hard on him. It was as if she were constantly probing him for the fatal flaw, and all because she thought she had caught him canoodling with Miriam once.

Upon reflection, I now believed that she hadn't, but there was no telling her that.

So, I hiked up my skirts and went searching for him, leaving his girlfriend pissed off in the bathroom. Eventually, I figured Mary would return there, and they would have a grand time bitching to each other. Or maybe they'd get drunk and have one of those college-era lesbian flirtations or something. I didn't care. I was sick of drama. I needed to have a drink with a man because all women were, by nature, drama queens. I even had my moments. Henry was the least-dramatic fellow I knew.

Unfortunately, he had no defenses against the little slut Miriam, and I was one of the few of us sober enough to have seen her strut drunkenly over to him and plant her ass on his lap as if it wasn't the most inappropriate thing she could have done. It was at that moment that I formed my child abuse theory of the Harrows girls and began looking at Mr. and Mrs. Harrows in a different, creepier light—it really was the only explanation for the Harrows girls' complete insanity. They were lucky to be so pretty.

Miriam draped herself on Henry and was practically making out with him, and my heart leaped, but for a moment I was frozen. I knew Denise was in the bathroom, and I was curious as to whether the Sub-Doofus, who I'd come to like quite a bit, would do something stupid or something gallant.

The joke was on me. The Sub-Doofus, displaying zero sentience or consciousness, didn't do anything. He sat there staring at Miriam as if she were a large and colorful bug that had chosen his lap as a landing spot. Which at least ruled out motherfuckery, I figured. If he was going to whoop in delight at this lucky event—hot drunk chick throws herself at you—he would have been halfway to the elevators by now, rummaging around in her bosoms. It was suddenly obvious that poor Henry was stunned and terrified. I felt an unexpected pang of sympathy for the Sub-Doofus and was startled into motion, intending to save him from her. But when I was just halfway there, Loathsome Tom popped from the crowd, plucked Miriam from Henry's lap in a surprising display of grace and coordination, and after what must have been a prize-winning conversation, bore her kicking and giggling into the dancing throng. Henry remained seated, looking like he'd just been kicked in the head.

I collected myself, took a deep breath, and smoothed my dress down. I walked over to the Sub-Doofus and waited for him to notice me and my amused smile. Maybe how good I looked in the dress too, but only a very little. I'd started out the day feeling fat and waterlogged, but a few glasses of wine had done me good. But he just sat there looking stunned.

"You're popular tonight," was the best I could do. He looked up, and I sat down.

"I was going to save you, but Tom beat me to it." He looked doubtful. "We're watching out for you, is all." He had no idea how much he needed allies by then. Well, some idea, surely, but not *enough* of an idea.

"Really?"

He could be adorable, that was for sure. I decided he needed to be reminded of his status as Sub-Doofus. "Denise is upset enough, you bad man."

That soured him, and I regretted it. He didn't seem like he was taking Denise lightly, and after watching Miriam at work, I thought it was pretty obvious he wasn't really doing anything with Miriam except not running away fast enough. I touched his shoulder lightly. "Listen, I sympathize. You didn't ask for this drunk coed to throw herself at you in front of your girl."

I thought that was pretty good, but he just leaned back and raised what I would describe as a pissed-off eyebrow. "The implication being that I wouldn't mind if Neesie weren't here."

Fucking Sub-Doofus. "You didn't exactly run away from her."

He snorted cigarette smoke from his nose. "Fuck you, Kelly."

I laughed at his cute little drama shtick—after the Big Sisters of Drama Queendom, he was just an amusing opening act. "Jesus, Henry, pay attention! We like you. The women are looking out for you. You can't get a better deal, baby."

He gave me an adorable wink and leaned forward with a casual, intimate sigh. "Where's Denise?"

"Nothing unusual. Bitching about you to Flo, probably."

He seemed pained by that, so I told him he was being an idiot again. He still refused to be comforted, so I stood up, holding out my hand. "Poor baby! Come on, dance with me."

He offered me a distrustful glance, but with a sly grin. I felt skinny and smart. I was not Mary, psychotic on my wedding day. I was not Denise, endlessly disappointed. I was not Flo, with Flo's unfortunate hair.

"Don't worry. I'm approved company. It's safe."

He looked at me as if he doubted me, and that made me feel good about the Sub-Doofus. I held out my hand, and he took it, shaking his head and smirking, but in a nice way.

. . . dreamy dreamy dreamy he smells like cigarettes but in a good way the room is spinning or I am spinning so soft so nice think I'll just

. . . hot breath oh that feels good. It's just his mouth and his hands, busy hands, and the spinning room and the sound of my stockings rubbing together Christ I'm so wet and the room is spinning or is it just me . . .

. . . swimming up and he's gone and I'm cold . . .

. . . I'm dreaming of an explosion, everyone is flying through the air and Tommy is carrying me again. Tommy is in the room. B is hiding behind the door, now he's yelling something over the wind and the rushing air. Then everything is quiet for a moment.

Jesus

. . . but the spinning isn't . . .

fucking

. . . so much fun . . .

Christ

. . . anymore . . . where's the dark come back . . .

are you two

. . . shut up SHUT UP . . .

fucking crazy?

. . . all they ever want I can't fight that kind of sustained effort and why bother when I don't mind they're so cute when they're stupid and anyway . . .

He's. I'm jupid.

Bill the goddamned door, you know.

. . . I used to lie in bed waiting for Mary to come home, climbing in through the window and I'd pretend to be asleep . . .

We're Mare's honor!

. . . and sometimes she was a real bitch but I liked the other times and she'd tell me how much fun she'd had . . . dancing . . . drinking . . . it always sounded so exciting. I loved hearing about it . . .

Hank? In for a moment?

. . . Henry, stolen from me . . . what he saw in the Ice Princess . . . he liked me . . . sweet . . . sweetie . . . Hankie . . .

Tom? Few minutes?

. . . Tommy . . . Loathsome Tommy Kelly calls him all the time . . . Loathsome Tommy, Loathsome Tommy, Loathsome Tommy . . .

Ugh. Sick. Sickarette.

s'cigarette

. . . she would climb in, red-faced and full of chatter, and she'd tell me about her boyfriends. Drinking beer in basements. Blowjobs in backseats. Hair-pulling the bitch who was chatting him up. Laughing about it all. I was so jealous of her . . .

Hoblem.

Jesus, Bick, you're a goddamn sister-in-law

Wah wah wah wah wah

. . . the whole room to myself now . . . away at school though, roommate silly girl cries all the time won't come out boys boys everywhere but I'm up on the third floor so no climbing in through the windows wouldn't be prudent . . .

Wokay, firoff shateen, shenunnerade

Okrist wrake ake

. . . ugh . . .

Swinging, not good. Motion, not good. Opened my eyes, and there's Henry, horribly upside down and all red in the face and I am swinging. Henry's good, calloused hands were under my shoulders, touching me. He glanced down at me.

"Hey, that's great. Please go back to sleep. Please."

So nice. I looked down at my dress, so wrinkled, and there's Loathsome Tommy, sweating, a cigarette dangling from his lips.

"Good evening, Ms. Harrows! This is all a dream, and Hank and I are angels."

Tommy laughed. When Tommy laughs it is as if his head has split open and a whole second set of teeth juts forward. It's all teeth.

"Hang on, Thomas, we're almost there."

"I'm buff, asshole, don't let the huffing and puffing fool you. Ms. Harrows, what in hell have you been eating? Lead pellets?"

"Weakling."

Tongue made of something bizarre and bloated. I opened my mouth but all that comes out are gummy sounds.

"I think she's trying to tell us something," Tommy said dramatically. "What is it, girl? Mike's trapped in a coal mine?"

"Let me down. I can walk," I managed. It sounded more like *lemme owne I calk*, but it would serve. Somehow my tongue had been broken.

There was a hotel smell in the air.

"No way, Mir," Henry said with a kind smile. "You'd fall and go boom. We're going to stretch you out on your bed and let you sleep this one off."

"We're noble motherfuckers, we are," Tommy said.

"Will you stay with me?" I mushed out. I wanted to have Henry near me in the dark, telling me his life story.

"She's a goer, I tell you."

"Shut up, Tom." Henry looked down at me. "Sweetie, you should just lie down for a while."

"You'll feel much worse when you wake up, trust me."

Swinging . . . swinging . . . I felt like a prize deer being carried back to camp.

"What the hell are you laughing at?" Tommy demanded.

"Are you going to gut me?"

He looked up at Henry. "What in hell did she say? It sounds like she's got marbles in her mouth."

"I hesitate to tell you what I think she said. It's kind of disturbing."

"Sexual overtures, eh? Miriam's a horn-o-plenty when it comes to entertainment. Here's her room, right?"

"Lord, I hope so." Henry was being very gentle and kind, taking time to bring me to my room like this. I wondered how I got here. I didn't seem to know.

"Christ, you're heavy, Harrows. Filled with liquor, I guess."

I was, that was true. Swinging . . . too much swinging, what was I a fucking rag doll . . .

"Let me down!"

"Okay! Okay . . . Tom, she looks a little green, let's get her upright."

"I'm sorry."

Henry, gorgeous, gorgeous Henry, smiled at me and flicked ash off his cigarette into the toilet, and then flushed it. "Don't sweat it, Mir. Happens to the best of us, eh? Come on, let's get you into bed."

I shook my head miserably. "Tommy's in it."

He gave me his best smile. "Don't worry, we'll roust him."

He started to stand up, but I pulled him down. I couldn't help it. "You think I'm an idiot, don't you?"

His brow creased in concern. "Hey! Hey, don't cry, for God's sake. Oh, jeeze, come on."

"I heard you guys. You aren't bad guys. You aren't."

I couldn't read his look; it was weird, kind of sad and careful. Then he smiled and gave me a nudge. "Tommy is, sometimes."

I love Henry. I love his way of getting so easily embarrassed. I love that I embarrass him. I love that he won't cheat on Denise. I love how he's so fiercely loyal, won't say a bad thing about Tommy no matter how obviously terrible he is. I love how he won't forsake me even when Denise wants him to.

"Come on. To bed with you."

"You don't really mean that."

I regretted it, the joke, because he made a sad face, and I knew I was being mean, and Henry deserved better, even if his worthless girlfriend didn't see it, even if her friends talk him down all the time. I see it.

"I'm sorry. Help me up? I promise to cooperate."

He helped me to my feet and walked me into the room, a hand just barely touching the small of my back, ready in case I passed out.

Loathsome Tommy was snoring on the bed, mouth open. Henry shoved him and he woke up with a start.

"Done yakking, then? Bedtime for Miriam. In you go, then."

"Come on, Tommy," Henry said. Sounding tired. Adult. Manly. "It's been a long night and we've got miles to go before we sleep and all that. Okay? So just let the girl get into bed, okay? Without molestation."

"*Hmmph.* No fun." But he got out of the bed and I crawled in, it only just barely smelled like Tommy, all cigarettes and evil purpose. I wriggled under the covers and instantly felt sleepy, too sleepy to ever wake up. I forced my eyes open.

"Thank you, Henry." I wanted to say more. To say everything. But Tommy was there. Ruining things. My head ached and my stomach ached and I felt hot and weak.

He smiled, and pushed some hair out of my face. "Jesus, Mir, don't *cry.*"

"Come on," Tommy said, "there's an open bar for another forty-five minutes. I haven't yet recouped my costs here."

They were fading away, and I rolled over anyway and wiggled my toes and thought of Scarlett O'Hara, for tomorrow is another day.

VI.

MONDAY

I've had a lot of Henrys in my life. I knew them well. The species.

Hell, I knew them all well. I arrived early and settled in down the block and across the street to wait. I was fuzzy and leaden. I'd managed to keep Bick at bay the night before, but my careful plans for a new sobriety had gone awry because of the new bartender at MacLean's. I'd quit my job and was literally walking around with the cliché cardboard box of my possessions—although my box only contained things I'd stolen off of other people's desks on my way out. I saw her through the big plate glass window of the pub. Young, brunette, skinny. Messy hair. My type. They were all my type, but her especially.

So I'd gone in and started ordering big. Johnny Walker Blue. Fat tips. I chatted her up relentlessly, every chance I got. Wallace Charm was powerful stuff.

I'd gone to bed bitter, with a dry dick and a pounding head. The morning hadn't improved things. Three donuts and a pitcher of black coffee had helped some, but it was still too fucking cold to be sitting on an Oldsmobile a half block away from Henry's apartment. Waiting for all of them to arrive.

I'd become an expert on Henry's block in recent days. I watched Hector emerge from his house across from Henry's building and juggle a travel mug of coffee, a newspaper, and a set of car keys as he walked to his car. Hector dressed like an important man, but his suits were cheap—though they fit well—and his car was fifteen years old and had a huge rust spot on the roof. He wore his money in gold on his wrists and around his neck. You saw Hector coming; you knew right away his soft spot was to belittle him, make him feel poor. The stupid fuck would start throwing cash at you just to prove you wrong, just to shut you up.

I glanced up at the second floor of Henry's building. The old woman was at her station, frayed pink bathrobe and crazy yellowed hair. She sat at the window most of the day, watching. I was pretty sure she couldn't see me, perched on the car. I was just out of her line of sight. There was a light cone of this block that Ida knew better than anyone, and I'd been careful to stay out of it.

It was early, because Kelly was some sort of fucking Olympian woman who never slept. Although there was a crude sort of cunning to it because there was no way a sodden mess like Henry would be awake at this ungodly hour, so it was a proper ambush. People were popping out of their homes, going to work, walking to the subway or hopping in their cars. I didn't worry about sitting on the Olds. I was the demi-god of Griffith Street. I knew everything, and this pale green Oldsmobile had not been moved in three weeks. Or even gazed at lovingly.

And there she was, our big girl, Kelly. In tight running clothes. I perked up. Black leggings, a green windbreaker. Hair back. Face scrubbed. She was red and sweaty and as I watched she doubled over with her ass in the air, pointed in my general direction as if she could sense me. Ancient feminine instinct telling her to show me her goods, let the chief have a sniff.

With her hands on her knees, she looked like she was going to just puke onto the sidewalk. New Year's Resolution, I thought. *I will lose those three pounds!* I was alarmed. I like a taut, skinny girl as much as anyone, but Kelly's best features were her tits, and weight loss fucked around with that. I'd worked out a complex flowchart for managing a girl's weight: You had to make her feel just fat enough to shed those unsightly inches, but you had to pull back at *just* the right moment and make her feel sexy before she went all fucking anorexia on you and got bony. And then when she hit that perfect middle ground where she had curves and tone coexisting you lost your best weapon in arguments, because if you made her feel fat in order to shatter her self-esteem, you paid the price in the form of thighs the size of your enormity.

I admired her ass.

Then Flo. Already dressed for work, wrapped in a thick coat. Stockings and sneakers. Ugly as hell, but then Flo had long ago determined that there were no straight, handsome men at her office she wanted anything to do with. She'd started the job a year ago and at first it had been hairdos and makeup, stilettos and blouses unbuttoned just *one* button too far. Now she was unimpressed with the talent and it was bags under her eyes, roots showing, and dirty running shoes.

I watched her and Kelly peck cheeks, pass a few grumpy words, and then stand around. Waiting for me. Me and Bickerman. All of us, playing our role.

I held back. I wanted Bick in my line of sight. I didn't want to be standing with my back to him, mesmerized by a pair of tits. Bick was run by his slithery underbrain. He'd stab you in the back in a flash of animal instinct and then regret it, briefly, stepping over your bleeding shuddering body to go get some pancakes.

When he arrived, it was with due ceremony. He glided across the street like a king in his expensive blue coat, throwing out his arms as he assaulted the girls with Bick's A-Game flirtation material, unchanged since grade school. His hair was too long and greasy. His face looked blotchy and red. I could see, even at this distance, that his socks did not match. His shirt was wrinkled albeit stain-free.

I sat for a moment more, imagining the smell of his breath.

Then I was up and on my feet. My headache, which had faded back a bit, came roaring back. I'd been Bickerman-free for a few days, but I was still drinking myself into an early grave. The man left deep grooves in you. I thought I'd be free and clear of him—just yesterday, sitting on a cardboard box in my emptying apartment, I'd congratulated myself for pulling his head out of my bloodstream. But here I was, walking back toward him. It was foolish. But I had no choice. I had to supervise.

He saw me first and pointed at me. As the girls turned to face me, his face split open.

"Where the hell have you been?"

I calibrated a smile for them. Tired. Manly. Unamused by Bickerman— I sensed the wind had changed in this shrinking world and Bickerman was no longer popular. He'd never *been* popular, strictly speaking, but he was bottoming out and I wanted to put some distance there. Which was just instinct. It didn't matter anymore.

"Ladies," I said, nodding to Flo and Kelly. "Anyone else attending Intervention Day?"

"Ignore me, then, you fat fuck."

I could smell him.

Kelly glanced at Bickerman, then back at me. No kiss on the cheek for Tommy. No hand on the shoulder, tippy toes, peck peck. No smile. I looked at Flo, but Flo was staring moodily at the sidewalk. I had a psychic premonition that none of us would ever see each other again. A length of rope, a syringe, a cold winter's day—this was how you broke free. This was how you reinvented your whole life.

"Just us," Kelly said. "Look, we're here for Henry, okay? Let's just go and talk to him. He won't answer calls, or texts, or e-mails. Last time I saw him he looked horrible."

She politely declined to mention the fisticuffs, or my own behavior on that day. I could still remember Bickerman's zombiefied amazement as he watched an Indian gentleman vomit prodigiously inside the diner. Good times.

I nodded cheerfully, starting to enjoy it. It was like I'd seen the movie before. There would be no surprises. And there were Kelly's boobs to enjoy.

"Let's go, then," Bickerman growled. "I'm *freezing*."

We trooped up the stairs. Leave it to Henry, sad super nice Henry, to live in a fucking walkup. I'd been up and down these stairs too often of late. They were familiar to me the way hospital corridors get familiar to sick people. I wanted to come up last but Bickerman was wheezing like he'd recently donated a lung and forgotten about it, so I ended up ahead of him and behind Flo. Her ass was hidden by her coat, but I imagined it anyway. You go drinking with people often enough you memorized them, or parts of them. Flo's wonderful ass. Kelly's boobs. Bickerman's wet slash of a mouth. Henry's vague expression of confusion. Denise's boobs. Denise's legs, for that matter. Miriam's little blowjob bow of a mouth. Mary's boobs.

I missed a step and almost reached for Flo's ass to steady myself. I started laughing.

From above me: "Jesus, *Tommy*."

Then we were crowded into the hall outside Henry's apartment. It was suddenly hot and damp instead of cold and dry. Kelly pounded on the door.

"Henry!" she shouted. "It's Kelly!"

And her marvelous boobs, I thought.

We all stood there in confused silence. I didn't know why they were all here. Kelly, I figured she was trolling for Henry now that Denise had dropped him like a hot rock. Saw in Noble Hank the genetic material for an army of children she could train in some forest compound. Flo, because Kelly had ordered her to. Bickerman, because there were girls involved and he was still under the impression that grief was an aphrodisiac. And that anyone believed he was grieving.

Me, because I had to supervise.

She pounded the door again. Repeated his name. Her name. Like it was a ritual.

"You just going to ignore me forever?" Bickerman growled in my ear. My suspicions were confirmed: His breath smelled like cough syrup gone bad.

"Are you kidding me?" I said. "You're not even here. You're hallucinating yourself."

Whatever else happened, I could not look into the Bickerman Void, or I would become the Void.

Kelly pounded the door.

"Jesus," I said. "Key under the mat, Kel. Spare me."

She knelt and retrieved it. Worked the lock. We flooded into Henry's kitchen. I didn't know what they expected to find. Something dramatic. Henry, in the bathtub, wrists slit, final letter to Denise clutched in one pale hand. Henry, drunk and raving, aiming a firearm at us, screaming about ants nesting in his head. Henry, sad and profound, sitting calmly, ready to tell us each our future.

I knew what we would find: An empty apartment.

A surge of energy buzzed through me as we stepped inside. The kitchen was warm, but it was just the warmth of being on an upper floor, all the farts and exhalations of your neighbors floating up and collecting against your ceiling. One upper cabinet open. Boxes of cereal, all stale. One box of cereal on the scratched-up wooden table. A bowl and a spoon. Crusted cereal, long-gone milk.

Something small and dark, skittering away under the stove.

The place smelled normal. Musty, but that was from all the windows being closed up. I ran my eyes over everything, seeking clues. I didn't see any.

"Henry!" Kelly shouted, moving off into the living room. "Hank, baby, we're coming in!"

I realized with alarm that I was left in the kitchen with Bickerman. Before I could move he'd sailed over to the doorway between the kitchen and the living room, blocking me. I glanced at the upper cabinet where Henry used to store his liquor. Mercifully closed. Finding myself trapped in Henry's apartment with Bick, I briefly questioned my intelligence.

I gave Bick my full attention for the first time in days. Regretted it instantly. Up close he was fat and sweaty; a few months ago he'd been sleek and skinny. Well, not *skinny*. But not this kind of booze-bloat horror show. He had, however, stopped floating around on a cushion of alcohol fumes. Graf Bickerman had docked with the real world again. I just stared at him, studying. He licked his lips with a liverish tongue, like he was some sort of human-shaped beetle, or intelligent fungus.

I liked to stare. It made people uncomfortable. People wanted noise, protective coloring. The longer you waited to say something, the more power you had over everyone around you.

Then, without warning, he made a break for Henry's liquor cabinet.

I watched in mixed horror and excitement. The slow, brain-damaged way he slid himself over to it. The familiar little tribe of bottles. The slight sway he had as he stood there, contemplating a stiff one at eight-thirty in the morning. I watched him swaying. I was mesmerized. Would he? What would I do?

I decided to go all Schrödinger's cat on him, and stepped briskly out of the room. As long as I wasn't watching him, I figured, Bick existed in both states. It was a relief to stop thinking about him.

The girls were emerging from Henry's room. Kelly looked confused. Flo looked irritated, fussing with her phone, thumbs punching tiny letters into the universe with nuclear force.

"He's not here. Hasn't been for a while," Kelly said slowly.

Confirmed: Kelly had a crush on Noble Henry. I fought back a grin that would have given everything away, leaving me in the familiar position of the recently kicked in the balls.

"Better go wrestle Bickerman away from the liquor," I said with forced casualness. "He looks thirsty."

She cursed under her breath and breezed past me, pulling Flo in her wake. Kelly was, I suddenly realized, the female counterpart to Henry. They'd been switched at birth. I was suddenly rooting for them as a couple, simply for the extravagant horror of their offspring.

Listening to the buzz of voices in the kitchen, I stepped into Henry's tiny bedroom. Cluttered. Dusty. More dusty than ever. The floor less dusty than it should be, but I thought a few more days would balance that out. I stared at the window. A single double sash window that let in almost no light, leading out onto the fire escape which fed you either up to the filthy, hot flat roof or down into the dense jungle of tree-like weeds that smelled like poison.

I looked at his bedside table. A dusty paperback book. A lamp. The alarm clock, unplugged. A row of unnoticed plastic bottles, the white caps off, on the floor. A sticky glass.

Through the dirty window, you could see the rusting iron of the fire escape. I squinted, studying, slowly walking forward. Scanning downward. Until I was pressed up against the sill, my nose almost touching the thick glass. I squinted and moved my head, but I couldn't see anything except the vague implication of thick, dark branches, a canopy of leaves. No one had tended to the backyard of Henry's building in years. It was a patch of natural growth in the middle of the city, a postage-stamp of jungle.

When I'd first seen it, through this window a few years ago, I'd thought it must contain some amazing things. Things lost completely to the universe, swallowed by those trees and incorporated into the roots, absorbed for nutrients.

"Tom?"

I spun. Heart pounding. Infantile smile immediately on my face. Kelly wasn't looking at me, though. She'd turned to look back over her shoulder. By the time she got back to me, I was normal again.

"He passed out on the floor? Graf Bickerman?"

She shook her head tiredly, leaning against the doorway. A pretty girl. Too tall, too broad, too much hair. But pretty, in a big way. "No. We kept him away from Henry's liquor, no worries." She paused, chewing a strand of honey colored hair. "Tom, I'm worried about him. Henry, I mean. Not Bick."

Never in life would it be *Bickerman*, I thought, and wanted to cackle. Bickerman did not make Noble Kelly dampen her panties quite the way Noble Henry did. I thought perhaps I'd missed an opportunity to take some DNA scrapings and scent samples from Henry, find out how it was that the least interesting of all of us was, somehow, the most popular amongst the ladies. The shallow pool of ladies available to us. The shrinking, shallow pool.

I needed, I thought not for the first time, a whole new set of friends.

"He'll turn up," I said, trying to sound comforting. Mature. It was foreign territory, and felt faked. Method acting, I decided, and some touching. There weren't many opportunities for me to touch Kelly in approved over-the-clothes ways, and I wasn't going to let this one pass me by. I stepped in close, quick, before she knew what was happening and pulled her in for a hug. Mashed that wonderful chest against my belly. Pushed my dripping red nose into her hair and inhaled. Sweat and yesterday's shampoo and cigarettes and something else indefinably *her*.

Just like that, I was turned on.

She pushed away. Gently. Looked at the floor.

"Uh, all right. I'll try him at work again later. Let's go."

Kelly's ass encased in black leggings led me back through the dusty living room. Everything preserved like a museum exhibit. Noble Henry's Habitat. Note the dust on the bookshelves; the man hadn't read a thing in years. Note the single flattened couch cushion where Noble Henry sat alone most nights, fondling a remote control. Note the slight smell of desperation in the air.

I knew my Henrys.

In the kitchen, the liquor cabinet had been shut up again, and Bick was still standing. I made a mental note about the liquor. It was dangerous sitting there, like an unexploded bomb.

I paused in the doorway, letting my eyes adjust to the sudden gloom of the hallway. Everyone else already on the stairs, heading down, escaping. Bick confused as to his location and purpose, no doubt. Flo relieved to be getting back to her busy schedule of Internet shopping and prick-teasing at work. Kelly chewing her pink lip in that adorable way she had, upset.

I glanced back at the still-life kitchen. I was going to have to get myself a new Henry. Fortunately, I was good at that.

VII.

NEW YEAR'S EVE

The door opened and Tommy's face, freshly barbered, peeked through the small opening. He looked us up and down.

"Leave the woman and the bottle," he croaked in a bad Spanish accent. "You go."

"You can have the woman," I replied, pushing the door open, "but the bottle stays with me."

Denise elbowed me in the ribs.

"As you wish, gringo," Tommy said, bowing us into the apartment. "We'll get it off you anyway. My dear! You're looking absolutely edible!"

"Can't you be normal tonight?" Denise suggested. "Try it as a resolution."

"Tomorrow, for you, I will. But resolutions are for the New Year. This is merely the Eve. So you'll have to put up with me."

I took Denise's coat and bundled it along with mine into Tommy's small bedroom, which was big enough for a bed and nothing else. You could squeeze your way around the bed, but only if you bent double to avoid the shelves he'd put up on the walls. It was best, I knew, not to enter Tommy's bedroom at all, since—

"Whatcha doin'?"

I turned to find Tommy, hands in pockets, smiling as if he were not making sure that I wasn't searching his room.

I tossed our coats onto the bed. "We the first?"

He nodded cheerily. "You're the least fashionable people around. Come to the bar area, I'll get you started. Got some nice bourbon, just for you." He winked at me obscenely. "I made Denise a wonderful gin and tonic. She'll be wasted in an hour."

I tried to match his wink for obscenity, but that was no easy task. "So I can use your bed later?"

He blanched. "Uh . . ."

I put an arm around him. "Don't worry, Tom my boy, we all know your weird little phobia concerning your bedroom. Fetch me a bourbon and all is forgiven."

The bell rang and Tom slipped from my embrace with feminine grace. "Duty calls. Make yourself at home!"

Unspoken, of course, was the caveat that *at home* did not now, or indeed ever, include his bedroom.

I found Denise by the bar, which was an overlarge thing that dominated Tommy's largest room, which wasn't all that big to begin with. I slipped behind her and wrapped my arms around her middle, lacing my fingers around her belly.

"Barkeep, I'll have a bourbon and soda."

She giggled warmly as I bit her ear. "Tommy told you he was getting me drunk for you?" she said playfully.

I paused and extricated myself. "Jesus, he said that to you?"

She turned her head to wink at me. "The exact phraseology he used was 'lubricating you for my pal Hank.' It's okay. I've known Tommy long enough now not to take him too seriously."

"Thank God for that," I said, slipping to the other side of the bar, where a wonderful bottle of Jack Daniels waited. I busied myself with making a drink as Tommy came back, leading Bick and Mary.

Fresh from the cold air and dressed up in passably classy clothes, Bick and Mary looked like the model Young White Couple: gawky, gorgeous, sure of themselves, and terrible in their ease.

"Ho, it's the Young Couple," I called out. "I thought the White House, Bickerman and Harrows?"

Bick threw his arms out, and Tom smilingly removed his overcoat like it was a royal robe. "Mary failed the security check. Something about sex with communists, whatever that means."

Mary slapped him lightly with her gloves and handed her own coat to Tom. I let my eyes roam her for a split, guilty second, then a quick look at Denise to make sure she hadn't noticed. All seemed well.

"I thought as much. Drinks? I know how to make anything with one ingredient."

Bickerman was, as always, disturbingly manic. I'd never seen him without a red-cheeked kind of excitement about him, as if he were always running up stairs. Or was always internally burning something off, a big meal, too many drinks. Mare was pale, next to him, and small, trapped in his immense gravitational pull.

"I'll take a Scotch, bub," Bick said, turning to kiss Neesie on the cheek.

"White wine for me," Mare said sweetly. "How are you, Hank?"

"Swell," I said, trying to be flashy as I poured alcohol for everyone. "Another year done. Looking to drown my sorrows."

"Sorrows?" she said archly, her eyes flicking to Denise. It had been two months for us. I had forgotten to make a big deal out of what seemed to be, to me, an arbitrary sort of anniversary.

I kept my eyes on the booze. "Now, now, let's play nice, Mare."

She laughed. I handed her her wine and Bick his Scotch, and the doorbell was ringing.

"Okay, everybody!" Tom shouted, sprinting for the door. "Act normal, for God's sake!"

I took his advice and drank fast.

For a misanthropic ass who pissed off everyone he knew on a weekly basis, Tommy had a lot of friends, and his tiny, oddly white apartment was filled to bursting with strange people. Denise had gone off with Kelly and Flo to the bathroom, and I leaned against a wall and watched the party flow. I hadn't spent a lot of time at Tom's place; we usually hung out at mine. Tommy liked to amuse himself by "disappearing" things into the jungle-like yard my bedroom window opened onto. Objects my friend Tom Wallace had *disappeared* into my dense, overgrown backyard included, but were not limited to: a bowling ball, several watermelons, a box of files from his job, two unopened bottles of middling Scotch, and, once, inexplicably, every pair of shoes I owned.

Tommy's place was fascinating.

First off, the whiteness of Tommy's apartment. I'd known Tommy for years, had done a lot of questionable socializing with him, but I'd been completely unprepared for his taste in interior decoration. The walls were white. The furniture was upholstered white. *Everything* was white, or close to it. Bick and I always referred to Tom's apartment as the White Castle, or *Casa de Blanc*. It was weird, but it had become entrenched weirdness, and thus almost ordinary and normal. Tommy's apartment was white, and always had been, and therefore was no longer remarkable, really.

I didn't know too many people at the party, aside from the Bicker-mans, Mikey, and Luis. The rest of the people might have been work friends or old school chums or random strangers plucked from the street—who knew? Not me. And I wasn't asking the right questions. I leaned against one of the white walls and sipped my drink and watched the party flow by. After a few moments I acquired a fellow wall-watcher, a guy about my age in a beat-up sports jacket. Noticing me eyeing him, he smiled and held out his hand.

"Phil Dublen."

I'd heard the name, and it must have showed in my face as I dug through dusty memories trying to place him. He nodded, as if reading my mind.

"I used to date Flo."

"Denise's Flo?"

He nodded again. "Long ago. Uh," he looked suddenly grim, "she isn't here, is she?"

"Yes," I said. "So step lightly. Do you know Tom?"

"Not really."

We stood there for a moment, surrounded by white noise, forgotten by the rest of the revelers. I struggled to think of anything at all to say to this guy, who appeared to be a mildly normal human being.

"You're the guy," I said with a note of triumph, "who quit his job, right?" Small bright portions of something Flo had said once when recounting her many failed relationships coalesced into coherency. "You came into some money and quit your job."

"I didn't quit my job. I *wanted* to quit my job. I did come into some money. But I blew it all. So here I am."

"You're here looking for money?"

"No—why, is there some here?"

I didn't know what else to say to this guy, and he seemed at a loss too, so after another second or two of staring we nodded and went back to leaning against the wall.

Tommy was across the room playing DJ with his tiny player plugged into his huge stereo. The stereo was gigantic, the speakers half as tall as I was, from a previous era. He was leaning toward crappy dance music in deference to the bad taste of his guests, who were a rowdy bunch. I was getting jostled on a regular basis and almost didn't notice when Mary began tugging on my arm. I turned, startled, and she grinned and leaned in to me.

"Henry! Are you having fun?"

My God, I thought, she's *so drunk*.

Mary was not much of a drinker. Which was to say, she drank like a surly longshoreman but had a stomach made of glass, resulting in several Black Ops missions to bring her home through torrents of vomit and verbal abuse. Number of times she had acknowledged this and vowed to be a better person: Hundreds. Number of times the evening had ended with Mary screaming and punching and puking on someone's shoes: Thousands. Number of times the shoes puked on had been mine: Four.

"Yes, Mary, and you?"

She was hanging on the lapels of my jacket, beaming up at me in red-faced excitement. "A great time! You know, Henry," she continued, pulling herself erect by my jacket and leaning against the wall next to me, "we never talk."

This was true, but I'd never thought of it as a problem: You didn't have to become best friends with your friends' significant others. Sometimes it happened, sometimes it didn't, and either way it was usually for the best.

Mary, after a consultation with what appeared by her breath to be a bottle of tequila, had decided otherwise.

What I said was: "Ask me anything." Then I struck a dramatic pose.

She giggled, and I noted with alarm that she still had her hands on my jacket. I had no illusions that Mare had suddenly developed an attraction for me; rather, it was an alarming indication of how drunk she was. I became frightened, and scanned the immediate area for Bick.

"Okay," she slurred, then wrinkled her brow in concentration. "Okay! Do you prefer Henry or Hank?"

"I prefer Ishmael."

This brought her leaning into me, shaking with laughter, hanging off my jacket. I scanned the room again, smiling helplessly.

"You're funny!" she gasped. "You're Dave's funniest friend."

I shook my head seriously. "That would be Tommy."

"No, no—he's funny but not funny like in humor," she said. "You're cute funny. I think Denise is lucky."

"Uh-huh," I said, a little floored by an unsolicited compliment. I decided to deflect before she started asking me all sorts of things about Denise that I had no answers for. "Where's Bick?"

She frowned a little. "I'm mad at him, the little bastard." She stumbled, and I had to grab her to keep her from doing a header into one of Tommy's icy glass end tables. She steadied herself and went on, unconcerned. "This always happens. He always pays so much attention to his friends, and I end up standing there alone."

I nodded wisely. "Denise says the same thing to me," I confessed and immediately regretted it.

She slapped me playfully on the chest. "Why do you men *do* that?"

Before I could answer, Mare was jostled from behind by a beefy guy in a golf shirt, wearing, inexplicably, shorts despite the inch of snow on the ground outside. Whatever he muttered with his head half-turned toward Mary might have been an apology. It might also have been a quotation from the *Tibetan Book of the Dead*, for all I could make of it. I opened my mouth to reply, but she whirled around, stumbled against me, then stumbled against our new friend as she tapped him on the shoulder.

"Excuse me, *asshole*, watch where you're *fucking* going, okay?"

I blinked dimly.

Beefy Boy turned halfway toward her, one of Tommy's known-to-be-deadly mint martinis in one hand. He murmured something that was not, I assumed, an apology of sufficient class.

Mary leaned forward and slapped him on the back of his neck. I flinched in sympathy.

"Hey, *asshole*," Mary snapped. I reached forward and tugged at her, looking around at all the people who were taking time out of their busy drinking/socializing schedules to stare in our direction. She ignored me and now had Beefy Boy's attention.

"What the fuck is your problem?" he asked, reasonably enough.

Mary, a foot his junior but obviously a few pints ahead of him otherwise, swayed and began screeching. I wanted to have a better word for that, a calmer word. But she was *screeching*.

"Who the fuck do you think you are, and why can't you watch where the fuck you're going?!" She pushed him hard on the chest. *"Shithead!"*

She turned away from him. He stared at her with a dumbly shocked look. I sympathized. I wouldn't know what to do in his situation, either.

Mare grabbed my drink out of my hand as Bick materialized out of the crowd.

"Fuckheads," the new Mary muttered, slamming back my drink and making a face.

"Honey?" Bick said with a wink at me. "You okay?"

"Your honey's a goddamn psycho, bud," Beefy Boy said, turning away.

Mary whirled. "Shut the fuck up!" She screeched before Bick got his hand over her mouth. He smiled at Beefy Boy.

"Sorry, man," he offered. "She's a monster when she gets fucked up."

"Whatever."

Bick turned his game show smile on me, holding his struggling wife-to-be as she grunted and kicked at him, red-faced.

"Sorry, man. Did she say anything crazy? Mare shouldn't drink. She becomes a monster."

I looked them over. Bick's smile appeared to be long-suffering. "Nothing to me, man," I said. "Don't worry. You gonna be all right with her?"

He nodded, the smile still bolted in place. "Sure. She can't stay this way forever."

Mary wriggled free, slipped under his arm, and stumbled into a group of people standing nearby.

"Get your hands off me, goddammit!" she snarled, righting herself at the expense of several other people. "I will not be *brutalized* in public, you fuck."

"Quack, quack, quack," Bick answered mildly, leaning next to me, all casualness. "Go pass out somewhere."

"Asshole," she slurred, stumbling off.

"Quack!"

Aside from the booming music, there was an odd silence in the room until Tom suddenly appeared, standing on one of his own end tables. "That concludes tonight's presentation of *The Troubles of Being Bick*, performed by our own *Days of Wine and Roses* players! A big hand everyone!"

Everyone laughed, and Bick even took a little bow. Then the buzzing of conversation welled up, and I found myself embarrassed, not sure what to say.

"Everything okay?" I asked lamely.

"Sure, perfect," Bick grimaced. "She just should never ever drink, but always does. That about covers it. I'll find her asleep somewhere later, and she'll be super nice to me for a few days, and then it's all forgotten," he smiled. "It's all right. Drunk chicks turn me on."

"Speaking of drunk, she took my drink."

He put his arm around me. "Let me make it up to you."

"There are many people here that I have never met before," Luis said, shrugging. "I am not sure I like them all. I wonder where Tommy met them? He is always with us."

"Not always. The man has a job. A past. Who knows what's he's doing in his spare time?"

In Tom's tiny white kitchen, there is room, perhaps, for a dwarf to relax comfortably. Somehow I was wedged in with Luis, a tipsy Denise, and three or four complete strangers. It was hot and loud. We were closer to the bottled beer, however. Small consolation, but lemonade was being made industriously.

"I had expected it to be just our usual group," Luis complained.

I had, too, and Tom's sudden wealth of friends and well-wishers puzzled me. He wasn't a cuddly guy who made friends and influenced people. His penchant for inappropriate cursing and mean-spirited insult comedy usually made him somewhat unlikable.

"Cheer up, Luis. We're here!" Denise offered.

In true Luis fashion, he *did* cheer up suddenly, grinning. "That is true! Have a drink with me, Denise."

I watched in some alarm as he unsteadily poured a shot of tequila into two shot glasses and passed one to Denise. She was already into her warm-and-moist drunk stage, marked by an attractive flush to her cheeks and a grabability she usually didn't exhibit. I had as yet never proceeded beyond this stage and wondered if there was a monster in Denise as well. It was frightening.

I pounded her back as she coughed, and she weakly clinked the little glass against Luis's.

"I have realized that being drunk solves all problems," he said seriously. "The trick, of course, is to be just drunk enough, but not too drunk."

I ran a finger along my nose. "You hit the nail on the head, chief. You'd do the world a good turn if you'd sacrifice yourself and find out how that can be done."

"Yes."

Denise and I waited a moment for the rest of his thoughts on the matter, and then, realizing that his thoughts had all been contained in that single word, we started laughing.

I realized it was the first time all night that I'd felt normal, which underscored how strange the whole evening had felt up to that point.

"What time is it?"

Denise was bopping around, doing a cute little in-place dance. I glanced up at the wall clock that was plain for all to see and then back at her. "Eleven-thirty-three." I pushed a stray strand of hair from her face. She was beautiful. Flushed and bopping, she was more gorgeous than I'd ever noticed. Or maybe I just hadn't been paying attention.

"We should start finding a good place to be for midnight," she suggested, rubbing her hand across her little nose. She was delectable. She wanted to be someplace romantic so we could have a kiss at midnight, and I didn't much care where I was, so it all worked out.

"I will have no one to kiss," Luis lamented. "I will be alone."

I put a manly hand on his shoulder. "You can kiss me, weirdo."

He nodded. "I accept."

We wormed our way out of the tiny kitchen and almost ran into Tom, who appeared to be a little frazzled.

"Hank! Thank God!"

"Problem, Thomas?"

He snorted. "I got red wine soaking into a couch cushion in the living room, some guy wandering the place trying to puke into the potted plants, and oh, by the way, your presence has been requested in the bedroom, where Mary has hidden herself in my closet."

"Excuse me?"

He rolled his eyes. "You heard me, Precious. Bick asked if you would step in for a moment. I've delivered his message, so if you'll excuse me, I have stain management to engage in."

I glanced at Denise, who waved me away in annoyance. "Go, your idiot friends need you."

Luis nodded. "Do not worry. I will kiss Denise in your absence."

The door to Tom's bedroom was closed, so I knocked lightly. Behind the door I could hear muffled sound: a female voice, Mary I supposed, and a general rumpus.

"Yeah?" Bickerman called out.

"It's Henry."

The door opened and I was pulled in. Bick closed the door behind us. I looked around, but saw no Mary, and gave him a perplexed look before I realized where all the Mary-related noise was coming from. Mary was, indeed, in the closet. I processed this slowly.

"How long has she been in there?"

Bick looked desperate. "Twenty minutes or so. She's trashed. She always gets this way after a certain point."

A moment of quiet between us revealed that Mary was cursing like a sailor from within the closet, her voice nasal and nasty and strained.

Bick looked back at me. "She won't come out."

I crawled over the bed and sat on its edge, near the closet. The room was so small and the bed so large that the closet door couldn't be opened all the way. "Mary? Mare? It's Henry."

"Go away!"

I glanced at Bick, who shrugged. "First non-curse words she's used in a while. Go with it!"

"Mary, honey, come on out of there, okay? You need to relax now," I said, staring at Bick. He waved me on, full of confidence.

"No!" she shouted. "Not until he leaves! I'm not coming out until he's gone!"

"Mary, sweetheart, come on. He's going to be here. You can't hide in there forever."

There were a few moments of silence. "Are you going to stay, Henry?"

I nodded, for some reason. Bick threw his hands in the air and stared up at the ceiling. "Yes, Mary, I'll stay here if you want me to."

The closet door opened and she stepped out, and I struggled to keep my face blank, struggled to not think about the ridiculousness of the scene: Mary emerging from Tom's closet, ready to fall over and pass out, and smiling at me as if it were the most delightful joke.

"We're going home," Bick said flatly. "Thanks, Hank."

He tried to be blustery and violent, but the dimensions of the room forced him to slowly side-step his way along the wall, bent over because of the shelves, until he could reach out and grab her arm. Just before she was pulled through, Mary winked at me, and then she was gone, pulled away roughly by the Bick. He left the door open, the party noise seeping in like fog. The wink stayed with me, and I just sat there, staring at the floor, feeling very tired. I felt like I could lie back on all the coats and just sleep. So much effort just to get through the day.

"What are you doing?"

Denise was in the doorway then, looking scandalous.

"Nothing," I said, standing up. "It's just sad."

"What is?"

I took her hand and we started walking back to the party, where everyone was getting ready for the new year. I squeezed her hand, and told her.

VIII.

CHRISTMAS

I was going to have to kill him.

If I never had to have a fucking cocktail with David Bickerman, the sole surviving Bickerman, I will be a very happy man. Having been dragged through every lame, holiday-themed and overstuffed bar in the universe, I was filled to the brim with cheap draft beer and even cheaper low-rent hooch, cigarette smoke, and swelling ennui. Being a slave to this bloated asshole, this hard-shelled beetle with his tiny human head, was what I got for being an asshole myself, I guessed.

It was my penance. The lesson: Never fucking try.

"Let's get moving," I suggested, slumping back in my uncomfortable wooden chair, a chair mended together by so many metal brackets and screws I knew it was just a matter of time before it collapsed under someone, comically, probably killing them with a sharp stake up the ass in the process. I fervently did not wish to be that person, which required that I get the Bickerman Zeppelin—Graf Bickerman, slow and floaty—moving toward the door within the next century.

We were in a place called—literally—Stinky Sullivans, an old bar filled to the brim with mouth-breathers. We'd gotten our table by sheer doomy luck, as Graf Bickerman was losing steam and needed to refuel and magically there was a damp, wobbly table and two chairs being abandoned by luckier folks just as we entered. Graf Bickerman required frequent refueling, as he'd made some sort of pre-New Year's resolution to be as fucking drunk as fucking possible continuously for the rest of his fucking short, sad life.

Which was pretty drunk, shattering previous scientific theories on the origin and nature of human life. Bickerman was some sort of alien life form that was based on alcohol instead of carbon. He was obsessed with finding Henry, but since we were searching bars this also meant he was obsessed with drinking at every place we stopped at.

Our waitress reappeared from the throng of denim-clad assholes, magically pushing her way through the lowing crowd with a tray of empties balanced on one hand. She was a pro. She was ugly as sin, with a humongous, nightmare-inspiring honker of a nose and a single ratty eyebrow over her eyes—which she'd outlined in heavy black liner—giving her a raccoon-like appearance that almost crossed so far over into hideous it was attractive. Almost.

Still, she was a damned good booze-slinger. I was halfway pissed myself thanks to Graf Bickerman's fuel requirements, and in recent months I found myself flirting on autopilot with anything with tits. Including some jolly fat men I'd run into at all-night diners.

"Need anything, fellas?" she asked, her accent sort of Boston-y.

"Sweetheart," I said brightly, half-shouting, "you're an angel."

She grinned. I had her pegged: She'd watched a lot of fucking movies, and in the movies rich guys in bars always picked up the waitresses and banged them like a piledriver. She'd been working at bars for years and so far nothing had happened. Just as she was beginning to wonder if maybe she wasn't as hot as her dancing-in-front-of-the-mirror-my-girlfriends-all-tell-me-I'm-cute self-image had suggested, she meets me: clever, handsome Tom Wallace, tipping well, drunk as hell, and being nice to her. I was going to end up a picture in her locker, no doubt, and I'd probably have to get the cops on her for stalking before too long. Such was the price you paid for being a Wallace man.

"Angel," Bick said, leaning back and grinning. "Scotch. Single malt. Neat."

The waitress looked at Bickerman like he was some sort of bug. A beetle, I wanted to say; he's a beetle! But I contented myself with a withering look at Graf Bickerman that he didn't notice. Bick wouldn't know single-malt Scotch from moonshine if we doused him with them and set him on fire, but I held my tongue—I'd sold myself to Graf Bickerman. We were conjoined twins, now, and I hated him.

"We gotta go," I shouted at him. "We got miles to fucking go before we sleep."

He managed a greasy wink at the waitress. "Scotch. Pronto."

She looked back at me and I shrugged. "M'lord says Scotch. I'll take one too, whatever he ends up with." This to keep Graf Bickerman from being poisoned by the bar staff, since I was too popular to be killed in his wake.

I let her slip back into the maelstrom of guts and haunches, fat people sucking down light beer and eating germy beer nuts. People always ate free food, no matter how disgusting. You could make nachos grande in your fucking toilet and people would sink to their knees in joy, sticking their whole heads in there.

I could feel the spotlight on me, my special glow, somewhat inhibited by Graf Bickerman's immense and grubby shadow. Every day I regretted tying my caboose to his engine. We were going uphill, and he was spluttering, and I was breathing his fucking exhaust.

"How are we going to find Henry," I asked, shaking out a cigarette and putting it in the corner of my mouth, "if we just sit here?"

Henry was out there in the world, and whenever Bick couldn't see him, Bick got nervous. As if Henry was at the police station right now, telling tales. As if Henry were working hard to undermine Graf Bickerman, maybe signing up for the Witness Protection Program—poof! He's gone. Never seen again, rumors of Henry in the wild post–plastic surgery, surfacing every now and then; and Bickerman would release the winged monkeys and the ninjas every time with orders to hunt him down.

Bickerman focused on me. It was an effort, obviously, a series of precise calibrations. "We'll find him, Tommy. Maybe he'll come here."

I sighed, shaking my head. "Hank hasn't hung out here in fucking *years*, man. Think: He's avoiding you. He's somewhere he never *goes*." This was so obvious my brain ached, boggling.

Graf Bickerman shook his head, fluttering his beetle wings and rubbing two hind legs together, making a sweet violin-ish noise. "No rush, man. Have a drink."

I lit my cigarette, wondering if he noticed I hadn't offered him one. I fucking hated this new Bickerman. Soft, drunk, spacey, bad-smelling. The fucking time of his life.

"Well, this is *much* better," I said. I didn't think Graf Bickerman, floating up above the rest of us like a Thanksgiving Day Parade balloon, could actually hear me. I had an urge to hold onto the hem of his heavy coat, to make sure he didn't just sail away, belching and farting for propulsion, never to be seen again. Aside from the tales about me—most incriminating and some downright criminal—the bastard might mutter in his sleep were I not around to stroke his hair and coo softly to him, I didn't want to lose sight of Bickerman because if I did, the whole endless, horrible evening would have been *pointless*.

This was a slightly more upscale-looking place, all black furniture and chrome, a trio of slender, buff male bartenders working the room efficiently, like some sort of East German Olympic Team of bartenders. I remembered coming here—it had always been our before-evening gathering place, a good spot to have a cocktail, read the paper while waiting for everyone else to crawl out of work. I didn't recall ever being here after hours, and now I was heartily glad of it, as the place was crawling with college-aged assholes, all hairspray and tight T-shirts and gold fucking chains and macho bullshit. Graf Bickerman and I stood out like sore thumbs in our middle-aged splendor—decent suits, nice coats, shined shoes instead of sneakers. Whiskey instead of tap beer made from piss and foam.

It was all fucking cocks, too. There were like three chicks in the whole place, none of whom were worth my time. I'd never been so bored in my life.

The brisk walk over had revived Bickerman a bit, at least, and he had something of his old red-cheeked bravado, drinking whiskey through a little red straw and eyeing the room like a wild animal waking up to find itself in a cage. My thumbs were pricking and I was cheered—maybe the evening was going to end well after all, instead of with me dragging Bickerman, soggy and heavy, through the city streets like a corpse. Or perhaps *as* a corpse, if he kept drinking the paint they were serving in this place.

"Dave," I said plaintively, "Hank is *never*—"

I was interrupted by the sudden intrusion of someone's elbow, jostling my arm and causing me to spill most of my drink on myself. I imagined the rotgut burning through my clothes, smoke rising up as I caught fire from it, burning alive while Graf Bickerman stared down at me with his bloated, slightly amused expression. This was no way to die, anchored to Bickerman, joined via horror and despair and guilt to his sinking ship, being dragged down. I hadn't had a night to myself in weeks. He was there, all the time, always inebriated and always leering at me, always worrying about Henry and terrified of sleeping alone. Motherfucker ought to be paying me rent the amount of time he spends in my living room, fluttering his beetley wings and drooling into my couch cushions, which would have to be burned, eventually. Along with the rest of my apartment.

I made a note to check on my homeowner's insurance.

I glanced at the elbow, then at the jerkoff attached to it. He was a big guy, sweaty, with a baseball cap on backwards and a huge tattoo of something gray and blurry on his forearm. Based on the disparity in size between us, I decided to let his rudeness slide, as nothing ruins my carefully cultivated image of cool indifference to the lowing crowds than having those crowds rise up and hurt me.

Without warning, the jerkoff turned and focused on me, his eyes small and dark. They were the eyes of a Roman emperor, one of the ones who'd lasted about thirteen days—glorious, lusty days, no doubt, but ended with a thorough garroting nonetheless. This guy wasn't a Roman emperor. He looked like a business major, though, which put him in the same general category: incredible asshole.

"What's your problem, nerd?"

I blinked. I was drunk enough that it took me a moment to realize the jerkoff was talking to Graf Bickerman, which was fine by me. I took a subtle step backward, giving the jerkoff a nice view of Bick, adrenaline racing through me. Had the jerkoff really called him a *nerd*? Eyeing Bick's slow realization that someone was speaking at him, I decided to table the issue.

Graf Bickerman was attempting a midflight course-correction, slowly listing over to orient on the jerkoff. "What?" he said, licking his lips. I had a sudden surge of energy. Henry, had we been able to locate the droopy bastard, would have identified it as the Glee in his usual irritating style. I had a sudden vision of Bick's nose once again getting smashed into a bloody pancake, and couldn't stop myself from smiling a little at the thought. Especially after the last month and a half, wherein Bick had become my own personal albatross.

Unfortunately, the jerkoff surmised Bick's general uselessness and with a disdainful tick of his lantern-like jaw, he turned back to his friends, none of whom seemed to have even noticed the blip. My hopes deflated and I contemplated having yet another watery drink here with nothing but a mush-mouthed Bickerman for company with the same level of enthusiasm I'd had for a broken nose a few seconds earlier.

And then, Graf Bickerman suddenly inflated and lifted up a foot or two from the floor, swelling up to his former glorious proportions for one shining moment of hope, and reached out across me to give the jerkoff a little shove.

"What?" Bick said wetly, lips shining, a familiar expression of stupid belligerence spreading like melting wax over his face.

I couldn't stop myself: I grinned. This was *excellent*.

The jerkoff glanced at his own shoulder as if seeking evidence that yes, he'd actually been touched. I clocked the jerkoff's mental speed at about *retarded* and considered ordering a fresh drink with which to enjoy the spectacle—I figured I could go to the bathroom, piss all over the floor and toilet seat, amble by the jukebox and choose a few songs, and get a fresh drink all in the time it was going to take the jerkoff to figure out what was going on.

"I said," the jerkoff shouted, "what're you looking at, fag?"

Bick, thus promoted from *nerd*, smiled, an expression of dopey happiness blooming on his face and making him almost pretty. "What?"

The jerkoff looked at me. "You better get your friend out of here, man."

Incredible assholes were always all piss and vinegar until someone actually shoved them back. Then it was diplomacy. I raised an eyebrow. *"Non mon ami, et vous sentez comme une femme."*

"Great," the jerkoff said, *"two* fags." He leaned in toward Bick—a rookie mistake, I knew. The jerkoff took a breath to say something he imagined would be devastating to Bickerman—imagining, naturally, that Bickerman was a human being with feelings, also a common rookie mistake—and Bickerman swung his arm up and smashed his tumbler into the jerkoff's head.

"Sacre bleu!" I shouted, pushing myself clumsily up onto the bar, knocking several tons of glassware onto the floor with a crash and thoroughly soaking my pants. This, I decided, was my chance for escape—Bickerman beaten to a bloody pulp by enraged assholes, and me sneaking off for a little vacation, Bickerman-free for the first time in weeks. I'd visit him in the hospital in a few days and when he got all pissy, pointing accusingly at his catheter and colostomy, I'd say *you got off easy, didn't you?* and there would be an awkward, ominous silence.

I tried to jump to my feet on the bar as a scrum formed below me, with an idea about shouting something dramatic as I leaped down and made a run for freedom, but the world skittered out from beneath me, sending me crashing down behind the bar right on top of all the broken glass I'd just generated. I waited a few seconds for pain, that weird burning-numb sensation when you'd been cut to ribbons and your body was just shooting platelets and endorphins and adrenaline everywhere all at once to give you a chance to escape whatever horrible thing has damaged you. The Wallace men have an incredible evolutionary instinct that kicks in, and we go all Alpha Male when existence is threatened, and take no prisoners. And my genes knew I hadn't yet spawned, so were in red alert mode.

Hell, if I stayed childless forever, I'd probably never age.

I was uninjured, however. A miracle, which I chalked up to the universe having an as-yet undiscovered purpose for me, like a Messiah. I leaped up and made a dash for the other end of the bar, pushing myself rudely into the crowd and clawing for the door. Everything in the place was dirty, it was all greasy hair and huge, gaping pores, blackheads everywhere. I didn't dare breathe. Red-faced and desperate, I burst out into the cold night air and doubled over, half-laughing and half gasping, taking in big lungfuls of air. I was ecstatic. I was the happiest bastard in the universe.

"What are you laughing about?"

The voice of Bickerman. He was like some sort of ancient folk tale, a demon who ate babies and haunted innocent men who were just trying to get laid without an albatross around their necks.

He was leaning against the facade of the bar, lighting a cigarette.

"How'd you get out here?" I demanded, outraged. I wanted to shake my fist at the sky in anger, but was suddenly afraid; the way things had been going for me, a lightning bolt would probably strike me in response.

He smirked at me like I was a moron, which was a favorite and familiar expression from Graf Bickerman. "All they did was get the bouncer to eighty-six me," he said. "I saw him lurking behind us anyway."

I nodded. Bickerman hadn't yet found a confrontation he couldn't run away from, but he often found these elegant ways of having fun and avoiding physical injury. The door to the bar jangled open at that moment, and Bick's explosion of fervent, terrified motion, all elbows and knees, amused me enough to bring some blood back to my brain.

"Fuck," he panted, "let's go."

I spun in place as he walked past me, throwing my arms out again. I was damp and it was cold and this was not the way the cosmos wanted me to be used, a lackey for a syphilitic half-wit. He was a two hundred pound cyst, and I yearned to do some home surgery. But he was filled with caustic pus, and I had to figure out how to remove him without him bursting.

"Where are we going now?"

"I just got a call from Mikey. I think we can catch Henry."

I sighed, deflating, defeated, and fell in step behind him. I saw myself, an old man, thinned and dried out, shuffling after Graf Bickerman as he climbed down into tar pits somewhere, because someone told him that the corpse of Henry was down there, preserved for eternity.

For the first time in fucking *years*, I thought: Fuck, I wish Mary were here.

"Well, this is fucking excellent."

"Shut the fuck up."

I considered hitting Bickerman for the first time in seven years, but eschewed the idea as dangerous considering his unpredictable state of mind. A few months before, it would have been a safe bet, as Bickerman's usual reaction to violence was to curl up into a fetal position and play dead. Recently, though, the boy had been under strain and had become reckless. While possessing a glass jaw and being unfamiliar with bravery of any sort, Graf Bickerman had swollen to heroic proportions, and he might defeat me just by using gravity and his own dead mass. I would suffocate in the folds of his belly fat, lost to history.

We were at Ice Station Zebra, otherwise known as Henry's apartment building. The Stupid Fuck's information about Henry had proven useless, of course—by the time we'd arrived at yet another fucking bar where the drunken inhabitants were wearing Santa hats and singing carols, there was nothing but the faint smell of puke and doom—a dotted-line outline of Henry in the bathroom, almost, like in those old cartoons—to mark that Hank had ever been there. Bickerman was a man of purpose, and had instructed me to lead him, sodden and squinty, to Henry's horrible little home. Where we now stood, freezing our balls off. I stared at the dirty, crusted snow that clogged the streets and contemplated my life, which had shriveled, recently, into something cold and dull.

Bick handed something to me. I looked down and stared. It was a flask, dull metal glinting in the streetlight.

"What's in it?" I asked. I'd been burned by Bick's beverage choices before.

"Whiskey. Not bad. Where is this idiot?"

I took a slug and liked it—not the greatest whiskey ever, but not moonshine either. I didn't hand it back. "He's out living his life, enjoying himself, stepping out on Neesie. Which is what we ought to be doing. Stepping out. Or living our lives. Or Neesie. One of those. Not standing here freezing our balls off at Ice Station Zebra."

"Waaa, waaa, waaa," Bickerman intoned, all nasal annoyance.

"I'm not your fucking wife, so don't make quacking noises at me, you fucking simp."

The icy stare of Bickerman, guaranteed to turn your balls into ice pellets. He reached out for the flask and I gave it back to him. I was pretty sure I wouldn't be offered any more, as I had offended The Bick. No, that isn't exactly possible—you cannot offend a mindless creature of pure energy, which is what Bick was.

I kept my mouth shut and stared at the street, a pleasant smile in place. I could keep a smile on my face forever if I wanted, one of many skills I possessed that you couldn't put on a resume. I was an untapped national resource. I started imagining myself in a better place—home, or a beach somewhere during Spring Break, lots of wasted chicks in bikinis staggering around, half of them already dosed with roofies and the other half in town to get laid in the first place. I wanted desperately to be anywhere else, because Henry was never coming home. He'd changed his name, gotten some plastic surgery, and was now living in Mexico under the name Carlos Elchacal, plotting against Bickerman. It would take decades and millions of dollars, but Henry was going to launch a devastating attack on Bickerman, destroying him entirely.

I slid my eyes to Bick. The bloated ass believed it, that was for sure. For weeks now, paranoid. *Where's Henry?* might have been his mantra.

Suddenly, Graf Bickerman threw out both arms, moving faster than I'd imagined he was capable.

"Henry!" he bellowed. "Thank God you're alive!"

I peered back across the street and there he was: Sodden, shivering, gray-skinned Henry. Gone was the bright-eyed, thick-haired kid we'd all voted Most Likely to Succeed Despite His Lousy Taste in Friends. This was Henry's Ghost. I told him so.

"How far did you walk like that?" Bickerman demanded.

He looked around like he was contemplating making a run for it—which would have worked perfectly, as I didn't think Graf Bickerman could get airborne in anything under an hour, and I had absolutely no intention of chasing Henry through the streets. Then Henry seemed to realize he'd been infected with Bickerman and there was no escape, so he walked tiredly across the street and climbed up the steps to stand in front of us. He was a pussy. Defeated. I had no idea why Bick was so worried about him—Henry would stand up for us, not because he was a stand-up guy, but because he was weak.

"How long have you guys been here?"

Ah, Henry, all outrage and disappointment. Henry had been disappointed by me for years, and I'd always borne it with good cheer—it wasn't his fault he thought I was a Normal and thus expected certain things from me, like respect and fair play—but after chasing him all night I was irritated. Why couldn't the shithead just stay put, be normal, make things easy on us all?

"Awhile. We heard you were all by yourself somewhere drinking like an old juicehead." I decided a little softening was prudent. "We were a little worried. We tried a few of your usual haunts but didn't find you, so we came here to wait." I noted Bickerman was just smiling vacantly at Hank, so I took the opportunity to grab the flask back. I offered it to Henry.

Henry glanced at me with his mouth slightly open. He knew better. I could see it in his sad, honest face—Henry was the worst liar in the universe. He knew we'd been tracking him all night. He looked doomed.

"Let's get inside," Graf Bickerman boomed, grabbing Henry roughly in what I was sure Bick thought was an affectionate, reassuring gesture, and which Henry probably saw as an assault. I realized suddenly that I was a lot drunker than I'd suspected. When Henry got the outer door open and we started making our way up the dark, narrow stairs, I had a vision of the rest of my life spent like this: With people I didn't like doing things I didn't want to. I had a quick urge to just reach out, overbalance, and take all three of us down, breaking necks and solving problems.

I'd finally docked Graf Bickerman in a subway car, and he sat silently, brooding. I could tell he was brooding because he looked constipated—as far as I knew, I was the only person in the world who looked good while brooding, managing a heroic, slightly tragic countenance that women under twenty-five found endearing. Over twenty-five and she'd likely seen it before, and hated it. We were both sobering up and not enjoying it, and I wisely stayed quiet, letting the subterranean rock slip past us.

After a few moments of blankness, I slid my eyes to Bickerman. This was intolerable. This was a movable hell, and I began thinking of ways out of it. Nothing could be done right away, it would take some time. But I'd left plenty of people behind in my life. You just did it: You found your way and you just kept walking and never looked back. Then when you got to a new place you burned your clothes and shaved your fingerprints off, and didn't answer the phone for six or seven months, and everyone you used to know just became someone you used to know, nameless. Worked every time.

Thinking of Tom's World Without Bickerman, I leaned back and closed my eyes.

IX.

SAINT PATRICK'S DAY

It was all going well, for a change. Neesie was pissed off at something vague, one of those things I certainly should know without being told what it was. Lord knows I liked a good mystery as much as the next guy. Who needs precise information like *this is why I am pissed off at you* anyway? Just makes life boring.

Aside from Neesie, which was no big deal because I knew in some ways I deserved a little attitude, and she wasn't really turning the screws, anyway—I knew what that felt like, believe me, and this was nothing. Aside from her, things were swell. Bickerman and Mary were tolerable, being very cute and very drunk, but at least she wasn't in Monster Mode. I still had mental scars from New Year's. Mike was being his typically inoffensive self, and Kelly and Flo were actually being nice to me, for a change. Well, Kelly was. Flo was on the prowl, that much was obvious. When chicks showed up for a friendly beer-guzzling gathering wearing a shimmery blouse with a low neckline and super-tight jeans, and their hair done up, you knew they were playing the odds that every single man in the area was going to be there to ogle them.

Then there was Miriam, who was troublesome as always, but at least she was misbehaving elsewhere. I was vaguely worried about how drunk she was, because she was underage, but then I assumed the presence of her older sister made it not my problem, and thank goodness.

I had to take a piss like nobody's business; Kelly could drink like a pro, I'd discovered, and my cheerful attempts to get her drunk while being ignored by my girlfriend had backfired.

"Anyone seen Mir?" Mary asked, looking around. She was pretty blotto herself, and hadn't thought much about her adventurous sister all night.

The men wisely pretended we'd never heard the name and had no idea who she was talking about.

"Just saw her by the bathrooms, actually," Flo offered. "Thought she was coming back this way."

I watched Bickerman stand up with dread. I knew what he was going to say and heard it echoed and translated in my head.

He said, "I'll take a look around, make sure she's okay."

I knew that meant, *I'll go hit on her if she's drunk enough, just for fun.* Bickerman always considered flirtation to be a harmless activity, no matter the circumstances.

I watched him go and wished for Tommy. Tom could have been trusted to be a witness of Bick's bullshit; he had no conscience, but he was practical. He would watch in amusement as Bick fucked everything up, but he'd have sense to stop it at the right point. Without Tom, it was down to me, and I had no stomach for it.

Once more into the breach, though. "And I have to go to the bathroom like nobody's business, so Mike, I leave you with four damned attractive ladies. Hope you're up to it, buddy."

The women, except for Denise, gave me a warm smile for the compliment. Mike just grinned his usual *I have no idea what you're talking about* grin. I waded out into the pond of swampy guys, trying to find Bick's slope-shouldered profile amongst them. Just to see him being innocent before I bopped on over to the bathroom, just to put my fears to rest so I could go get drunk in peace and not have to worry over him being shitty somewhere, in some way that would eventually gleefully boil over into my space.

Still, in a room filled with soft white men getting drunk, everyone looked just like Bick. Like me too, I guessed. I decided to not think about that so much and concentrated on just getting to the bathrooms before my situation became an urgent one. And then, suddenly, my situation *was* an urgent one, because there, bathed in fake light by the cigarette machine and swarmed past by all the people in line for the bathrooms, was Bickerman the Great, and he was being attended to by his newest courtier, Miriam, squint-eyed from booze and all over him like a blanket.

I looked up at the smoky, darkened ceiling and asked, silently, for my burden to be lifted from me.

When I looked back, he was kissing her neck.

Throwing a silent curse at the cosmos for not removing my burden, I made my way through the noise and the smoke and the people and tapped Bickerman on the shoulder.

He froze and looked over his shoulder at me.

"Fuck, man," he said, collapsing into Miriam. "You scared the shit out of me."

"Uh-huh." I jabbed my thumb over my shoulder. "Beat it, asshole, before the womenfolk catch you."

"Yes, Mom."

"Hey!" I slapped him lightly on the forehead. "I'm doing you a favor, you dumb fuck."

Bick gave me his smoldering stare, which was meant to convey a razor-thin space between Peaceful Bick and Kicking My Ass Bick. I was too pissed off to be amused by this from Bickerman, a man who had not broken a sweat in five years. If he took a swing at me, I knew I'd have to end the evening resuscitating him, breathing his digested booze fumes and tasting his dinner. Then he grinned and grabbed me up in a sudden, inexplicable bear hug, like tendrils of alcohol reaching out to envelope me warmly, a dear lost friend, newly found again.

"Henry!" he said into my ear. "You're the best of us, you know that?"

"Jesus Christ," I answered, catching Miriam's eye as I struggled to hug him back properly. "How sad."

Miriam burst into laughter as Bick and I separated. Bick patted my cheek with oddball affection and turned away from us. "Gonna take a leak, have a smoke," he muttered.

I watched him stagger off, then turned to look at Miriam. Miriam had been sixteen when we'd first met her, and my entire association with her had been one of trying not to stare. It wasn't that Mir was so amazing a beauty. She was pretty, but not in any Grace Kelly, immortal kind of way. She was just suburban pretty, with a good body that showed no signs of eternal greatness. What it was about Mir was that she was a teenager, and she was hot, and she was frequently drunk around a bunch of middle-aging guys who'd never had enough hard-bodied teenage girls when *we'd* been that age. It was twenty years of frustrated lust, standing in front of us in a constant parade of baby-doll T-shirts and cutoff shorts.

Feeling as witty and urbane as I had all night, I stood there and struggled to keep my mouth from falling open.

"Henry," she said with a giggle. "I think it's cute how you and Dave and Tommy get along with each other."

"Oh yeah?" Witty and urbane to the end, I put a cigarette into my mouth to protect myself and felt myself up for a light. "So you haven't realized that we're all part of a secret homosexual conspiracy to marry hetero women and not breed?"

She pulled a Zippo from her jeans pocket and smiled at me. "Gosh, Henry, you're strange."

I leaned forward and put a hand on the cigarette machine to balance myself as I lit up. Putting a wall of smoke between us, I felt safe, and kept my hand where it was.

"You should leave Bickerman alone. He's getting married, you know."

She made a wide-eyed show of shock. "No!" Then she smiled up at me. "You're not getting married, Henry."

I smiled ruefully. "The way I piss off Denise, no, not any time soon."

"You guys fighting?"

I shrugged. "Not really. I just seem to be able to annoy her, and she can't seem to believe it's unintentional."

"I don't think she likes me."

I didn't know what to say to that. *No, but none of the women here do* didn't seem like a nice thing to say at all. I just shook my head. Miriam seemed to be looking at something just over my shoulder.

"Anyway, Henry, I think she's nuts. I can't imagine anyone being annoyed with you. You're too cute."

I could tell when I was being had, and I gave her the fisheye on that one. I'm a sucker, and a fool, but even I wasn't that dumb. Or that drunk, maybe. I looked over my shoulder as I straightened, and I gave Miriam my eyebrows and said, "I should get back to Denise before she gets even more pissed."

"Yes," she said back, grinning widely. "You should."

Fucking teenagers.

I struggled my way into the bathroom, a truly grotesque display of puddled gray water, cigarette butts, empty bottles, and other, less definable things. Some guy was in the stall, moaning and cursing. There would be this horrific watery noise, and through it, *simultaneously*, he would moan *fuuuuucccckkkkk*. I stood at the urinal staring at the graffiti on the tiles and tried to keep a straight face.

There was no sign of Bick. I went about my business and made my sweaty way back to the bar.

Mike, Bick, and Mary sat glumly and watched me approach. I stood before them in shame and just sighed.

"Ah, fuck," I managed. "How long ago?"

Bick seemed almost humanly awkward. "About ten minutes, 'cording to Mare."

"They didn't say much. Kelly and Denise came huffing through, grabbed up Flo, and were out."

I looked at Bickerman. He looked at me.

"Fuck 'em," he said heartily, holding my eyes. "Let me buy you a drink, Henry. You can plumb the mysteries of that woman tomorrow."

And I let him.

In my dream, I was lying on my back looking up at Mary, who was the Most Beautiful Girl in the World. The Most Beautiful Girl in the World was stroking my hair and holding my hand and making cute little comforting noises from deep within herself. The Most Beautiful Girl in the World was miles above me but could still reach me. The Most Beautiful Girl in the World smelled like beer and cigarettes. Beer and cigarettes were making me nauseous.

I turned my head slightly and surveyed my world, my kingdom. Bickerman and Mike, Mike and Bickerman. The last guy in the world who needed a Yes Man and his own personal Yes Man, grinning around as if his head were broken, lolling wherever gravity took it.

Gravity was weird. I kept getting pulled in odd, often opposing directions.

Mike and Bick were speaking in an odd language I didn't recognize, full of mushy vowels and stretched-out consonants. It was a secret language only they understood. I resented that because they were talking about me, me and Denise, Denise and me. Denise, who had been mad at me, it seemed, since before we'd met, and me, who'd been apologizing since the day I was born. The world lurched and stopped, lurched and stopped, and I was pushed into Mary's soft belly, which smelled like cigarettes and alcohol, while Bick and Mike spoke softly in their mushy secret language about me and Denise and how Denise had left me in the bar because she thought I was either fucking Miriam or wanting to fuck Miriam or somehow instinctively seeing fucking Miriam as a possibly pleasurable option or what have you.

I tried to mount a defense, even though my defense team was my only audience. Still, I thought it best to practice my summation anyway, despite a lack of prosecution, judge, or jury. I tried. But the defense team hadn't wanted to hear it, and shut me up with booze.

I looked up at the Most Beautiful Girl in the World and said, "You're beautiful."

"Can we please get him home? He's drooling on my skirt."

More mushed language from the boys, reassuring, calming.

"If he yaks on me, David, I'm going to punch you."

Mush, mush, mush.

The world stopped, and there was commotion. Mike was getting out of the cab. Bick was getting out of the cab. I was getting out of the cab, pushed from behind by the Most Beautiful Girl in the World, who made little grunting noises as if I was a huge weight, impossible to think that a small girl like herself could move my immense mass, and pulled from the real world by Bick and Mike. I lurched into a semblance of uprightness, a dead arm thrown around each of them, my feet working feebly against the sidewalk, dragging more than anything else as the two men pulled me forward.

Mush, mush, mush.

"Chums," I said, feeling that this special moment required some sort of speech, "thank you for escorting me home after all this tragedy and drama. You are the truest of friends. I love you both, very much."

It didn't come out right.

Mush, mush, mush. I wanted them to speak clearly.

"English, dammit! *English!*"

Mush, mush, mush. Bick's greasy laughter.

I was propped up in front of a door, not my door, a door I recognized, and it filled me with foreboding. I was propped up against something, I didn't know what, but it supported my weight and I rested against it, relieved, and I did not fall. The door was troubling. Bick and Mike stepped up to it and simultaneously rang the bell and pounded the door.

Then they ran away, cackling to each other: Mush, mush, mush.

I regarded the door quietly, just listening to myself breathe, listening to my heart pound troublingly. A moment later, the door opened, and Denise stood in it, wearing just an old, oversized T-shirt, her hair up, her face clean and tired. She looked around before catching sight of me.

"This wasn't my idea," I said by way of defense. "But I seem to have lost control of my legs. I had to have them cut off, you know."

She sighed loudly and put her hands on her hips. "I ought to leave you out here, asshole."

"Don't yell at me. I didn't do anything."

She stared at me for a moment. Her face softened. "Christ. You okay? You going to be sick?"

I shook my head. "I couldn't possibly." Then I proved myself wrong, and she moved forward, took me onto her shoulder, pulled me into her place. She smelled good, like soap, like home, and I closed my eyes.

I was dreaming, I know. I was dreaming that Bick and I were having a talk. We were sitting in Denise's small kitchen, at the card table she kept in there, living like some frat-boy bachelor or something. Miriam was bartending, standing on the other side of the table. She was wearing tight black jeans and a tight black *Too Much Joy* T-shirt. Bick ordered a gin and tonic, and she produced it from under the table as if she had had it ready for him. Then she turned her attention to me. She was pretty, I realized, but not gorgeous, not beautiful, like Denise was.

"What'll it be, Henry?"

She said it like a poem: *What'll it be / Hen-ree?*

"I'll have a glass of milk."

Miriam didn't say anything. She produced a tall glass of milk, with a wedge of lemon, and placed it in front of me.

"Fag," Bick said genially. He was always full of bullshit homophobia like that. You got used to it.

"Where's Denise?" he asked.

I shook my head. "She's mad at me."

Miriam started to giggle. I gave her my most annoyed face and then looked at Bick. He was laughing.

"Dude, you know what I'd do if the Monster started pulling that shit on me?"

I knew I didn't want to hear the answer, but I shrugged, playing it cool while dread crawled up my spine. "What?"

"Kill her."

I looked at Bick, and he nodded as if I'd said something. "Make it look like an accident. I swear to God, I'd kill her. You and Tom would help."

I thought, *No way*, but I didn't say anything.
"Sure you would. She'd deserve it."
Miriam was still laughing.

"What's wrong? Are you going to be sick?"
I sat up, sweating in the cool air of Denise's bedroom.
"Yes."

X.

MARY'S FUNERAL

This was the second time in my life I'd wanted to fuck a corpse.

The first time, I was little. Ten, eleven, I forget exactly. Ms. Keller had been my teacher the year before. Not a pretty woman, looking back. Not *ugly*, but not beautiful. But, and this was the important part, she was easily fifteen years younger than the other teachers. Thirties, I guess. Thin and wore skirts just above the knees with stockings or pantyhose, whatever. Her legs made this wonderful dry noise when she uncrossed or recrossed them. I'd spent the year before in her class listening to those legs until I had to ask to go to the lavatory and then masturbate in one of the stalls. This probably three, four times a day. She wore a skirt every goddamn day, and after a month in her class I had red, scaly skin on my prick from tugging it to her.

Wallace men develop fast. We have to, because we're unlikely to reproduce under normal circumstances, so evolution has widened our potential breeding window, to give us a decent chance. And for thousands of years we'd made a go of it. I was there as living, breathing, masturbating proof of that, and for a while Ms. Keller starred in my quick fantasies. She wanted to teach me things, all right. She wanted to teach me *so damn bad*.

And then, she died. It was mysterious.

That was my first funeral. I wanted to go. I'd spent months fantasizing about this slim, flat-chested woman with kinky black hair and a vague flowery smell, and I wanted to put on my tiny Sunday Mass suit—rarely worn—and go marvel at a person who I'd known, now dead.

So my mother, whose name escapes me, bundled me up in my starchy suit and took me to the funeral home where Ms. Keller was laid out. I guess we did not, actually, go to the funeral, now that I'm resurrecting this ancient memory. We just went to the viewing. The wake.

My memories are like that. They disappear, go hidden. And then I'll think of something I did once, long ago, and it'll be thin and gray at first, gruel, and then as I think on it details will fade in, slowly, reddening up until it's dripping with juice.

I remembered the pale green carpet of the funeral home. The silence. The smell of flowers. The open casket, and there was Ms. Keller, looking *fantastic*. Better than she'd ever looked alive. Her face made up, all the imperfections covered up, spackled over. Her hair done and not just pulled back with an elastic band. Her boobs pushed up and out in a way that seemed like voodoo—she *had* boobs, which was a revelation. In my fantasies I'd often given her the gift of boobs, like a genie charitably handing out miracles, but there they were, somehow. Bloating, maybe. Gases building up, inflating her tits. I didn't know how, I didn't care. I was immediately aroused.

Mother encouraged me to walk right up to the casket and kneel there, say my final farewells. This seemed like a trick. I was suddenly certain my mother had figured out my dirty little secret and was prompting me to do something terrible in public, something she could punish me for. Which was a trick Mother liked to play on me. I crept up to the coffin and knelt down. Incredibly close to her. In class I'd often tried to get close to her, sidling up to her desk and leaning in, or asking her for help with classwork so she would lean in over my desk, her smell filling the air around me, brushing against my arm.

She was perfect. A doll. No wrinkle or imperfection marred her. As I knelt, I got a hard-on right there, and wanted to climb up into the coffin with her and do things. What, I wasn't 100 percent sure, because even in my masturbatory fantasies this was sort of muddy ground. Things. Play with those improbably expanded boobs, if nothing else.

It was years before it occurred to me that this was not a normal reaction.

Now I was leaning over another coffin. My back to all of them, I let my face relax. Studied Mary, who looked fucking *fantastic*. Better than she'd looked since the wedding. She was a cupcake again, perfectly frosted, sculpted into the absolute wet-dream image of a girl who'd been a blond cheerleader-cum-sorority girl since her inception, emerging from the womb with pom poms and kneepads, ready for her calling.

Before I could become inconveniently aroused again—and we Wallace men find it difficult to hide our immense, civilization-founding erections—I stood up and made a vague approximation of a religious gesture, spinning and putting my game face back on. And there they were. My friends. My albatrosses. Bick, drunk but looking sober and playing his part well, but Bickerman always did well on stage. It was in private that he transformed into a beetle and scurried around eating dead skin and dung. Miriam next to him, and the other Harrowses, all fair and vaguely Norwegian or Swedish or something, diluted through years and years of good old American crossbreeding.

Miriam was a knockout in a black dress that covered every inch of her skin except her puffy face and her bitten-down nails. If her dead sister had not looked so absolutely edible, I would have been scheming to get her drunk later and peel her like a ripe fruit. She'd been crying since she woke up, it seemed, and that didn't bother me at all. I'd incorporated it into my fantasies: Miriam pinned under me, an ankle in each of my hands, weeping ceaselessly in deep depression.

Then, of course, everyone else. Luis looked great in a dark blue suit. Mature. Serious. Successful. He looked like he worked at the funeral home. I realized I did not actually know what Luis *did* for a living, and was suddenly certain he *did* work for this funeral home.

The potential of that concept filled me with excitement.

Next to him, Henry. Next to Henry, Kelly. Next to Kelly, Flo. Next to Flo, Denise. Denise and Henry, not speaking. No one looked at me, and I looked at no one.

We were at the Harrowses house. Harrows House. Harrohouse. I was drunk. Not my fault; the elder Harrowseses, who were tiny little people with white hair and the kind of clothes that cost some money but were meant to last for decades, completely neutral in style and coarse to the touch, had put out a spread of booze that answered many of the questions concerning the Harrows daughters and their behavior around alcohol. With so much liquor in the house it was certain the two sisters had been drunk since grade school. They probably went to bed at night and found bottles of rye stashed under their pillows.

Denise was talking to Kelly. Denise was not breathing. Denise spoke continuously, a drone, her words washing over Kelly in a repetitive loop. Henry. Motherfuckery. No listening. Vile Tommy. Henry. Motherfuckery. Denise was moistly tipsy and Kelly had a stone-faced expression of resignation on her face. I was not Kelly's favorite person, but I suspected she would gladly let me touch her boobs if I offered to rescue her from Disapproving Denise at that moment.

I was invisible. A pariah. Everyone was pretending they couldn't see me.

Luis was talking to Henry. They were standing by the food, trays of simmering bacterial infections. Luis was telling Henry that in his home-town back in Spain, the people have stopped holding funerals because they regard the local church as corrupt and greedy, so they just break into the graveyard and bury people themselves. He's telling Henry that an old man everyone regards with affection because of his adorable alcoholic adventures throughout town always gives the eulogy, rambling on drunkenly until he just sort of stops and wanders off. Henry keeps nodding as if any of this makes any sense to him at all, which is impossible. I watch Henry carefully. He doesn't look good. Secrets weigh Henry down.

Luis tells Henry that this may be the basis for a new religion, that a thousand years from now this old man might be revered as a new prophet, that this makes as much sense as any religion, and Henry nods, seriously. His glass is empty and I can almost feel the gravitational pull of the bar on him.

Bickerman is talking to me. We're standing in the damp grass at the cemetery. Bickerman is just a hair too loud, but this is because he is a hair too drunk, having been sipping from his flask since waking up that morning, the morning we buried his wife. Who fell down the stairs.

"He's going to break."

Henry, he means Henry. I shook my head. "No."

Henry liked himself too much. Everything Henry did was, by definition, morally okay. Because he was a good guy. It was a circle. He was a good guy, so everything he did was good, because he was a good guy.

"We should talk to him."

I shook my head. "No."

I realized I was going to be having a lot of endless conversations with Bickerman over the coming weeks. I was not looking forward to it.

Denise was talking to me. This was unusual.

Denise was kind of drunk, which wasn't unusual and which explained a lot. She was still too fat for her dress and was popping out of it, as if she'd been baking all this time and was now rising like good bread. Bread with awesome tits. At first I'd struggled manfully to keep my eyes off her chest while she slurred at me, at least when she was looking at me, but then I realized she didn't seem to care so I just lost myself in her overflowing boobs.

Denise was unhappy. This was not unusual.

People always thought they were deep oceans of secrets, mysteries wrapped in enigmas and such. Never true. Maybe Luis. But, generally speaking, never true. Denise felt that Henry was not truly *with* her. That he was still with Bickerman and me. I tried to offer him back, but she wasn't listening to me. She was just complaining.

I was listening. I didn't like what she was saying. Henry. Chatty, open, honest, stupid Henry. Noble Henry.

"Thanks for listening to me ramble," Denise finally says, touching my arm. I look down at her hand, then back at her.

Miriam was talking to me. Except replace "talking" with "weeping." For the first time in our association, I did not find Miriam at all erotic. She was the same pretty girl with the same hot little ass, in a passably tight dress, and I was still sporting a semi-erection from Mary's coffin cleavage earlier, but she was just a soggy, sad mess. She'd come up to me with a saucy little smile and a glass of wine in her hand, and I'd been encouraged and glad to see her. Then her face had done some sort of remarkable collapsing thing, like a special effect, and she'd pushed her head into my chest and just burst into tears. She'd also spilled red wine on my jacket.

I stood there patting her back and letting my eyes roam the Harrowseseses fussy living room, plush carpet and dark wood and bric-a-brac everywhere, exhausting to look at. I had to get free of them. All of them. This had gotten boring.

"I miss her so much, Tommy," Miriam wailed into me.

"Sure, sure," I murmured.

"I was a fucking *terrible* sister."

"Sure, sure."

I stared around the room, seeing nothing. I had to get free of all of them. Starting with Henry.

Bickerman was talking to me. The Harrowseseses standing there with vague, painful smiles on their faces. They'd been talking to Bickerman, and then he'd called me over. His insane tractor beam latched onto me and I floated toward him, limp and helpless. Bickerman was talking to me like the Harrowseseses, the parents of his dead wife, were not there.

"Henry's avoiding me," he said.

"No, he isn't," I said, anxious to be away, to be free. I had no idea if I was lying or not. I didn't care. I felt the million threadlike legs of Bickerman's body enveloping me, heard the clicking of his pincers. The rattle of his stinger.

"He *is*," he said authoritatively. "We need to keep an eye on him. We need to be sure of him."

I looked at Mr. Harrows. He was shrinking. He'd shrunk since the last time he'd gone clothes shopping, because his elegant and expensive black suit was a little too big for him. He was pink-faced and had the World's Largest Tumbler of Whiskey in one gnarled hand. I fully expected to be able to look that up in *The Guinness Book of World Records* and find a picture of Mr. Harrows, scowling. Mrs. Harrows was grinning. It wasn't an expression, which implied intent or emotion. It was just a tug of muscles. The way cats sometimes looked like they grinned. They'd lost their daughter, and now they were maybe realizing what, exactly, their daughter had married.

I didn't remember seeing them at the wedding. Which was odd.

"He *is*," Bickerman repeated, drifting, losing focus. "He *is*."

Denise was not talking to me. Her eyes were closed. The top of her dress was down. Her bra was still on. Her brow was beaded in sweat. Her hair had come loose in a mess of lazy curls. Her hands were on my chest, pushing down. Her knees dug into my sides. Her throat made little grunting noises, like chirps.

Afterward, we lay next to each other in her bed and I tried to figure out if I was on Henry's side of the mattress or not. The ceiling was cracked.

Denise was crying. I became aware of this in stages. Jesus fucked, she was *crying*.

"Just go," she said in a wavery voice.

I sighed, staring up at the ceiling. I had this effect on people.

XI.

THANKSGIVING

"What's wrong? Is something wrong? Was that Bick?"

I slid the phone back into its cradle and sat in the cool air of Denise's bedroom. I nodded, then realized she couldn't see me.

"It was Tom. I'm not sure. They want me to come over."

"Now? Henry, it's three in the morning."

"Yes."

There was dark silence for a moment. "And you're going?"

"Yes."

"Fine."

A lot of words hidden within that one. A loose translation, I thought, was "Your sad devotion to these immature friends of yours is pissing me off mightily right now." To dot the Is and cross the Ts, she rolled over so her back was to me.

I sat there for a moment, hearing Tom's voice in my head. He'd only said a few words. He'd said, "Hank, it's Tom. I'm at the Bickermans'. Something bad's happened. We need you to come by." His voice had been muted, strained. I hadn't heard Tommy sound that way, ever. He sounded panicked. He sounded like he was sitting in the dark, alone, for the first time in his life.

I could feel Denise icing over next to me, the frigid tendrils of the glacier spreading outward from her tense shoulder blades. It pushed me, gently but inexorably, out of the bed, onto the floor.

I dressed in her small bathroom, pulling on dirty clothes amidst the slight mildew smell that filled it. I dressed quickly and silently, my own breathing loud and grating, rapid and acidic in my throat. Tommy's voice, it was sitting, stagnant and unfamiliar, in my head. The more I thought about it, the more my hands shook. I stopped and pushed them into my pockets and stared into the mirror for a minute. My hair was standing up in odd ways, my eyes looked sunken and darkened in the glare of Denise's makeup lights. I looked yellow and plastic.

I buckled my pants on and opened the door. Denise stood in the doorway, looking sleepy and annoyed.

"So, Bick calls at three in the morning and you just run over there?"

I shrugged, pushing past her. "There's trouble."

"What kind of trouble? They having trouble drinking everything in sight? Those two are fucking alcoholics, Henry."

"Tommy's there."

"That doesn't make me feel any better."

"I'm not trying to make you feel better."

A moment, then, of icy silence.

"So you're going to drive over there?"

"Jesus, *yes*." I regretted the nasty tone and swallowed my annoyance. "Look, it sounds like trouble. They're my friends. They ask for help, I show up. It's that simple."

"Uh-huh." She sat down on the bed and watched me hunting for my shoes. "You're always doing their shit work, you know that? They fuck up like the retarded booze monkeys they are, you scuttle over there to clean it up for them."

I found my shoes and sat down on the floor. For a moment I just looked at her. "Jeez, you're giving me the idea you don't like Tom and Bick."

She nodded. "Or Mary. They drink too much, and they're mean."

I nodded. "Okay." I pulled a shoe on, began tying it.

"So you're going?"

I clenched my teeth. "Yes."

"What if I ask you not to?"

I looked back at her. I tried to broadcast despair and weariness to her. I tried to get it across, invisibly, through the air that I was completely unamused by this. "What's this, power games? Right now? Does it have to be right now? There's absolutely no better time to fuck with me over this?"

"I am *not* fucking with you."

"The hell you're not," I snapped. Standing up, I tried to adopt a moderate tone and expression. "Can we please just talk about this later?"

"Sure."

Her attitude was pissed-off.

"Don't do that. It's blackmail."

"What's blackmail?"

"*This.* This sudden demand that we discuss something. If you're bothered by it, why now? Why not earlier? Last week? Tomorrow? *Why now?*"

She lay down and pulled the covers over herself. "Sorry if my timing isn't convenient for you. Just go, then."

I stood there for a moment, and then I thought, fuck it, I could stay here and argue until it was too late to do anything, which is what she wanted. So I turned and left the room. I wondered if I'd left anything there I was going to have to fight to get back.

The roads were icy and the car's tires were bald, so I took it slow, playing talk radio and smoking cigarettes. I was in no hurry to get to Bick's. I didn't know what I was gonna find there, but experience told me I wasn't going to like it.

I thought about Denise. I wondered if we'd just broken up or if it had just been a fight or if I understood anything about her, really. Or maybe it was the other way around. Maybe she didn't understand me. But I was a fucking simpleton: It was just beer, baseball, and sleep with me. What was there to understand? Don't forget to buy something pale and domestic for me, don't change the channel when the game was on, and don't ever wake me up before eight in the morning. I was a simple guy.

I opened the window and let the cold air in, the smoke out.

The guy on the radio was saying that children who were caught buying or dealing illegal drugs ought to be put in jail like any other criminal, no matter how old they were. He sounded very sure about this.

I pulled up outside the Bickermans' apartment building and put the car into park. Listening to the engine click and cool, I looked up to the sixth floor and saw a light on. Every other window was dark; only my friends were sufficiently fucked up to be awake. I sat and finished my cigarette, staring up at the window and the odd shadows that appeared there, sudden and quick-fading. I couldn't tell who was who, but I had an idea that the blurry form that stood before the drapes as if posing for a shadow-watching world he knew was out there must have been Bickerman, and the elusive splotch that quickly made its way was Tommy. I didn't see anything that looked like Mary, and I wondered if she'd up and walked out on him. They were the kind of married couple that made you wonder if the cosmos was fucking with you, to show you a couple like that.

And Tommy was sitting in the dark, and staring at me, by himself. He had a tumbler of whiskey in one hand. I didn't know where David was. Getting help, maybe. Why was Tommy just staring at me? I wanted to ask him, I wanted to shout at him. But I couldn't. I couldn't raise my head, I couldn't move my lips, I couldn't even breathe. I couldn't even move my eyes from Tommy. He was sitting in the dark, and staring back at me.

It's so cold. Tommy looks cold too, but he's got something nice in a glass to keep him warm, but I'm on the cold wood floor. I'm not shivering, though. I can hear David. He is talking to Tommy.

"Is he coming?"

"Yeah." *Tommy sounds weird. He sounds quiet. I've never heard Tommy without the high-pitched whine of mania in his voice.*

"Why do we want him to come again?"

"We need help. We can't do it alone. Someone's got to watch our backs."

"Maybe we should call the cops."

"Go ahead."

"Oh, go fuck yourself, then."

"Go fuck *yourself*, Bicky."

There's a stillness, then, with Tommy staring at his glass as if something were happening within it, and David standing behind him, hands at his sides but with that gangly bent-elbow look that hinted at a readiness to do something.

"Ah," *David suddenly spat, throwing up his arms.* "To hell with you, then."

"To hell with you."

"You think I wanted this to happen?"

"Bickerman, you don't want to know what I think right now, okay?"

David threw his arms up, but Tommy wasn't paying him any attention. "Well, then thank goodness Hank's heading over because you're useless."

Tommy just sits there and stares at his glass for a moment. Then he takes a really deep breath and says, "You didn't need my goddamn help pushing her down the fucking stairs, did you?"

A shock went through me. Or, I expected a shock to go through me, and was pretty surprised when nothing did. David walked a few steps out of my frame of vision, and I couldn't move my eyes to follow him.

The doorbell rang, and David and Tommy got very still. The blurriness around them stopped, and I could see them clearly for a moment. They looked old. Tommy had some gray hair on his temples; I'd never noticed that before. David's slumping had gotten worse—I'd been trying to get him to stand straighter for some time, but it had never worked.

For a moment, neither of them moved.

"Go get the door," *Tommy said, draining his glass.* "Your servant awaits."

David just waved a hand at him in disgust and left the room. Tommy got up and crossed to the bar, where he refilled his drink. I was terribly thirsty, too, and wished he would bring me something to sip. Maybe if he lifted my head and held the glass to my lips, he could get something in me. When David walked back into the room, Tommy didn't turn around, just stayed at the bottles, one hand on his glass, busy bringing it up to his mouth, the other on a bottle.

Henry walked in behind David and stopped, looking at me. Poor Henry! He always looked about to cry, I thought.

David was being quite rude, too, and stood with his back to Henry.

"Oh," *Henry said.*

"Jesus, is that all you got to say?" *David said, running a hand through his hair.*

"Welcome, Hank," *Tommy shouts, spinning around, spilling booze all over the cream rug we just bought!* "I know what you're thinking. You're thinking: This is some fucked-up joke we've cooked up for you, that maybe we've been in here blowing rails all night again and we thought this would somehow amuse a fucking saint like you. But it's no joke. Sorry, man."

Henry stepped backwards, seemed to lose his balance, and caught hold of the couch. He looked damp. Poor Henry!

David finally turned around. "We were arguing," *he said, understating it as always, the fuck.* "And I admit I was intimidating her, coming at her. She didn't look where she was going, and she backed onto the stairs. I dived for her—Christ, I did! But she just went over. We . . . we haven't moved her."

"It's true," *Tommy sang, choking on the rest of his drink. He was bright-eyed and red-faced again, drunk as hell.* "I know you'd believe that Bicky pushed the bitch, we all would, but that isn't what happened."

"Shut the fuck up, Tom. Keep drinking."

Tommy held up his finger at David and went back to the bar, listing a little.

Poor Henry was still holding onto the couch as if gravity had shifted to the left. He licked his lips. "Did you call . . . someone?"

Tommy was pouring different liquors into his glass, mixing them into something horrible. "The cops, Hank? Hell no. We're concerned because they've been here once tonight." *He turned to look at Henry, winked.* "Domestic violence, you know."

"Tommy, I swear, if you don't shut the fuck up—"

"Bicky, we're on the first floor of this place, so I figure I'm safe from you."

"Christ," *David swore. I hated when he used the Lord's name like that. He did it sometimes in front of Daddy, and it killed me. He looked up at Henry. Henry was still staring at me. I wanted to make him feel better, let him know I was okay, really.*

"We were arguing, I told you. One of the neighbors called the cops, and we had to sweet-talk a fucking uniform who stopped by. Took a fucking stroll through the whole place, too."

Tommy had a dark glass, filled to the rim, which was bourbon and gin and tequila and who knew what else. He turned, smiling, filled with something, some spirit I'd seen him with before, something like . . .

Glee. It was the Glee. I saw it in Tommy and felt nauseous, because there was something else going on here. Something other than Mary, which scared the shit out of me as it was. Something cold was growing inside my stomach, and the floor was trying to buck me off, and Bick and Tommy were standing there like the Worst Fucking Rat Pack Ever, boozy and open-collared and assholes assholes assholes.

"Come on in, Henry!" He shouted at me. "Bicky's got nothing to hide, right, Bicky? We're inviting everyone over for an open house. A party! We'll drape something stylish over Mare and she'll be the ultimate conversation piece."

"Shut up," Bick snapped.

I opened my mouth to tell Tommy the same thing, but I couldn't make words.

"Jesus, Hank, you okay?"

She was lying on the floor at the foot of their stairs, one arm twisted behind her in a terrible way. She was dead. I thought of every time I'd pictured her naked and felt nauseous. The cold thing in my stomach got bigger.

Bick was Sinatra, freaked out and wasted. Tommy was Dino, red-faced and indecent. I was Joey Bishop: No one gave a fuck about me one way or another.

"Call the motherfucking cops, Bick," I croaked.

"He *can* talk!" Tommy shouted, drinking recklessly.

"Sit down, Henry," Bick ordered, shoving Tom aside and heading for the bar. "Let's talk," he added over his shoulder.

"Talk?" I couldn't breathe and my legs had broken again, snapped silently and numbly. I could hear the gravel-like sounds of the bones rubbing together within.

"Sit down."

I closed my eyes because it looked like Mare was staring at me. It even looked like she was smiling. "Fuck you."

"Too late!" I heard Tommy sing out. "He's already fucked himself."

I heard, somehow, nothing but a tense silence. Then Bick.

"Tom, I swear, shut the fuck up."

I opened my eyes again. Mary seemed to be encouraging me. I struggled to remain on my feet with a cannonball of ice in my belly and no air in the room, finally wobbling on my feet. "What the hell is there to talk about? Jesus, how long has she been lying there?"

Bick let out a frightening laugh, a single derisive note. "Hank, focus, okay?"

"You're here to be a witness, Henry," Tommy said. He was extremely drunk, which you could tell with Tommy because he passed through slurring and stumbling into a sort of stone-faced impassiveness, where he appeared steady and sober, if expressionless and bitterly sarcastic. "Bicky's afraid that with the domestic complaint and my general unreliability and habit of coming off as a liar, people might get the wrong idea. So we want you, as a mildly upstanding young man, to back us up."

"That's the most fucked-up thing I've ever heard. You want me to say that I saw it happen? *Why*, for God's sake?"

Then I knew why. I saw it in the way Tommy could barely keep the Glee at bay. He wanted to whoop, he wanted to run around with the joy of it all, the excitement, the security of knowing that someone else had fucked up.

Suddenly Bick was right in front of me, his boozy breath all around me and his hands on my shoulders.

"Hank, Hank, it was, I swear it was, an accident. I swear to you. On our friendship. I didn't mean it to happen. I swear. I wouldn't have ever hurt her. I swear. I was so fucking angry, Hank, so angry you just don't know, I pray you never know how it felt, and I didn't see where she was, and I reached out and fucking Jesus—then she was falling and hitting her fucking head on every goddamn stair."

He let go and turned on Tommy, his shoulders tense, and he hissed at Tom so low I almost didn't hear him.

"And you fucking made me drag his poor ass over here, asshole. And now we've got more problems."

"We?" Tommy seemed to be fighting with physical force for control over his own amusement. "We? Bicky, I was down here scheming to go through her underwear drawer, listening to you two bitch and moan at each other like a proper married couple. Don't fucking tell me *I'm* in trouble."

Bick was back to me, hanging off of me. "Jesus, Hank, you can't think I'd do it on purpose. Look at me, Hank! Look at me! I've known you forever. Forever, Hank! I'm just asking for some help. It just doesn't look good, you know? And I need your help. That's all."

And for some number of seconds, I don't know how long, we stood there, with Bick's hands clutching my jacket, our eyes on each other, with Tommy standing in the background vibrating with suppressed Glee, with Mary staring at me, and me staring back, begging to know what she wanted me to do. I was pretty sure Tommy actually wanted me to refuse, *wanted* this to get worse and worse, to spiral down into blackness and horror. The Glee was fed on blackness and horror, and Tommy was willing me to tell Bick to go fuck himself. I could almost see him mouthing the words for me.

Finally, I focused on Bick again.

"Okay," I nodded.

"Great," Tommy said immediately. "Here's what we want you to do."

"Hank? You with me?"

Mary's eyes looked dusty. I sat on the couch with a drink in my hand, which was wet from melting ice and sweat, and stared back at her. She kept her eyes on me, a filmy stare of accusation and resentment. It was, I realized, the same way she'd always looked at me. I could see Miriam in her. I used to think they didn't resemble each other beyond minor things. But I could see they were sisters.

"Hank? You been listening? Are you okay with all this?"

"*Now* you ask him? Jesus!"

What bothered me about it, I realized, was that she'd been lying there, all twisted up and staring, and none of us had done anything for her, no sign of empathy or respect. No covering, no dignity, no attempt at comfort, whether she could feel it or not. I'd been sitting here listening to Tommy and Bick tell me how they wanted me to lie so no one got "the wrong idea" about what happened, and I was exhausted, and I think standing up was the hardest thing I'd ever done.

"Henry, what's up? You understand? Where are you going?"

Tommy seemed disinclined to let me past him, but I just went around. I'd known Tommy long enough to know that he wasn't one to take a swing, at least not without a clear exit and a lot of running room to work with. He smelled, up close, like sweat.

I could hear them both like pigeons behind me, a lot of bobbing and weaving and ruffling feathers, a lot of preening. I walked over to her and looked down. She appeared to be staring at my feet, intent on something. I'd never really liked her, I realized. Still, I swallowed back something resembling regret, something that tasted vaguely like sadness. I knelt down and pushed her hair away from her face a little.

"Jesus Christ," I heard Bick say.

I shrugged off my jacket and held it before me, feeling static, momentarily at peace, but maybe it was just an illusion, just blankness, someplace where I was supposed to be feeling something and was misinterpreting nothing as calm. I snapped the jacket out like a sheet and let it settle gently on her, covering her face. I kept kneeling for a moment because I didn't want to turn and face them. I wasn't ready.

"Well," Bick said quietly, "Thanks."

I closed my eyes.

"Jesus," I said, surprising myself with the levelness of my voice. "Hasn't one of you called the cops yet?"

I wanted to move, I wanted to move badly. I was sick and tired of being still, and Tommy was saying horrible things. Vile Tommy, we hated him, we did, because whenever he was presented with a choice between saying something nice and saying something vile, he always chose vile. Always. Vile Tommy.

I tried to concentrate on what he was saying, but I couldn't do that and keep trying to move, to break my stillness. I gave up trying to follow Tommy's annoying little nasally voice and pushed everything into my fingers, pushing, I just wanted to move one finger, and if I could move one finger, I knew I'd be able to stand up and tell the boys to go home, to get out and leave me alone. David, too. I wanted to be boy-free for the first time in my life.

The first had been Maury, Maury whatever his name was, in seventh grade. I'd made out with him at Kelly Dessent's party, in the basement after half a lite beer and one puff of a menthol cigarette. He never spoke to me again. I always thought it was because I wouldn't let him touch my breasts. I learned my lesson.

Six months later, I let Carl Sweeney touch them as much as he wanted, and squeezed him until he came in his pants. We dated for six months. We never removed a single piece of clothing. I got him off dozens of times. I don't recall him ever touching me under my clothes.

Throughout high school there had been Jeremy Hannon, who said hello to me in homeroom on my first day and who had been my first real actual sex seven months later after a pint of blackberry brandy in the backseat of his rusted, broken-down Mustang that I thought was the coolest thing in the world. I remember he cursed every time he came. Nothing that made sense. Just random fucks and shits and then he would bury his face in my hair and sob.

I dated Jeremy for four years. I cheated on him a lot, though. It always just sort of happened. Plus, we were forever breaking up and then I would be at a party and trying to enjoy myself and put him behind me and then we would get back together again—was that my fault? Who knew we would end up back together? You can't predict these things, and you can't go through your life feeling blue and depressed all the time, either. Jeremy was okay, though, and he never acted all possessive or bugged me about some things I might have been rumored to have done. He was usually really sweet, but he got too weird near the end of high school, calling me all the time and asking me to move to New York with him. As if. As if I didn't have my own life to worry about. It was hard breaking up with Jeremy. He came to my house and cried and begged me not to. It was one of the worst days of my life.

I had already met Billy by then, but hadn't really done anything with him. Made out a little with him at a college party me and my best friend Eileen had gotten invited to. I dated him freshman year, or most of freshman year. Then there was Sam, who was a brother at Phi Theta; he was fun. After Sammy there was Ralph, and then another Jeremy, although Jeremy Two didn't really ever go anywhere because his name freaked me out all the time and he kind of looked like Jeremy One too. So while I was seeing Jeremy Two I was also kind of messing around with Ralph, who I didn't really fully break up with until after school. Even then we kept running into each other and sleeping together a lot until I started seeing David One.

David One was my boss at my first job. I was an assistant in the marketing department, making like twelve thousand dollars a year, but it was a start. David was forty-three and married, but he made me weak in the knees anyway. I guess David and I never really dated. We slept together; we had an affair. It was great fun, it was breathless and exciting, and it was the best sex I'd ever had. After two years he changed jobs, and I sort of lost touch with him. It just kind of happened. Since we'd never really been dating, I'd sort of been going out here and there, with the girls, to bars and stuff, meeting people. I think when you're under twenty-five it's just natural to be out meeting people. I have my whole old age to sit at home with my cats and a cup of tea. So I'd had a few dates with this guy Kenny, who was wild. Liked drugs, stayed out all night, showered and would come in to work. Knew everyone and was constantly getting into shows and clubs that made my friends jealous. He was wild and fun and a little scary, and I was still dating him and just starting to get tired of his act, of nursing his hangovers, when I met David Two, my David, my husband. By then I was twenty-five and willing to settle down.

David Two was great. He was fun and a little wild, but not like Kenny: He was smart. He was older but not married-and-getting-a-gut older, like the first David had been. He made me feel like he was in charge without making me pissed off about it. He had a magic about him. He dazzled me at first, and even after that dazzle faded, I still felt breathless around him.

His only downside, I thought, was Vile Tommy, who came along like a disease, and Droopy Henry, who slouched around like a fucking rainy day in human form—but they were okay, really, and I even came to like Henry a little.

But no more. No more boys for me. I was declaring my Independence Day. I was shedding the skin. Look where boys had gotten me. Look where David had gotten me. I was going to be rid of them all.

And it was dark, and I imagined that it smelled like Henry, who I remembered somehow smelled like cigarettes and cologne, some kind I'd never identified. It was a tired smell, an after-a-night-of-drinking smell, not bad at all. It was weird: I was almost touched by Henry covering me with a jacket, which was just a weird thing to do. But there had been such niceness in his eyes when he'd done it, I couldn't think anything bad about him.

I could hear them talking, the kind of not-yelling volume that I used to hear from Mom and Dad when they "weren't fighting," back in the day. None of the words made any sense, and I became so sleepy, suddenly, so tired. I would have closed my eyes if I could have, but it seemed beyond me, too *much strength required. Could you be too tired to close your eyes? I was, though. Too tired to close my eyes.*

Henry was being melodramatic, though, talking about calling the cops. An ambulance, maybe. Someone to find out what was wrong with me, but the cops—that was nuts. I didn't want David to get into trouble. I just wanted to be boy-free, and I didn't need police to do that for me. I could handle David Bickerman all right.

"What's wrong? Is something wrong?"

I kept unlacing my shoes and didn't turn to look in the direction of her sleepy voice.

"Yes. I'll tell you about it tomorrow." I wanted nothing more than to sleep. To close my eyes, have a quiet heart attack, and never wake up. I pulled one shoe off and set it carefully on the floor.

"I'm mad at you," she said, sweetly. She pushed her feet against me, though, and somehow, by some magical human communication, I knew that I'd been forgiven. "You were gone a long time. What's up?"

I unlaced the other shoe. "Tomorrow, okay?"

"Okay."

Quiet. Lightening dark, because the sun was coming. I set my other shoe on the floor. I was beginning to be able to see.

The phone rang, and I shut my eyes. I started to cry, silent, just welling tears dripping down because I wasn't even going to get this night. This one fucking night.

XII.

MONDAY

I knew Lindsay the Doctor from high school. I knew this, although I didn't remember much from high school. My childhood at all, really. My past faded. A few years down the line, it was like stuff never happened. People would show me photos—Tommy in a cowboy costume, Tommy screaming at some concert, Tommy playing guitar with a cigarette in the corner of his mouth at some frat party—and there was nothing. No glimmer of recognition. Like it was a different me doing all that, all those years ago.

I was a perfect organism. Unencumbered by past failures or triumphs.

It was all still there, though. If I concentrated, if I had a reason, I could pull it all back out of the dark moldy folds of my brain, the complex chains of acids and chemicals that formed memories. I rarely tried very hard. There was nothing for me there.

Lindsay, I remembered. She was useful to remember. She was pretty but not beautiful. The kind of girl you chatted up energetically at a bar and then spent the morning wishing fervently would leave. Super smart. Fucking Bond Villain smart. In high school, she'd been insecure and desperate, got high a lot, always had drugs, put out like a French Quarter prostitute, and spent a lot of her time crying. Naturally, I stayed in touch.

In college, she'd done well. Professionally. Pre-med, good grades piled up. She was fucking brilliant. Could read a book in an hour, remember everything. Said she hated her brain, because she couldn't forget. Anything. It all stayed there. Every insult, every backseat date rape, every humiliation and menstrual cramp, burned in. If we bred, our children would be Supermen.

She was already making money selling. Pills, mainly. Pills were plenty. She also sold gear. Syringes, ampoules, whatever. She got contacts to write scripts for a premium. Her dorm room was fucking party central, something out of a movie. People everywhere, getting stoned, Lindsay always stoned, but always somehow showing up for finals and getting fucking perfect grades. And when she went on to med school and I went on to a lowly perch in corporate America's gut, I kept in touch. I remembered her. I forced myself to, because she was too good a resource.

And she *appreciated* being remembered. Most of her old friends had moved on. Most of her customers forgot her the second she shut the door behind them. I always reminded her how cool she'd been in high school. A rebel. A smart, pretty girl who liked to party. I told her high school story like a fucking teen comedy film, leaving out the crying jags except when I'd been there to manfully put an arm around her—a bonding moment for the main characters—and the occasional six-month depression. I shaped her adolescence into a fucking magical time of freedom and triumph, so she liked having me around.

She told me people wore her out on OxyContin. Wore her out. That's all they wanted. She was fucked up to the gills all the time herself. Handfuls of pills, a bottle of vodka in her locker, in her glove box, in her backpack. She was thin and yellowed and her hair got brittle, she looked like fucking death but she pulled through her residency with flying colors. Told me she maybe killed two, three people by accident, but seemed kind of surprised by that stat. Like she knew it should have been more. Told me doctors killed more people than you would imagine but covered for each other. Invented symptoms, scotched up test results. She said most doctors were shit, they fucked up *all the time* but covered it all up so they could continue killing us.

She also told me doctors earned shit. Until they were out of residency, at least, and then only if they were specialists. And *then* only if they were fucking incredible. Most doctors made decent livings, but weren't rich.

I didn't do drugs often. I liked drugs fine, but the quality control issue bothered me. You buy something from some asshole, who the fuck knew what you were getting. Booze was safe. Regulated. Your chances of drinking a bellyful of antifreeze instead of bourbon were essentially zero. Your chances of blowing a rail made up 65 percent rat poison were essentially 100. But pharmaceuticals, from a fucking *pharmacy*, passed on a scrip? Fuck all. Why not.

Time had not been kind to Lindsay. At her messy, tight apartment downtown, she paced and chewed her nails. Her apartment had a layer of her dust on top of the dust that had been there when she'd moved in. A sublet. A sweet sublet, rent-controlled. She was paying practically nothing for a one-bedroom. And treating it like her dorm room. Shit everywhere. Hadn't been cleaned, period. Like, since it had been *built*, first not cleaned by the Italian or Irish immigrants who packed into it, desperate and unwanted. Then not cleaned by generations of increasingly upscale slummers who could have afforded some shitbox studio in midtown but chose to beat the system and pay pennies on the dollar for a place with atmosphere. The place smelled, and felt tight and hot, like we were buried under ash.

Her apartment made my skin crawl. I sat there with a theatrical smile on my face.

Lindsay had a small path to pace in. Eight feet, spin, eight feet. A canyon formed by piles of boxes and books, clothes and plump, swelling garbage bags I suspected should have been taken to the curb months ago. She smoked and chewed and spat little pieces of herself on the floor, telling me about it. Pills to wake up in the morning, pills to stay sharp during the day, pills to go to sleep at night. Dark bags under her eyes. Lindsay fucking up almost too much for even her fellow doctors to cover up. Dozens of people, now, she said. Dozens dead.

She kept telling me this as she paced, smoking a cigarette, hands shaking. Dozens. She'd killed dozens now. Nodding off during procedures, getting all blurry reading tests, writing out preposterous prescriptions that were filled without question, making hearts explode and livers fail.

Sure, sure, I kept saying. Soothing. I felt like I was back in school, trying to fuck a Sad Girl. You had to coax the Sad Girls. You had to listen and listen and listen and rub their backs and tell them they were special and beautiful and of course you understood and then you had to listen and listen and listen *again*, and rub their fucking backs and murmur kind words of support. And again and again, endlessly, your appetite for it directly proportional to how hot she was, how big her boobs were, how long her legs were. If you did it long enough, if you put in the time, the Sad Girls would lay down and spread their legs and you got in. And then you made them more sad, but that was the next asshole's problem.

Lindsay was like that. Pacing, making me dizzy. Smoking and talking. And talking. She was being watched. She was going to lose her license. She was being sued by *so many people* now, and she was going to lose her malpractice insurance. She was fucked. All I wanted to do was buy some pills from her, heavy-duty stuff that you could calm a gorilla with. But I had to sit there and rub her back and say *sure, sure* and tell her she was beautiful so she would lay back and put her ankles in the air and sell me some fucking pills.

She had a plan. She was selling everything. Everything Must Go. Caution to the wind, she was moving more fucking drugs out the door than she'd ever dared. She was going to sell everything she could, fucking bankrupt the hospital, screw all of her doctor friends, and put together a tidy amount of money. Move to Mexico. She knew an American doctor with a license in any state could buy a license in Mexico for a few grand. She'd set out her shingle in some shithole town and make burrito money stitching up cuts and diagnosing asthma, and live off her wad.

Except, except, except, as she paced back and forth back and forth, smoking and picking at a scab on her arm, except she wasn't piling the money up. She didn't understand it. She was selling so much shit, like really setting records with it. Call the Guinness people: a doctor who sold more prescription drugs than ever before in history! It was her. But she didn't have a ton of cash. It just melted away.

I rubbed her back. I told her, *sure, sure.* It was a fucking mystery. Unsolvable, unless you put a face on the cosmos and made it all angry and mean. The universe, fucking with her, stealing her money. I watched her scratching at herself. A real mystery.

Suddenly, she spun and asked me if I wanted a drink? Some music? Suddenly we're on a date. She smiles at me. Tomwallace, she says. She did that, said my full name as one word. It was a thing. Tomwallace, she says, thanks for sticking with me.

Panic swept through me. She's going to cry. Jesus fucking Christ, all I want is a bottle of horse tranquilizers, and now I'm starting to worry I'm going to have to fuck her to get them. She's giving me that dewy look. Like she actually believes we are some epic love story. She's the Ungettable Girl, super smart and pretty and successful, and I'm the nerd character, the puppy dog loser who's always there for her but never noticed. Until that one fateful night when something epic and tragic happens, and the Ungettable Girl looks over at me, the pop music swells, and I *get* her.

Holy fuck.

Failure was not an option, however. I rubbed her back. I told her, *sure, sure.* I was prepared to dive in. To peel back those sweaty panties and wear three rubbers and do whatever it took. I said I'd love a drink. I said I'd love some music. I retold an old chestnut about us in high school, showing up for a dance humming to the gills on brandy and mystery pills she'd doled out, everything slippery and hilarious. How she'd caused a sensation by dancing with abandon with a series of boys. I left out the part with her ending up in some jerkoff's Mustang, getting felt up until she puked suddenly, an explosion of puke with no warning signs sprayed all over the jerkoff and his upholstery. I edited it. I cut the end and faded out on her dancing, dancing, dancing, everyone clapping and excited.

She raced around the place as I talked. Handed me a dirty glass of sour red wine and raced around. Put the radio on, the old-fashioned over-the-air radio. Swing music. Jazz. Sophisticated. Raced around, disappeared into the bathroom. Terror seized me. I pictured her doing a hobo bath in there, wiping herself down, spritzing on deodorant over the old deodorant, taking the five birth-control pills she'd forgotten this week all at once. Sweat popped out on my face. I told myself I could do this. Wallace men had fucked some pretty horrifying things in their desperate quest to pass on their genes; one mildly skanked out junkie doctor was nothing to write home about. My ancestors would laugh at me and mock my fancy ways.

I stood up, setting the glass of not-precisely-wine-anymore on the filthy, cluttered coffee table, and started moving toward the bathroom. If this was going to happen, I was going to take control and do it in the best possible way for me. As I walked, I tried to ignore the persistent smell of body odor, the thick feel of the air. I didn't think about what was crackling under my shoes like desiccated beetles. I was going to go in. I was going to rub her back. I was going to say, *sure, sure.*

I knocked. No answer. I pushed the door in and stood there for a moment. Lindsay was sprawled on the floor. Passed out. I saw her chest rising and falling. For a second my ancestors crowded around me, urging me to fuck her anyway, a deal was a deal was a deal.

I looked around the bathroom. It was, of course, a level of disgusting I'd never encountered before. I was going to have to check into a hotel, burn my clothes, take a shower that was about one degree less than lethal, and possibly shave my head, before I could go back to my own apartment. The only thing that could be said in Lindsay's favor was that she appeared to still be using the toilet for its assigned purpose instead of just shitting on the floor.

I decided to leave the bathroom search for last, and thank God, because she hadn't even hidden anything. It was just piled up on her gritty bed. Pills in thick clear plastic bags, piles of them. Syringes, rubber tubes, small glass bottles—everything the ambitious drug user could

want. I took a single bag and examined it, noting the cute little OC
stamped on one side of the little pills. I stuffed it into my pocket and
sifted through the syringes, all packed in neat little sealed plastic bag-
gies. I'd no idea how many fucking types of syringes there were. I sorted
through them until I found a nice long one, thin like a bit of wire. It
looked sturdy enough to be pressed down through a cork. The Bick had
become recently snobby about wine, quoting entire descriptions from
books and magazines. Fucking unbearable. Somehow appropriate.

I paused and looked around her bedroom. Dirty clothes everywhere,
junk food containers, dust. On her dresser she'd arranged an implausible
number of framed photos. Of herself. Other people, but always her.
Always her from years ago—smiling, young, with healthier hair and
fewer bruises. I saw myself in one, a smaller one, faded and blurry. Me,
skinny.

I walked over and picked it up. I had no photos. I didn't keep them.
People sometimes sent me pictures; I threw them away or deleted them.
I stared down at it. It was my lines, my shape. But it wasn't me anymore.
I put it back where it had been, right exactly into the clean spot on her
dresser, turned and went back into the dark, stuffy living room. I paused
and listened. I looked around, thinking whether I'd left anything,
sloughed anything off I was going to regret later. There was nothing.

I stepped out into the hallway. Music, somewhere, soporific and
muffled. Ten thousand dinners stretching back to the nineteenth century crowded into my nose. I shut her door behind me and thought
about calling an ambulance. Then, didn't.

XIII.

TODAY

An enormous something, just beyond the tree line. And me, sitting in the grass, small, fragile, and just beginning to feel the hurricane winds of its approach. Soon to be blown away, then to be crushed beneath it, unnoticed. But an awesome feeling of insignificance, and resigned, impatient curiosity. About to be destroyed, but in the moment just before, at least about to *know*.

My beard is itching me. I open my eyes, flick ash into the ashtray, pick up my coffee cup. Around me, Pirelli's Diner bustles, taking no notice. It is the first day of the year, and I am sobering up. Coffee and nicotine, and, eventually, when I'm feeling up to it, pancakes. It smells like coffee and cigarettes, and the noise is wonderful. I'm wearing jeans and a flannel shirt and I haven't shaved in three weeks now. I'd drank myself into a spot where I felt terrible all the time, and, satisfied, it was time to move on.

The waitress stops to fill my cup of coffee, and I beam up at her in gratitude.

"Jesus, Hank, you look fucking terrible."

I look left, and there's Kelly: white T-shirt, faded jeans, a scarf wrapped around her neck and chest. She looks fresh-scrubbed, clean, which probably translates to hung over.

I smile. "Hey, Kel, Happy New Year."

"You too. Missed you last night."

I shrug. "Denise here?"

"I am 100 percent Denise-free, I swear."

"Have a seat."

She pulls out the chair across from me and sits on one leg, leaning forward slightly in her seat. "So? No invite last night?"

I pull out my pack of cigarettes and nod, holding it out to her. After a moment she takes one delicately. "Oh, I was invited all right. I just didn't go."

She squints to inhale as I light her cigarette. "What'd you do?"

I shrug. "I don't remember."

There is a moment of quiet. Kelly just studies me. I sip coffee and enjoy this feeling, completely wrecked physically. I am congested, nauseous, weak, shaky. Ungroomed. It is wonderful. I look up, smiling, and meet her gaze.

"Jesus, Hank. You're taking this pretty hard. If it's any comfort, I think Denise is taking it just as badly. She was putting on a brave face last night, but she was bummed the whole time."

I try to stop myself, but self-control has been sanded thin of late and it slips the wire-thin bonds. I throw my head back and laugh, it comes rushing out of me like a torrent, a river of amusement.

"Oh Christ, Kel," I say, wiping my eyes, "I'm not thinking about *Denise!*"

She seems a little taken aback, straightening up in offense. I hold out my hands placatingly, palms up, trying to look nonthreatening. "No, no! I'm sorry. I don't mean to laugh at you. It's just funny, probably to me only. I haven't thought about Denise in days. Really. She left me, I left her—we both got things to cop to, with that. I got bigger fish to fry."

I'd always liked Kelly. She is a big girl but light on her feet and really attractive. It's her eyes, at once amused and steely, determined but willing to laugh. Through the smoke rising up from her cigarette, she stares at me, considering.

"If not Denise, then what?"

I shrug. "Do you believe in evil, Kelly?"

"What?"

I lean forward slightly. "Evil. Badness. I used to think it was some foreign thing, that only Nazis and terrorists were evil, you know? Now I think it's something we all carry inside of us, all the time."

She appears to think about that, but then she says "Henry, maybe you ought to go home and get some sleep."

I shake my head. "I am here for coffee, pancakes, and butter. I'm not leaving until I get them."

"And to contemplate evil, right?"

"Nope. I've *been* contemplating evil, sister. This is my re-emergence."

The waitress comes and I have my order ready: I've been dreaming of buttermilk pancakes, sausages, and toast all morning. The waitress turns expectantly to Kelly, who considers for a moment, and then orders a Denver omelette and coffee.

"I haven't scared you off?"

She makes a face. "Eh, I'm here with Flo and this guy she picked up last night, young discomforted post-sex fuckups. You could eat the friggin' tension over there. No thanks, I'll take your insane ramblings about evil any day."

She smiles, but it fades. "This have something to do with Mary?"

There are cigarette ashes on the table, mixed with coffee spill, ugly and muddy. "Always a woman, huh?"

"We're always at the root of it," she says easily. "Wanna tell me what's eating you? We all miss her."

"Yeah?"

I look up and Kelly is giving me the stink eye. "Mary was a challenge, okay? But we all loved her. She was a child. When she was sober, she was great. We all have our moments."

I swallow thickly. "I'm sorry."

Suddenly, she is touching my hand. "Hey, what's wrong? Come on, Henry. Talk to me."

I wave my hand. "I can't, Kel. Don't ask me to."

There is silence then, and I stare out the greasy windows into the parking lot, squinting in the cold sun. I had just managed to leave it behind. I'm not going to be dragged back again. I know I wouldn't survive another round of poison.

I put a smile on my face and lean forward as her coffee arrives. "Enough of that. Tell me about Kelly. What's up with Kelly?"

She laughs. "Oh, you are *such* an insincere bastard!"

"But charming."

"But charming, yes. In a dissipated, hung over kind of way."

I lean back as a plate of food is placed before me. I'm starving. "So? What's up with you?"

She wraps both hands around her coffee cup and stares into it with a serious expression. "Nothing much. Work blows; I have a totally chauvinistic boss who keeps making me type his fucking letters even though the word *assistant* doesn't appear anywhere in my title. Still single and have recently sunk into the final, humiliating level of being set up by my mother, who leans toward thin, neat men with lots of money."

She looks up at me. "Don't you want to know about Denise?"

I shake my head and swallow. "She's fine. Denise is stronger than me, than anybody I know. She'll leave me behind so fast my head will spin."

Kelly laughs. "Wow. You're so wrong. She's devastated."

"She'll get over it before I do."

I feel her eyes on me, but keep eating.

"It's complicated, isn't it?" she says at last.

"Always is."

"Yeah, but . . ." She let it drop as her own plate arrives. For a moment we sit in silence as she arranges everything the way she likes. She has a precise, bird-like way of eating that I found attractive, in an odd way.

"Who did Flo hook up with last night, then?" I ask finally. "I am so behind the times."

Kelly laughs, snorting with her mouth full. "Oh, God! It's actually quite amusing. You remember the guy she dumped? Phil?"

I think for a moment. "Dublen. The millionaire."

She nods. "Not exactly, but yeah, him. They both crawled inside a bottle of Southern Comfort and came out the other end in bed, each saying something about how they should never have broken up," she smirks. "Man, I could have written the script this morning, except he won't go away. It's like this guy has no sense of shame or embarrassment. She's being really mean to him, and he just hangs on." She sips coffee. "I'm gonna be in purgatory for months for leaving their table. He's probably asking her to marry him right now."

"The excitable type, huh?"

"Yep. Not like you. You I have to keep resisting the urge to check for a heartbeat."

Mary. Eyes open. Dust and Bick, and a drink cooling in my hand.

"You okay? I'm sorry, I say things—"

I shake my head. "I'm fine."

"You're a fucking guy. Everything's fine until you're bleeding out, right? God, I hate that about guys. So much would be avoided if you'd just talk. Just talk."

I shake my head. "That's chick bullshit. I'm fine. I say I'm fine because I'm fine. You have no idea what kind of shit I've been in. You don't know. And when I refuse to tell you, you get pissed off. This is just gossip mongering. You just want to know what's been going on. It's emotional blackmail, because we're friends."

"Not fair!" she says fiercely. "I mean it, baby. I stick by it. If you men would just speak about what's bothering you, we'd all be better off."

I consider it. I do. I think about what might happen if I open my mouth and tell her all about the Tom and Bick and Mary show. My own shabby involvement. My own shabby capitulation. I hated most the idea that I'd been intimidated. Somehow. It was hard to explain. I'd been intimidated by Tom's good opinion of me, as ridiculous as that sounds. I wanted them to like me, to respect me. As shitty as that sounds.

I am an asshole.

"Jesus," Kelly says, hand on mine. "What's wrong?"

I don't mean to say anything. "Oh, Christ. I'm an evil fucking bastard, Kel."

I am horrified.

"Forget it. I didn't mean to say anything." I swallow coffee and force a grin. "Bet you didn't expect to get fucked-up Henry here today."

Miraculously, she smiles. "I *always* expect fucked-up Henry, are you kidding?"

It feels good to laugh.

"Come on. What's wrong?"

I shake my head. "Nope, sorry. I take this to the grave." Because I'm not one of the good guys. Because I'm as bad as they are. "Stick to Flo and the millionaire. Or tell me something juicy about yourself. That would do."

"It would, huh?" She gives me a sly look. "Why, Henry, you're gossiping."

I stuff a sausage into my mouth, feeling more and more human as time went on. "Not yet. Give me something."

She picks up her coffee mug and strikes a pose, looking thoughtful. "Well, there is a story concerning the younger Harrows sister."

I nod. "Go on. Gossip about Miriam will do nicely."

"Miriam and Tom had a . . . moment."

Ice in my stomach, but I clench my teeth against it. "Get out!"

She nods smugly. "Nothing serious. More of an unexplained loss of time, you know, like when people are abducted by aliens? There was a small gathering of intoxicants at Tommy's. Mir needed a ride home after too many rounds of Beer Poker, and the ride home took two hours. Much ragging and speculation, but Tommy insists it was a flat tire on the way home and that the buzzed little darlin' Harrows was safely between her flannel sheets, alone, within twenty minutes."

"But you can neither deny or confirm, eh?"

She nods again. "Interesting how nothing changes, even when you've been away for a while, huh?"

Been away. She made it sound like it had been years, a mysterious disappearance.

"Time stands still," I say, then wink. "At least for Tom and Bick."

"But not for you. You've moved on."

I linger over my coffee and an empty plate, the wonderful feeling of obese leisure, stuffed like a toad and nowhere to go for a while.

I study Kelly, and she stares right back at me, like it wasn't weird at all. She was what, thirty-two? Three? A young girl. Great big green eyes. A lot of fine brown hair, up in a neat, practical bun. Great skin, fresh, and I always imagined she was one of those girls who smelled good no matter what, even three days without a shower, a night spent smoking cigarettes. She stares back at me without any attitude, just curiosity. She was one of those girls you suddenly and forcefully wished you'd known as a kid. I desperately wanted to be Kelly's oldest friend, loved and trusted without thought.

I say, "Want to have a smoke outside?"

She grins. "You picking me up, Henry?"

"Maybe."

"What the hell." She stands up and pulls out a bunch of crumpled bills. "I smell like a brewery, my hair could be used as a wire brush, and I'm wearing men's underwear. My prospects are not good. Can't be picky."

"Thanks."

Out in the parking lot, it's bright and cold, hard-edged with winter. I light us each a cigarette, and we sit down on the curb right outside the diner.

"Flo's right behind us, isn't she?"

I glance up at the window. Flo is staring at us, sitting across from a bland-looking fellow I dimly remember from a party somewhere. I wave. Flo lifts a hand weakly in return.

"Yep."

"I am in so much trouble."

I shrug good-naturedly. "Fuck it. Life's short."

We smoke.

"I didn't think you liked Mary very much," she says. "But ever since . . . listen, don't kill me for asking this . . . did you and Mary, ever, you know, hook up?"

Dusty eyes, accusing.

"Jesus, Kel, no. And you're right: I didn't like her much. She was a loud drunk and a pushy bitch, most of the time." I pause and fight a smile. "She was perfect for Bickerman, actually."

"It's just, you were so weird right around when she died, and you've been . . . gone ever since," she exhales fiercely. "I was just speculating."

"Jesus, you miss me?"

She turns and punches me in the shoulder. "Fuck you. I thought we were friends. Of course I miss you. You broke up with Denise, not *me*, bastard."

I'd stopped listening, a horrible thought suddenly blooming in my head. "Christ, does Denise think I slept with Miriam? Holy shit, that's why she dumped me."

"Well, shit, yeah, that's what we all think. You certainly didn't deny it."

I blink. "Fuck, Kel, I didn't think . . . I didn't, first off. And it never occurred to me . . . she never said that, she never told me that she thought that."

"Everybody thought that, Henry."

I nod. Of course they did. But then Denise had not been an angel either, but fuck it, my days of arguing with fate were over.

"We all miss you, you know," she says sweetly.

"Listen, Kel," I say, looking down, staring anywhere but at her. I didn't know how to start it, how to dress it up, make it sound better. I couldn't. So I just say it: "Bick killed Mary, Kel. He killed her." I wanted to finish with *and I think I let him get away with it* but my throat closed up and I gagged on the words.

I couldn't say what I expected. When she reached out and put her hand on my arm, squeezing gently, I was surprised.

"Hank," she says, "*everyone* thinks that. Bickerman's like a plague rat around here. No one will touch him. He keeps sniffling around with Tom anyway."

I felt like crying. I just let that hang there, staring down at the pavement until two pairs of penny loafers appeared in their own pools of shadow.

"My God, it's Henry, back from the dead."

I look up. With the sun behind them, they are just inky human shapes looming over us, one slouching with a cigarette, one taller and looking over his shoulder. I squint up at them both.

"Jesus," I said, my voice a croak, "it's Mr. and Mrs. Bickerman. I knew I came out too soon."

"And the lovely Miss Kelly. How are you darlin'?"

"Thomas," she nods her head with dignity. "And Bick."

"Henry, you amaze me," Tom went on, thrusting his hands into his pockets and rocking back on his heels. "Out of stir for mere hours, and you're already on your way to bagging one of Denise's ladies-in-waiting."

Kelly holds up a middle finger at him.

"I'm hurt!"

I lean back on my elbows. "How's married life been, Bicky?"

There is a moment of silence. Bick is still looking around the lot as if he had no idea anyone else was around. Without looking at me, he says, "Shut the fuck up, Henry."

I felt Kelly tense up next to me. I didn't look at her.

"So Pirelli's still the venue of choice for post-party grub amongst the glitterati?" Tom says musingly. "And Henry. The glitterati and Henry."

Bickerman scans just over Kelly and me, his eyes skimming away from us as if we were too slick to gain purchase on.

"Wow," he says, staring into the diner. "Some weird-looking Indian guy just barfed spectacularly, all over his friends."

"Sorry I missed that," Kelly mutters.

Bick resumes looking around as if his head had become dislocated, bobbing about in a creepy way. He seems to be bouncing to rhythms only he could detect. Tommy, on the other hand, is all smooth bullshit, as always.

"Kelly, you're looking beautiful this morning. And is that the lovely Florence in there with an unidentified and somewhat dank-looking bachelor number three?"

Kelly couldn't help but grin. "Yep. Go on in and say hello. She'd love to be rescued."

"Isn't that why you were lugged along?"

"Probably. But I'm in the middle of a conversation."

"Well, now, so am I, so I guess Flo will have to survive somehow with the gruesome . . . man, for want of a better term, she has in there."

"No one's having a conversation with you," I point out. "We're just waiting for you to move on."

Tommy laughs, the old familiar braying setting my teeth on edge. "That's okay, Hank," he says, scuffing his shoe against the asphalt. "That's all my conversations. I've learned to take what I can get and make the best of it." He strikes a pose. "I'm really a hero, in many ways."

There is a moment of quiet. I squint up at them. "Bye, Bickermans."

Tom snickers. "Yeah, okay, we're not wanted. Steak and eggs, my squire?"

Bick is looking into the diner intently again. "That table where the guy just yakked? Man, I just saw this tubby little guy do a fucking pole vault over the back of a fucking booth like he'd been training for the event his whole life. It's fucking unbelievable."

I stare up at Bickerman. He is hard to see, backlit and all negative anyway, but he looks like hell. Unshaven. Thin. Disheveled. He stands with a cockiness, though, a strutting posture. He is fucking with me, he is still fucking with me with his bullshit, ignoring me, acting like I had done something rude, something amateurish, something to lose the careful faith he'd placed in me. I lay my half-smoked cigarette on the curb carefully, the burning coal suspended over air, and stand up. I stand in front of him, and slowly Bick drags his eyes to me. They are puffy and reddened, hung over.

"There was a time," Tom says jovially, standing next to us, hands still in pockets, "when I would have handicapped this sort of confrontation easily: Bickerman, while frail and sickly on his best days, is a ferociously dirty fighter, and Henry lacks what we scientifical types call *balls*. In the Golden Age of Bickerman, I would have given Bick the advantage without thought.

"Now, however," he went on, because Tommy was never one to be cowed by the disdain of an audience, "we see two changed men. Hank has the lean and hungry look of a man down on his luck, and Bick is Elvis-bloated and somewhat senile, by all appearances."

Bick's shirt is stained. It looks like he'd thrown up on himself.

"Come on then, boyos, let's see some action. Don't just piss-stare. The crowd wants blood."

I turn to look at Tommy, glistening in the sun, his hair wild, his sunglasses cocky. He looks prosperous. Fat. In fine fettle.

He smiles at me. "I bet you could knock him over pretty easily, Hank. He's a bit on the sorry side of sober this morning, if you catch my drift." The bastard is enjoying himself immensely, which wasn't too surprising, since he enjoys just about anything that didn't bother him.

"It's amazing," Bick says, his eyes focused just over my shoulder again. "They're all just standing or sitting there, staring at the puke, like stock-still. It's like a painting."

Tom suddenly reaches out and hits Bick on the shoulder hard enough to turn him slightly. "Jesus, punchy, what the fuck are you going on about?"

His voice is suddenly mean and angry.

I turn, making a fist, rear back, and hit Tommy a sucker punch right in the nose. Something cracks, and he goes down like someone had cut his strings. I knew Tommy; I knew he was a dirty fighter, and once you had him down you had to keep him down, or he'd pop up like a fucking animal. I circle around him fast and kick him in the stomach, once, twice, making him curl up like a potato bug exposed to light.

I could hear my own ragged breathing. Then, slowly, I become aware of clapping.

"Well done," Bick is saying, slowly and carefully, as if the pronunciation was getting hard for him. I stare at him. He looks like he was made of plastic, melting slowly in the sun.

"You're a bastard, Bick," I say slowly, as clearly as I could. It was all I had in me. "And everyone knows it."

He orients on me as if seeing me for the first time. "But Hank," he says with a grin, "no one *cares*." He starts laughing again.

I look at Kelly. She wouldn't look at me.

"Sorry," I say. "We're bad guys, you know? Don't forget that. None of us are any good."

I straighten up. Bick is still clapping and laughing this creepy, slow-motion laugh. I take a deep breath, scanning the parking lot: bright, cold, sunny, filled with sharp points of light. And Tommy writhing on the ground. And Bick applauding something only he could see. And Kelly looking at her tennis shoes. I close my eyes and take another breath.

The subtle rumble of something truly huge, trembling the ground, so loud you can't hear it, so loud you're ostensibly deaf, swallowed whole and reliant on the dull vibration in your bones for a gauge of how loud it is, nearby. The trees, swaying first one way and then another, chaotic and frenzied with the approach. The wind whipping through my hair, the air clear and free of bugs because they've all fled a long time before.

And me, sitting there, about to be crushed, unnoticed, under the approaching thing's heavy tread.

XIV.

LUIS'S BIRTHDAY

"Do we all have to hide in here?" I asked, reasonably enough. "And is it me, or does this whole place smell like Luis?"

Kelly shoved me. "Shut up, Tom."

I rubbed my shoulder. "Christ, just asking a question, and it seems like a reasonable one. Hank, this whole place smells like Luis, doesn't it?"

Hank grinned, an arm loosely around Denise, who looked edible in a pair of tight jeans and a green top. "Well, first I'd have to ask you to quantify what you think Luis smells like, and then I'd be able to say."

"Shush!" Kelly hissed. "Hank, don't encourage him. Be quiet!"

We were crowded into Luis's small kitchen. Kelly and Flo had finagled Luis's keys from him somehow and arranged to get us all inside his apartment without him knowing. So there were ten people crowded into the room, which I swear smelled like Luis. Not a bad smell, I wasn't trying to be insulting, but if you blindfolded me and asked me what I was smelling I would reply, "Luis, or possibly his kitchen." We'd been in the kitchen with the lights off for ten minutes. I was beginning to wonder if Luis was ever coming back.

"Does Luis smell like wet shoes?" Bickerman Alpha boomed from the back of the room. "If so, I agree with you."

"Shut up! He'll hear you!" Kelly snapped.

I twisted around to face in the general direction of the Bickermans. It had only been two weeks, and they were already beginning to resemble each other. Bickerman Alpha was the larger of the two, his girth having swelled to unexpected levels in the recent years of indolence and beer consumption. Bickerman Beta retained her girlish figure, it was assumed, via an exclusive diet of booze and the life force of Bickerman Alpha, sucked out nightly. Alpha had been very reticent regarding the joys of married life, and Henry had surmised that the horror of her pincerlike mouth sucking the sweet life out of you every evening would leave any man contemplative and distant.

"Quiet, Bick," I commanded. "Even Luis would be able to figure out what's going on. Probably. Do they even have birthdays in Spain?"

"No, they have a national birthday once a year for everyone. They're socialists, you know," Henry said.

"Fuck!" Kelly hissed. "Will you shut up?"

I grinned. "I have to go to the bathroom."

"No! He could be back at any time, dammit!"

"I'll be careful. If he comes in before I get back, I'll hang back, I promise."

I left them in there, breathing the sweet air of freedom. I'd only been in Luis's apartment a few times before and only had a vague idea of where the bathroom was. I poked my head into a few rooms along the way; if the rest of them hadn't been there, I would have taken the opportunity to go through some of Luis's stuff—why not, good clean fun and all that. I didn't see anything interesting in a cursory search, but then that was Luis: nothing very interesting on the outside, but plenty of dark, damp things going on just underneath.

I'd known lots of people, and most *thought* they were unique, unusual: special. None of them had been, and eventually they'd all turned into the same thing: People I used to know. I'd even forgotten their names, the knowledge fading out of my brain like dust in a wind. Didn't matter—they were boring anyway. Luis, though—Luis was maybe the first truly strange person I'd ever actually known. Years after all the rest of these morons were just vague concepts teasing my syphilitic brain, the name *Luis* would still be rustling in my ears like a summer wind, mysterious and fascinating.

I headed for the bathroom and poked my head into the open doorway right across from it, where I found Luis lying on his bed with earbuds in his comically large ears, reading a book. The tinny sound of muffled music filled the air around us.

"Hello, Tom," he said calmly, as if he'd expected to find me there. He always pronounced my name with a long O, like *Tohm*.

I waited for him to ask me why I was standing in his room, but he just stared at me, waiting for me to say something. I didn't have any remarks prepared, so for a good ten seconds or so we just looked at each other.

I put a big smile on my face. "Happy birthday!"

He removed the earbuds. "What?"

"Happy birthday!"

"Thank you."

Luis seemed satisfied to stare at me. "Okay," I said. "Gotta go."

I turned and walked briskly back to the darkened kitchen, and took my place quietly. I held my mouth clenched tightly shut, resisting laughter as best I could.

"Uh, Kelly, this *is* Luis's apartment, right?" Henry wanted to know. Everyone laughed, and suddenly Luis was standing in the doorway.

"Is this a party?" he asked, smiling.

"No," I said back, still keeping my face as straight as possible, "it's a surprise."

Everyone broke into laughter, a weak cry of "surprise!" went up, and we all broke ranks to slap Luis on the back or kiss him on the cheek. I did both.

Birthday cake and bourbon. I did my usual party dance: I prowled around gauging the general attitude toward meaningless casual sex amongst the lady attendees. Since almost all of the ladies in attendance knew me too well, my chances were slim, but it never hurt to stay in practice, I thought. You never knew when you'd find some previously cool-to-you bird unexpectedly drunk, or wanton, or temporarily confused or insane.

I followed my old Boy Scout rule: Be prepared. I'd been an Eagle Scout. Somehow getting shitfaced in the woods and tying other kids to trees had helped, not hindered.

Flo had just broken up a few weeks before with some guy she was now referring to as the Schmuck, which was Flo's way. When she'd dumped that loser Dublen last year, she'd stopped using his name and started calling him the Shithead. Flo took no prisoners. I figured I had an advantage because she already disliked me and referred to me, when I wasn't in the same room, as the Ass. I wasn't sure if she knew that I knew this, but I wouldn't have been surprised if she didn't much care.

Based on my encyclopedic knowledge of television situation comedies, that made Flo an obvious choice for seduction. They always end up banging the ones they hate.

And Flo was hot, in my humble opinion. Not conventionally pretty, like Bickerman Beta. Bickerman Beta was a cupcake. Flo was better, and while Bickerman Beta looked like she didn't perform any sex acts she couldn't spell, Flo gave me the impression of being very skanky, in a good way. She was a goer, I thought. She was always dyeing her hair—I didn't even know what its actual color was—and was perhaps the tallest woman I knew. I had developed a theory over the years concerning the height of a woman's heels and her willingness to have sex. The connection, I thought, was obvious. Flo didn't need the heels, which had tantalizing possible interpretations when you applied the scientific method. Eventually, I would compose my theory into a printed report and share my breakthrough with my fellow man, but for now I had lots of testing to do.

The thing with Flo was, she was easily distracted. While that worked in your favor, it also worked against you, because as soon as you had her paying attention to your carefully manicured false charm, someone else caught her attention and hours of charming were forgotten. Thus, the thing with Flo was being in the right time and place. Preparation and effort meant nothing; it was all about timing. So I just always kept my eye out for Flo opportunities but didn't put much effort into her.

Then there was Kelly, who seemed to really, really hate me. Flo just disliked me, which was okay. Everyone—except maybe Bickerman Alpha—disliked me. I was a dislikable person. Kelly, though, really seemed to have something against me, and it was weird because back when Bickerman Alpha had met the future Bickerman Beta, Kelly had initially taken a shine to me, I thought, and disliked Henry. Now the pendulum had swung the other way. I didn't know what the pasty bastard had done or said to get into Kel's good graces, but I was curious.

The wanker would never tell me, though. Hank was a great guy and I could generally tolerate his presence, but his sense of fair play was just too much sometimes. Still, if things ever went bad, I'd want Henry in on my side. He was the type to keep promises, no matter how stupid or how callow I was.

So Kelly was a logistical nightmare. The amount of booze and insincere posturing that nailing her would require was prohibitive, and the chances of it blowing up into an international incident were high. While I held as a personal philosophy that nothing was impossible, the cost just seemed too great. So despite the fact that Kelly was, in the right light, a big dumb knockout promising big dumb sex, it just wasn't worth it.

There was always Bickerman Beta, who was, as I've said, a cupcake. Getting into those French-cut panties wouldn't be a problem. Extricating myself from them might be. As evidence, I give you Bickerman Alpha, who still had a dumb look of mourning on his face. Best to leave her be until a magical combination of memory-erasing liquor and the absence of Bickerman Alpha fell into my lap.

Which brought me to Denise, Henry's prickly peach. I had good reason to think that Denise was my best bet, back to New Year's Eve, when I think only the problematic presence of Henry kept the Tom Wallace

Magic from operating at full strength, corroding metal and melting women. Denise had been simmering at a low boil about Bickerman Beta's kid sister, and it was common knowledge among the Wallace men that the easiest woman to seduce was a woman pissed off at her mate for suspected mental infidelity, because her mind was already constantly on sex, because she was already looking to feel attractive both to make her guy jealous and to make herself feel young and perky again, and, finally, because they tended to be brooding and drunken. This had been passed down from father to son for generations, all part of the survival instinct, because we Wallaces all knew we were despicable and unlovable and so we had to breed wherever we could.

While everyone gathered around the cake the girls had created through some means, obviously, other than baking—the misshapen thing was making everyone nervous, as it did not seem to have the normal properties of "cake" and we all wondered if someone shouldn't have the hospital's phone number partially dialed while we ate it—and sang in honor of Luis's continued existence, I studied Denise. She was clearly out of Henry's league. While not quite the cupcake that Bickerman Beta was, she had an air of confident attractiveness: This was a lady who knew that men surreptitiously turned to watch her ass when she walked by. As opposed to Flo's breezy casualness and Kelly's ballsy disdain for the social niceties, or Bickerman Beta's wide-eyed cheerleaderism, Denise was the girl who always looked like she'd spent two hours picking out her clothes and an additional hour doing her hair. Nothing was ever out of place.

Of course, nothing was ever by accident with this girl, so when generous portions of cleavage were doled out for us to gawk at, it was on purpose. Ditto the skin-tight jeans, the subtle perfume. Some men would shrug and say she was gussying up for her man, but I eschewed that in favor of a more Tom-favorable scenario: Denise's underbrain had already decided it was time to test the genetic waters for better material than Henry. She didn't know it consciously yet, but Denise was looking to get laid.

As we sang in the dim kitchen, illuminated by candlelight, I looked her over. A green sweater, tight and fuzzy against the chill. Low V-cut, drawing the eye. Old faded jeans, tight and whisper-thin. A little bit of belly showing when she stood straight, and Denise had good posture. Chunky heels, not quite in Flo's league but still an important lust indicator. Her hair was up in messy curls, and she had big hoop earrings in. She smelled like leaves in fall.

"Speech!" Bickerman Alpha shouted when the singing was done. "Speech!"

Luis smiled as the room quieted. "I would like to thank you all for coming," he said in his precise way. "It makes me feel very special. I was very homesick today, remembering my birthdays at home, and this has made me very happy. You are all great, great friends to me."

It was a surprisingly touching speech from our usually bizarre Spanish friend, and everyone clapped. Denise hugged him and pecked him on the cheek. I burned with jealousy.

The cake was sliced and eyed nervously, but everyone elected to start drinking rather than take chances with the Frankencake. The plan was to have a bit of cake and a cocktail or two and then head out to one of our favored watering holes, Rue's Morgue, where it was crowded and loud and none of us would be able to hear a thing the other said, but where the drinks were affordable and strong and the juke had lots of midtempo rock-and-roll to sing along with. Not a very complicated plan, but we weren't complicated people.

I slipped an arm companionably around Luis. "Happy birthday, *amigo*."

"Thank you. I am relieved to discover you were not here to rob me."

"I was contemplating a quick ransack of your place, but you were inexplicably here."

"Inexplicably?" he asked. "I live here."

Talking with Luis was often an existential nightmare. I moved on. "How old are you now? With that George Hamilton tan, you could be anywhere between twenty and seventy."

"I am thirty-one."

"Huh. I'm thirty-three."

He nodded gravely, and drank some beer, staring at me.

I suddenly wondered if I'd turned into a roach overnight and failed to notice in the morning. It would explain plenty, including this conversation, I thought. I decided to brighten my day with alcohol. "We ought to get you a drink, Luis. It's your birthday, and you should be drunk throughout your birthday."

"Is this an American tradition?"

"I always thought it was worldwide, actually." I opened the fridge. "You have a choice of three beers, none of which appear distinctive."

"I know what is in my own refrigerator," he said seriously.

I pulled out a pair of bottles. "Gotcha, buddy, I'm right there with you. Here, take this and go in peace."

Luis wandered off with a beer, somewhat gratefully, I thought. I know I exhausted him. I exhausted most people. Just as I was getting interested, they were getting bored. I leaned against the fridge and ran my yellowed eye over the girls again, resting finally on Denise, whom I caught staring at me. She looked away hastily, flushing, and then looked back. I smiled for her benefit. She was too far away from drunk for me to safely brace her, but a little jollying along never hurt. Besides, in a room of fifteen people there's no privacy, so flirting with her would quickly become a diplomatic disaster. But a little jollying along, what the hell.

We continued to stare at each other. I went back to New Year's, the smell of her, backed against the wall, pale and eyes half-closed, and Christ, if Henry'd been somewhere else or if there'd been less light in that room, I swear I'd have had an ankle on one shoulder and a hand over her mouth, humping away happily. Since then, she'd been avoiding me. Wallace wisdom told us that women did not avoid you when they were *unattracted* to you. They avoided you when they wanted you badly. The logic went like this: If she experienced nothing but a brief pang of revulsion when you walked in the room, you generally got nothing more than a sneer in your general direction. If she was dripping about you all the time and hating herself for it, she'd stay as far away from you as possible because your mere presence would be causing her skin irritations.

Finally, I winked at her, and she looked away. I waited to see if she would look back at me, but she didn't. I glanced at Henry and jumped a little, because he was staring at *me*. I did the only thing I could do: I winked at him, too, which made him laugh. I liked Henry and wanted to fuck his girlfriend without him knowing about it, if I could. I flicked my eyes back to Denise and she was looking at me again. Denise tried to act hard-assed, but I knew better.

Reading my mind, she flushed again and looked away, saying something sweet to Bickerman Beta, for whom she had little use, to distract her. I leaned against the fridge and imagined them together.

Then a brisk, healthful walk to the restaurant, a rundown dump called Casual Spain, in honor of Luis, who seemed underwhelmed, as if he wouldn't be caught dead in a place named Casual Spain but was too polite to say so. Fifteen of us, looking like a clothing commercial—I could hear the classic rock chestnut in the background as we cavorted—walking in small, careful groups. Except me, who was alone. The scent of danger, I assumed, all the minnows making way for the big fish. Or perhaps I wasn't as popular as I'd always assumed, which was unthinkable.

Sangria all around and I am sitting, magically, between Kelly and Denise, and across from the Bickermans and Luis, with all the Others, the vague friends of the Others, on the other end of the table. I leered at Denise again, but she ignored me and Henry caught it, and the simple soul thought I was funning with him again. Someday soon I was going to sell Henry the Brooklyn fucking Bridge and that would be the end of me and Henry, wouldn't it. I had lots of Henrys behind me, though, and Henry had hung on a lot longer than I would have imagined. He leaned across Denise, one hand around his glass of wine, which you could tell you were going to have to pry out of his death grip.

"You making eyes at me?"

"Your girlfriend, actually."

"Buck a throw, big boy."

Denise smacked him on the back of his head. Must have been pretty hard, too, because Henry threw her a resentful glare. Trouble in paradise. I mentally encouraged Denise to drink more, and faster.

Across the table, Bickerman Alpha was struggling heroically with our waitress to acquire shots of tequila for everyone. Surly and pissed about having fifteen people to deal with on what was usually an easy shift, she wanted nothing to do with us and scowled as Bickerman Alpha laid out his requirements. Next to him, Bickerman Beta was already getting that puffy, defiant look that precipitated her liquored rages, lighting a small flame of hope in my breast, and next to her, Luis was looking completely buggered as to what was going on, which I suspected had to do with a difficulty in keeping up with our slurred English in crowded situations. I'd witnessed Luis's bar catatonia before. At first I thought it was due to a simpleness on his part, then I realized even I could only understand half of the inane mutterings of my friends, and it was my native tongue. Lord knew what Luis was hearing. I upgraded him to wise and left it at that.

I didn't like sitting at tables. You were trapped. I liked being able to get up and walk away. I sucked weak sangria sullenly, wishing it were over, or at least *my* birthday.

Then came out the appetizers and the parade of gifts and cards that people had smuggled to the restaurant. Luis seemed genuinely touched at this display of affection, gasping at every package thrust into his hands, and reading every card out loud in his precise diction. Henry, being a nicely warped guy when he put his mind to it, had written out "Jabberwocky" by Lewis Carroll just to confuse the poor foreign national.

"Mim-sy were the . . . the Borogoves?" Luis read, squinting at the card carefully. He looked up. "That is correct?"

"Luis," Henry said seriously, "I don't understand a thing you just said."

It was a little mean, but with everyone laughing and putting their hands on him, Luis couldn't be angry. I'd never seen him be bothered by small-minded jabs at his lack of English mastery, although it was pretty shitty for supposed friends to do to you. Getting the joke, he smiled and read the rest of the poem in a Speedy Gonzalez accent thick enough to float.

I hadn't brought anything for him. I didn't buy people gifts, I bought them drinks. As the rest of them beached themselves on the shores of sobriety in the quest for eternal life, I said, screw them. If you didn't want a cocktail, I didn't want to buy you one.

More sangria all around, and several conversations I wanted nothing to do with erupted around me like tepid pools of lukewarm water. I kept a pitcher of wine for myself and began drinking recklessly out of boredom while Henry and Bickerman Alpha chatted about football scores and Luis gave Denise a fascinating travelogue about his native Spain. I let my eyes wander, looking for an attractive waitress to molest, but found nothing. I settled back in my chair and balanced my glass on my belly, which was growing large and powerful as I stumbled into my dotage. I resigned myself to boredom and set about falling asleep with my eyes open, uninterested.

So when a stockinged foot wormed its way into my crotch, I stiffened to an instant mode of readiness and assessed the situation.

I looked at Luis, who appeared to be engrossed in his conversation with Denise, or perhaps in his inspection of her chest. Anyway, his body was at the wrong angle.

I glanced up at Bickerman Alpha, but he was literally jumping up and down in his chair, hooting like an ape, much to the amusement of Henry.

I looked at Bickerman Beta, and the tart winked at me salaciously. I leaned forward, grinning, back in the game.

Dinner arrived and huge plates of food obscured Bickerman Beta from me, so I amused myself with a quick reminisce concerning my often-troubled relationship with the Beta, while multitasking a complex fantasy involving Denise, a bottle of vodka, and some unconsciousness—her leg kept rubbing up against mine and she smelled maddeningly good, and I hadn't given up on her yet—just put her aside for a more obvious possibility.

There had been, in the beginning, a paradise of bachelor men. Henry, saintly and soiled; Bickerman, the asshole who was useful in that he did and said things you wanted to do and say, and thus took the heat for doing and saying them; and then me, adroitly using both of them to maneuver myself within putting distance of all the great pieces of ass in this world. When chicks were hard to come by, as they occasionally were during droughts, they also served as good conversation. All trios are politically explosive, of course, and you end up pairing up into various combinations for sanity. Bick and I went in for worse shit than Henry, so I left him behind sometimes—he understood that and let it be. Henry and I amused each other better, and we often didn't mind each other's company. Bick didn't like anyone, at least not back then, unless he was loaded, so he never hung out with Henry alone if he could help it.

The three of us drank and smoked and picked up chicks. It was great.

Then, of course, came the fateful evening we descended on the old college town and the old college bars, ostensibly on a tour of teary memory, but really to see if a crop of freshmen chicks might be about, untrained in liquor consumption and ready to be impressed with our paycheck-inflated wallets. We didn't find any freshmen chicks, but we did find the Cupcake, the future Bickerman Beta, along with Kelly and a few other maidens-in-waiting. Bick and Henry were content to sit and drink in the back, while I made an assault on Mary, an obvious former sorority chick. Vague memories told me that back in the day I'd been catnip to sororities. I figured ten years, give or take, couldn't have faded me that much. I put my all into it—every Elvis crotch thrust, every mysterious I-know-more-than-I'm-letting-on laugh, every subtle hint that great and serious pain hid barely beneath my cheerful exterior. At first I suspected success because the Cupcake touched me a lot and laughed a lot and let me buy her several drinks. Now I know that Mary lets *anyone* buy her drinks.

The Cupcake remained unmoved. Eventually I retreated, confused, to the comfort of men, where they slapped my back and fed me booze, and soon we had such a cloud of manly testosterone about us, the women, despite apparently (and inexplicably) disliking me, had drifted over to be nearer the scent and soon joined us. The Cupcake, in a sign of things to come, was quickly bombed and had taken an obvious shine to Bickerman. From that moment on, paradise was lost, and we were forever changed.

It had been three years, and in essence, my relationship with Mary hadn't changed much. She disliked me, intensely, and yet seemed to enjoy flirting with me. Then again, it had once been suggested to me that I thought *everyone* was flirting with me due to an innate arrogance. I'd never believed it, of course. And it might have been the sangria, but she was eyeing me appreciatively enough over her glass, and I began to plot. Why not? Bickerman Alpha spent a lot of his extra energy going after Beta's sister. I figured he had no moral high ground to nail me on. And it took two to tango. And I was bored.

My choices of conversation were terrifyingly banal. On my right, Luis, Henry, and Denise were discussing something that sounded suspiciously like politics, with serious, pie-eyed sincerity, and the Bickermans were reliving wedding moments with Kelly, who seemed to be calculating how much energy would be required to slit her wrists with butter knives as opposed to the energy required to continue listening. She nodded in all the right places, but then, she'd been there, she'd seen it all—how hard was it to predict where the pauses were?

I started eyeing the butter knives myself and took comfort in the familiar action of getting stinking drunk. After a few moments, though, I caught Bickerman Beta looking bored and caught her eye. I winked.

"Not much of a birthday, is it?"

She smiled. "Poor Luis!"

Luis heard his name and glanced at us. "I am quite wealthy, actually," he said in his precise way.

I waved at the waitress. "I say Luis should start drinking more seriously."

There were groans from everyone, but they were just playing innocent, I knew. Kelly alone could drink me under the table. Everyone had been sitting there wondering when in hell the drinking was going to start in earnest, and, as usual, a Wallace Man had to step up and take the sneers of society just to get the debauchery started.

"Slow down, Tommy, we're not even at the bar yet," Denise said.

"I want eight shots of tequila," I ordered the waitress. The Others could fucking fend for themselves, I thought, especially since none of the booze already ordered had made its way to my end of the table.

Groans again.

"Thomas," Luis murmured, "I must pace myself. It would not be right for me to not survive the evening."

"Why not?"

"I am the man of honor, tonight."

"He's upgrading himself." I winked at Beta, who seemed perked up at the prospect of hard drinking, as I suspected she would be. I kept waiting for her foot to reappear at my crotch.

"All right, then, a toast," Henry suggested, as usual finding some graceful way for me to get my way. Thank God for Henry! He was my enabler, my social lubricant. Denise, of course, gave him a look that said, *You ass, stop encouraging him, he's a deviant.* Denise knew the truth, but thankfully no one could hear her at such high frequencies, like dog levels of sound.

"A toast to what?" Bickerman Alpha said, salivating visibly at the prospect of real booze. "Just to Luis?"

"Boring," I decided. "Although certainly," I added, catching disapproval all around, "it should involve Luis in some fundamental way."

Fucking proles. So literal.

"How about we toast Luis's continuing toleration of our middlebrow company?" Henry suggested.

"Yes," Luis said, nodding seriously.

The shot glasses arrived. The Others glanced our way jealously, but fuck them. They had money, buy their own shots. I made sure everyone had one and held mine up. Looking at Bickerman Beta, an opportunity for some fun bloomed in my mind—private fun that no one else would enjoy, of course—and I looked at Beta and held her bubblegummed gaze.

"Luis's loyalty to his undeserving friends, then," I said, holding up my glass. "To faithfulness!"

Beta's look soured a little, and it was worth it. Everyone shouted, "Faithfulness!" incoherently, unsure what I meant but used to that and amused by my bizarreness. Beta could have shriveled my balls with one look, I thought. She looked like she'd swallowed a pit.

I was cheered and thought I might be able to survive the evening without killing someone. I also figured I'd still be able to jolly Beta around in the end, so it would be a perfect evening.

Walking to the bar, Henry fell in beside me. "Quit it," he said.

I affected innocence, but that never seems to translate correctly for me. It's like I'm speaking Esperanto; I think I'm saying "innocent," but what seems to bubble up is "smug disdain for normal rules." It's a flaw I keep working on. "What do you mean?"

Henry snorted. "You're plotting. I can smell the Glee."

Henry had an annoying habit of talking in capital letters, which he'd gotten from me. "The glee? Hank, I think you've been playing *Dungeons and Dragons* on the sly again."

"What are you up to?" he said, trying to sound bored. Truth was, Henry was fascinated by me.

"Just sowing the seeds of love as usual, my friend. Getting Luis crocked as he should be on his birthday, throwing some manly vibes to all the ladies, keeping everyone entertained, informed, and fortifying everyone for the trials ahead."

"What trials?"

"What I'm up to, obviously. It'll be quite a test of our friendships."

"Quit that, then."

"Can't do it, chum. Like to help, but it's impossible. Tell you what: I'll buy you a drink and give you the high sign when it comes down so you can get out of the way."

Henry shook his head, I could see from the corner of my eye. "C'mon, Tom, let Luis have his night."

"Lighten up, Henry. Luis won't even know what's going on, y'know?"

I glanced around. Denise had fallen in with Kelly, the two of them a mildly glammed up pair. Women always glammed up to go out drinking. The men were a crapshoot: Henry had a sports jacket on, me and Bick jeans and old T-shirts, Luis in a European mix of nice shirt and crappy jeans—but the chicks all hotted up as much as they could. Women glammed up when they went out in case better men came along, even if they were married or spoken for.

I was always amused by the way women pretended that once they mated they reprogrammed all their libidinous ways to focus on the man of their choice. The fucking whores spent their lives looking for a husband and then spent the rest of their lives wondering if they'd shortchanged themselves. And they kept their tails in the air just in case something better wandered by, no doubt.

I didn't mind. It kept the sights interesting. And my own ambitions realistic.

Bickerman Beta was hanging onto her hubby for dear life, listing heavily under so much booze so early in the evening. Flo and Luis appeared to be talking soberly, much to my irritation. And we were three blocks from the bar of choice.

"You're staring at my breasts."

I lifted my eyes to Kelly's face. "No, I'm not."

She laughed, her hearty-big-girl laugh, jiggling the globes in question. "Sure you were. Tommy, it's okay. If I gave a shit about you, I'd be offended. But you're such an ass, I'm not even going to pretend to be surprised."

"Let me buy you a drink, then, to make up for my shocking lack of manners."

"You're just trying to get me drunk."

I nodded. Why not? Only idiots pretended that the people around them didn't see right through them when they obviously did. Lies were powerful weapons, but when they're perceived, it's best to go with the truth.

"Standard operating procedure," I said.

"You're staring at them again."

I looked back up at her face. "They're nice."

"Thanks. But stop, okay?"

"To being the smartest men in the room, Tommy Boy."

I clinked my shot glass with Bick's and drank, gagged, and sucked beer to survive. He was half-right, anyway. Knocking back beer, I let my eyes find Bickerman Beta, who was talking, glassy-eyed, to Henry, one hand on his arm. What was it with the Harrows chicks and Henry? Her kid sister practically wet her pants every time he entered the room, and now Mary was giving him the old covert-touching thing.

Oh well, a little professional competition was healthy, I guessed, and Henry wasn't really competition, with Denise lurking on the edges like a dark cloud.

"How's married life?"

"I'm living with a monster," he belched, looking red-faced. "But I'll tell you this much: Since we got hitched, she's been a fucking groupie in bed."

"Really?" I lifted a professional eyebrow.

He nodded. "The biggest turn-on in her life, apparently, was putting that white dress on. She's been a wet dream since then," he grinned. "I'm a little dehydrated as we speak, actually."

"I wonder if that white-dress thing works without the wedding ceremony and all that. Maybe I should just give them away as gifts."

He shrugged. Bick had no imagination. "Sure. All I know is, it works like a charm with Mare." He winked. "I'm thinking of loaning it to Miriam."

Bick's sexual fantasies about the Harrows sisters bored me because I'd had them myself many times. We were both unimaginative when it came to that: tan legs, anklets, cheerleader uniforms, and the accidental interruption of one sister by another leading to a mutual shagging. If you overlaid Bick's fantasy on top of mine, the only difference would be the color of the cheerleader uniforms.

I was familiar and unconcerned with Bick's reptilian designs on Mary's younger sister. I just hoped there would be videos.

She smelled like peppermint, I thought, and bar, mint, and nicotine, and tasted like lip gloss and cinnamon liqueur. I pushed her up against the wall next to the pay phone by the women's room and she grunted, firm and yielding at the same time. I pushed myself into her, as people flowed around us to the tunes of Jimmy Buffet.

"What is it with you and the Harrows sisters, chum?"

Henry pretended he didn't know what I was talking about, making faces at me and sipping his martini, very grownup.

"Come on," I spat, "there must be some sort of genetic link between you and the Harrows women. Harrows Minor has to change her underwear every time you walk in a room, and now Harrows Major is giving you the googly eye, too. What gives?"

"Tom, man, I don't know what you mean. Mir has a little crush on me, maybe, but she's got a little crush on a lot of guys."

"I don't know. I was there with you last week. Sounded like little Mir is mighty sweet on you."

He shrugged, uncomfortable about the whole episode. "Doesn't mean anything. Besides, I'm not shopping for Harrows love, like some of us."

I winced. "I'm not being subtle enough, eh?"

Henry gave me his twinkly eye, always amusing. "Why not dry hump her while we stand around and clap? It'd be more 'subtle.'"

Henry did have a way with words, sometimes.

Henry seemed vaguely embarrassed, as if he knew what I was thinking and didn't like it. Henry had an active imagination, though, and probably did know what I was thinking, the prude.

"Does Denise have a similarly approving attitude toward your flirtation with a Harrows-a-trois?" I asked, giving him a boyish grin.

He scowled back at me. "She's getting drunk on purpose and throwing attitude, of course," he said darkly. "I didn't *do* anything."

I shrugged. "That's like saying you were just *vollowing erders, ja*? You know by now that excuse doesn't cut much with the ladies, right? My advice? Quit speaking to either of the Frau Harrowses. Save you lots of headache on the home front, and you might even escape with your sanity."

He sipped his martini and winced. "Great advice, Tommy. Of course you're just trying to get the talent off the field so you can plow Frau Mrs. Harrows yourself, right?"

By God the kid was entertaining. "I am simply an audience to that one's little passion play. If the play becomes interactive, who am I to complain?"

"Bick won't mind?"

I glanced over at Bickerman Alpha, who had a possessive arm around his wife and a roving eye out for everyone else in panties. I turned back to Henry with my serious look. "Hank, man," I said carefully, "Bick and I have been through stranger things, with stranger people. I think he'd slap me on the back." I considered again. "Maybe hit me, once or twice. But nothing serious."

She reached down between us and grabbed hold, hard, her breath whistling through her nostrils. Peppermint and skin lotion, now, up close and personal, and the soft hairs on her upper lip tickling me. I could feel her bra, underwire and satin, and the hard pebble of nipple between my fingers. She mashed her lips against mine, grunting. Dry humping by the bathroom, and I thought to myself, *Why would I ever want to be anyone but me?*

"You're shtaring at them again."

Kelly was looped. I'd been plying the crowd with shots of hard liquor, which had sent Denise outside to get some air as a pre-emptive strike against heaving up the delicate contents of her stomach, and had everyone else surrounding the jukebox, singing "American Pie" with an off-key gusto I was horrified at and refused to take part in. Kelly was slowly sliding off her barstool, hitching herself back up a bit, and then sliding again. The whole process made her assets bounce encouragingly and I was frankly enjoying them. It secretly pleased her.

"You don't mind, huh?"

She shook her head and leaned toward me, smelling of cinnamon liqueur, of which she was inexplicably fond. "I know you guys look at the Girls," she confided. "It's okay. I'm proud of 'em."

I smiled. "That's good, Kel, because they're really spectacular. You should show them off more."

She smirked. Not drunk enough yet, I figured. "You're scummy, Tom, you know that?"

I blinked. *Definitely* not drunk enough. "What's that now?"

"You're a scumbag. I've known it since I met you. That's okay, though, it's actually charming when you're kept at arm's length."

"As long as it's charming, then." *Fucking whore thinks I'm a scumbag*—I settled down. I was perverse, I knew this. It was often misunderstood.

"So why are you talking to me?" I asked with a grin.

She shrugged. "You're an amusing scumbag, Tom. And I'm drunk. And you appreciate the Girls, so you can't be all bad."

I winked. "I do appreciate the Girls."

She laughed. "Tommy, the thing about you is, you're harmless, you know? The more you talk about being weird and nasty, the less I believe you actually are. I mean, I think you go home at night, pop open a beer, and watch bad horror movies on TV. You talk a good game is all."

"Lady," I grinned, picturing my fist knocking that knowing smile off her face. "You're talking out your ass."

Some sixth sense I guess, Spidey Sense, maybe, the doors of perception—I pulled away and turned. She's so drunk she doesn't see him at first, she's just putting herself back together like nothing happened, red-cheeked and disheveled. Unhappy women are so fucking gorgeous.

He was giving me his hard-on stare, but I just spread my hands. It wasn't me he should be pissed at, after all. I was a free agent.

I turned to follow his thousand-yard stare. She was still fixing her hair, like she was fooling anyone.

I thought I had a miserable piece of bar to myself, hunched over with a cigarette and bourbon, looking myself over in the mirror and feeling pretty sexy, but then there was a heavy hand squeezing my shoulder and the smell of a light dusting of aftershave. Luis grunted into a stool next to me, resplendent in skin-tight jeans and a bright red shirt. He leaned his head on his hand and smiled at me for far too long without saying anything.

"My friend," he said seriously, a sure sign, usually, that Luis was very drunk. "We are getting older."

I distrusted the simplicity of this statement and raised a skeptical eyebrow.

"But," he said at last, and I relaxed, "how do we know this? I do not feel different than years ago. I do not feel older. I do not think I look older. Do you?"

I considered my suspect back, the sweaty, panting mess I arrived at work as every day, and then shook my head. "Not a bit."

He smiled. "See? We are told things, how things are. We are informed that we are born and will die. But we do not know. Perhaps we will not die. Perhaps we are being lied to. For what purpose? Perhaps so we will think death is inevitable, and thus will be willing to die, for causes."

I blinked. This was my usual response when Luis got philosophical on me. "Maybe you and I are the only real people, and everyone else here are actors, humoring us."

He nodded. "I have considered this, yes."

I turned away to hide a smile and found Denise's breasts, tightly contained within her green sweater. I lingered a bit and then looked up. "Hello, Neesie. Luis and I are getting paranoid. Want to join us?"

She oriented on me, red-eyed and upset. "Sure."

I summoned my concerned face, stiff from disuse, but there were those breasts, wasted on Henry all this time. "Hey—what's wrong?"

She got the bartender's attention and ordered a vodka tonic. "Ask your shithead friend Henry, huh?"

"I'd rather ask you." She drank her cocktail breathlessly. I hadn't seen pretty girls drink like that since college, the memories of which warmed me on cold nights. "Here, I'll get you another."

I wondered if Luis had left but didn't want to risk looking.

I resupplied her glass, paid the bartender, and tried to look soft and gloopy like her boyfriend. "C'mon, tell me about it."

She took another gulp, but left some drink in the glass, much to my dismay. "No, Tom, I don't think so." She was apple-cheeked. I glanced around for Henry. He was being lectured by Kelly and Flo and looked miserable.

"C'mon. I promise I won't take Hank's side. I swear. I might have some insight, you know? I'll buy you another drink."

She drained her tonic recklessly and slammed the glass down. "Done!"

"That's my girl. Unburden yourself."

I could have, of course, dictated the entire conversation to someone, almost verbatim:

Her: *I hate Henry. He's always looking at other girls and acts like I'm an impediment to him.*

Me: *Uh-huh. I'm guessing the bra is pink, right? I'm right, aren't I?*
Her: *Pig.*

After a while, though, as she sank into the stool and began playing with her hair and flirting with me out of drunken, ancient habit more than anything else, we started to make some progress. I played the friendly sympathetic man to the hilt, she told me some juicy stories demonstrating Henry's shitheaddom that I would get to use against him someday. Nothing really strange, of course, Henry being Henry, just the usual bad boyfriend behavior, and it would have been boring if it weren't for Denise's red cheeks, heaving jubblies, and that hair-twirling finger that indicated she was enjoying, perhaps for the first time in recorded history, a conversation with me.

Things were going so well that when she suddenly puffed out her cheeks and swayed a little, I stood up immediately to steady her.

"Ugh," she gasped, clinging to me in a wonderful way. "I think I need to yak."

"Nonsense!" I said cheerfully. "Come on; I'll walk you to the bathroom."

I slipped an arm around her waist, and she hung off of me. "Why are you being so nice to me?" she asked miserably as I nodded to everyone as we passed.

I considered my reply. I gave her a companionable squeeze. "I'm a sucker for hot chicks, let's say."

She wasn't so bombed she couldn't giggle a little at that. We made it through the crowd, past the cigarette machine, and I held the women's room door open for her. No line, miraculously.

I lit a cigarette and paced while she did whatever it was she had to do, vomit, belch, eat magic beans, whatever chicks did to themselves. The girl's room was in a little grotto off the main bar, hidden until you turned the corner to approach it. Not much traffic—no line at the women's room in this dick-heavy bar filled with Luis's odiously male friends. It was strange that even though Luis was such an adorably confused Latin man, the girls never seemed to flock to him as I would have expected. The whole thing made me think that maybe my carefully considered understanding of the universe was faulty. Maybe it was the poofy shirts he favored.

I looked around. Around the fake-wood corner there was noise, smoke, and people. Where I was, it was me, a cigarette machine, and a bathroom door.

Denise emerged looking unsteady but smiling. "Yay for me, I seem to have settled."

"Must have been the whiff of urine and ammonia. Always perks me up."

She laughed. I flicked my cigarette to the ground, winked at myself internally, pushed her up against the wall, and kissed her, hard and fast, hands roaming.

I'm perverse, and I know it, and that's fine.

I spread my hands and smiled and walked toward him. I hadn't been hit in the face since seventh grade, but figured I must be as close to it as I could be without already picking my teeth up off the floor. I thought better of the smile and wiped it off my face as I drew even with him. I paused, watching him from the corner of my eye, ready for sudden moves.

"Henry, sorry man."

I didn't know what else was expected of me. I waited a moment, to be hit, for him to say something, and then I just kept going and I let my smile creep back onto my face. I found Luis still sitting at the bar where I'd left him, only moments ago. I slapped him on the back and tossed a bill onto the bar.

"Luis, let me buy you a drink because after a brief period of confusion, life is good again."

"Bick and Mary have left," he said seriously, pronouncing their names as *Beek and Maree*. "There was some fighting."

"Isn't there always?" I said brightly. "It wouldn't be right in the world if there weren't mean words bandied between those two. Don't worry, grasshopper, someday one of them will kill the other and that will be that."

He looked at me very steadily, and for a moment I thought I'd offended him somehow. "What," he said ponderously, "is this grasshopper you speak of?"

I laughed and kept laughing. That's fine.

XV.

TOMORROW

I shifted Bickerman's shoes to one side and sat down on the bed. The whole damn place smelled like shit. I wanted a cigarette and took out my pack, then thought better of it and retrieved Bick's pack from his jacket pocket. Sitting back down, I sat there for a while with the cigarette in my mouth, but didn't light it. For a while I just sat there and contemplated Casa Bickerman, which was decorated in a style known, apparently, as Abandon All Hope.

It was a split-level condo, two bedrooms on the second floor, living room, kitchen, bonus room on the ground. Not bad bones, really, and before the ruinous involvement of the Bickermans it probably had potential as an unexceptional living space. Post-Bickermans, however, it was a structure fire in waiting, nothing but a pile of insurance money. It was hideous. I'd been in it many times, and was now winding down six hours straight in it, sweating and absorbing its carcinogenic atmosphere. I could identify the Bickerman place by smell at five hundred yards: Old Spice, bourbon, the rusty wire-scent of tension.

I worried that the smell was going to stick with me, and that years from now someone I'd never met before would do that air-sniffing thing, bobbing his nose up and down, and say "Does anyone else smell failure and ennui?" and everyone will look at me. And there would be a lengthy uncomfortable silence.

The thing about the Bickerman condo is that it was decorated and furnished and terraformed by two completely classless people. You hear about people like the Bickermans, idiots with a bit of scratch and the docile, empty certainty that the world was created just for them. It was a sticky, dusty jumble of patterns and styles, a mix of Bick's old college furniture spruced up by desperate, amateurish refinishing and a host of abortions in furniture form, all of which arrived with a fucking Allen wrench in order to be assembled by the uncoordinated Bick. They all ended up looking like sculpture: The title of the works, invariably, would be *Almost*. They all had at least one unfinished screw, or unsanded edge, or a slightly unbalanced nature. None of the pieces were tied together in any kind of coherent way—it was a fucking garage sale.

And the colors! The colors made me angry.

How people who liked to pretend to be smart could choose such an ugly palette was beyond me. The whole house was chaos. I'd often daydreamed of burning it down, although that wouldn't have helped much. The Bickermans would have just bought another concrete box and remade their abortion, except this time with more money to start off with.

I stood up, and with an unlit cigarette between my lips I took my handkerchief from my pocket and looked around the bedroom. This was the master. Everything had a master bedroom these days, like we were all nobility heading out every day to whip the slaves and dock the renters, instead of mouth-breathers earning paychecks. Master bedroom my ass. It was fifteen by fifteen, with two grimy windows on one end and two closets, shallow and disorganized. Beige walls and a carpet an inexact shade of pink that might also believably be called any number of bizarre and meaningless names. *Melon. Picot. Rouge. Salmon. Scallop.* Whatever you called it, it resembled puke. This had somehow escaped the Bickermans' attention, and when they'd taken possession of the house they'd failed to immediately rip the carpet out, with their bloodied fingers if necessary. Maybe they were colorblind. This was possible, as the last time I'd asked either one a personal question was about seventeen years in the past.

The bed was nothing special. King-size, of course, because royalty such as the Bickermans could not be expected to sleep on anything less, and their unerring eyes had brought them the ugliest fucking bed ever created, a triumph of Bickermanism. I dragged my handkerchief along the square, brown pressed-wood headboard, taking off a thick pelt of dust. Small, basic nightstands on either side with matching digital clocks. I wiped down the one on Bick's side, sending more plumes of dust everywhere, the fucking pigs. I imagined they'd made a blood oath to not clean the fucking house until they were rich enough to afford a maid.

I scanned the crappy dresser opposite the bed with the big mirror over it, but kept my eyes moving. I walked over to the cave-like bathroom, an avocado dream. Avocado being a main color in hell's palette, and probably matching most of Bickerman's stools over the years, since he'd been staying one thin step ahead of scurvy due entirely to the lime wedges you got with certain beers. I stepped inside, breathing through my mouth. Fluorescent lighting, the absolute genius choice of green accent rugs—because only Bickermans would choose green to accent avo-fucking-cado—and sweet lord, there it is, the fuzzy, carpet-like toilet cozy. While the Bickermans had not descended the final step into insanity signaled by a carpeted bathroom, they had festooned their crapper with something that could only be called a crapper carpet. Filled, I was sure, with minute butt hairs woven into the loose pile, it glowed radioactively. I sometimes dreamed of Bickerman's crapper carpet being stuffed into my mouth, suffocating me. I didn't know why, and didn't want to know.

I wiped the faucet and handles carefully, and then gave the sink a quick run around the edges. I hadn't touched the toilet. Whenever I had to piss when over at Bickerman's I did it in the sink. There was no way I would ever touch that toilet. I winked at myself in the mirror and headed back into the bedroom.

I hadn't been in the spare bedroom, which was just a collection of random extra furniture, including Bick's old semen- and puke-stained SRO mattress from his younger days. I didn't think anyone had been in the spare since they'd bought the place. If you opened the door the ghosts of winters past would hiss out of it, howling and swirling, smelling vaguely of stale disco moves and flat beer.

I walked down the stairs, rubbing my handkerchief down the banister as I went, and pictured Mary on her way down, hitting, every, damn, step on the way—from my vantage point at the top of the stairs I'd seen her perfectly, her amusingly amazed expression and the way her head whipped around waaayyyy too far right there at the end, with her limp husband standing there, mouth open and dick in his hand. Mary: a more graceless woman had never been created. She'd been born to look good in short skirts and spend half her life rubbing out bruises after she tripped—definitely the sort of girl who needed to have someone take hold of her ankles and move her around, show her what to do. A fucking waste of ass, that was.

The kitchen was a fucking mess. On the surface it was okay—a quick glance and you might make the potentially deadly decision to prepare a meal there. A closer look, though, and you could tell that the people who'd lived here were subhuman. The white tile was not so much grouted as caked with grease and ancient dirt, and the countertops—cheap laminate that was never designed to withstand the onslaught of two people who were like two gorillas in a cage when it came to hygiene and housecleaning—had been faded from their natural beige to a sort-of yellow, which was probably just light refracted through a layer of grease. The appliances had been here when they bought the place. They worked, and that's all the Bickermans cared about.

Two empty beer bottles stood on the counter next to the sink. I couldn't recall which was mine, so I took both and slid them into my pants pockets, damp and awkward. I rubbed my handkerchief on the fridge handle and the countertops, imagining the layer of Bickerman grease being rubbed off, knowing that I'd have to burn the handkerchief now. That was okay—I was pretty much going to burn everything: bridges, my apartment, my clothes, and myself. I was going to rise from those ashes, and be someone new and exciting. Exciting to *me*, at least. No one else mattered.

The living room, I was pretty sure, hadn't been cleaned or touched in any way since the night she had died. I was pretty sure he hadn't done more than move through it quickly, probably with his eyes closed, in that time. He'd considered the room haunted.

I moved through it quickly, entering the bonus room. The bonus room was in reality a den or an office—it didn't have a closet, so they couldn't call it a bedroom—but some douchebag of a realtor had sold Bickerman on the term *bonus room*, so a bonus room it was. When you were talking about a huge McMansion with four bedrooms and a media room, a bonus room might make sense as a fucking room they built but can't think of a single fucking thing to do with. But when your condominium has exactly five goddamn rooms, that fifth room is not a bonus in any way.

As a personal fuck-you to me, I'd always assumed, they'd even left the fucking room more or less unfurnished. Of course, this made some sense: The Bickermans didn't read, so there was no use for a library. They didn't do anything requiring an office. They didn't have any appreciation for art or entertainment beyond consuming it with groups of other people, so a media room would have been wasted. They probably couldn't think of anything to do with the room except use it as storage.

Personally, if your whole life fit into four fucking rooms, you weren't living.

I stood amongst the cardboard boxes and random furniture—a card table piled high with coats, two old wooden chairs that may have grown, organically, inside the room itself, and a weird, nonfunctional floor lamp that had a strange little table affixed to its middle. The room was dark and dusty, and filled with shoes, endless rows of her shoes, gleaming like something alive, seeming to pulse with respiration. I hadn't been in the room, but I liked to glance into it every time I was over at the Bickerman place. It made me feel happy to think of people living in such self-imposed squalor.

In the living room, I wiped things down randomly. After a few minutes I put the handkerchief in my back pocket. I'd have to burn everything. I looked around the terrible earth tones of the living room, the scratchy cheap upholstery and the dark rug that looked like it held every known pathogen in a desiccated, preserved state, just waiting for some idiot to spill water on it, bring Pandora's Box back to life, wipe out the planet. Millions of years later some alien scientists will trace the end of life on the planet back to this room, and reconstruct a spilled glass of tap water.

I went back upstairs.

It was nice and quiet. Finally quiet—I appreciated silence, and this place was usually always filled to bursting with noise. TVs on everywhere—they had five fucking rooms and four televisions, including ones in the bathroom and kitchen. All while the owners themselves were ranting and raging and puking and cursing each other. Coming over here had always been torture, but Tommy had brought The Silence and it had settled in on everything like baffles, making even this hellhole a tiny bit contemplative. Padding on the dry, corrupt carpet I went back into the bedroom and began going through the drawers: Her silky underthings, his permanently crusted underthings, an envelope containing five hundred dollars in small bills which I left in place, assuming it was crawling with small, microscopic parasites.

I glanced up. All around the big mirror were photographs. I stared, fascinated. I'd never noticed before, and would never have assumed that either one of them had a sentimental streak, but there we were, all of us in happier times. Me, looking stiff and awkward, like I'd just wandered into the photo and paused when someone said *cheese*. The droopy one, casual and sincere, my fucking God *painful* to look at. His old girlfriend with the cans, looking especially tasty in a pair of tight jeans and a T-shirt, fuzzy pixels hinting at all of her curves, curves sadly lost to me forever now. She would age and sag and wither, all without ever knowing the joys of Tommy, which were considerable, no matter what my other flaws might be. The black kid, an epic waste of my time. Then him and wife, looking fresh and clean in what must have been an old, old photo. They looked like a fucking beer commercial, good, clean white folks having a good time with their good, clean white friends and token racial characters.

I reached out and plucked the photo from the edge of the mirror, bringing it in close. For a second I wanted to ask him where in fuck this was taken, because I thought I ought to remember Droopy's girlfriend dressed like that.

I started taking the other pictures down and stuffing them into my pockets, folding and wrinkling them. That was okay. They'd burn too. Here was one of just Droopy, whatshisname, and me, looking young and fresh, just out of the oven. Maybe some yellowing on the edges— *maybe*—at least for me and whatshisname. Droopy still hadn't ingested as many chemicals and screwed as many pooches as we had. Based on my last interaction with Droopy, I doubt he ever would. He'd remain perpetually youthful as I aged into my dotage, getting scaly and leathery. Here was one of the wife and the girlfriend pretending to be lifelong friends, and I experienced a stab of regret that those two hadn't been college roommates who'd experimented with each other's bodies one fateful evening—they were born for the role, awkward slippery sex they'd never speak of again. Or at least in my mind it was awkward and slippery, with a lot of inexplicable bubbles and smoke and heavy metal music. In reality maybe they'd be giggly and joyous, or angry and grunting.

Here was a picture of the Spaniard, alone, eyes too wide and smile too broad, looking insane. I left that one where it was.

Here was a photo from the wedding, a candid, taken with one of the disposable cameras left on the tables. We're all in a group, looking happy and dapper, a little blur of motion as we're talking and moving about. You can't really tell who's who—we're just well-dressed people, one of whom has a wedding gown on. Might have been a photo that came with a frame, for all you could tell, but I stuck it in my pocket anyway.

There were photos around the mirror that didn't have anyone I recognized in them, which was disturbing. Where did whatshisname and wife ever meet anyone else? As far as I could remember I'd spent the last seven hundred years with him, every minute of it. Woke up and had him lying next to me, spooning. Showered with him leering at me from his perch on the toilet, like a vulture. Ate lunch with him stealing fries from my plate, had drinks, went to work, puking, fucking, living, breathing him. Where in the world did they meet other people? I stared at the pictures for a few minutes, silence buzzing in my ears, wondering about these strange other people. They looked like fun, wholesome types, his other family. Fucking polygamist.

Turned and stared at his shoes. Scuffed. Something brown and crusty on the tip of one. A bit of brown sock, the slightest glimpse of hairy, pale ankle. He'd always been one of those secret slobs, who looked pretty shiny in the distance but turned out covered in cruft when he got close.

Moving through the condo back toward the stairs and freedom, I kept my eyes on the floor, the faintly dirty rug scrolling under me as I moved. I felt good. Light, empty. Hungry—I was fucking starving. I was heading for Frankie and Johnnies and ordering a porterhouse, a Scotch, and one of their chopped salads, and I was going to have a bowl of ice cream and a cup of coffee to wash it all down, all while I listened to the tinkling piano and the dull, brown chatter of morons around me, overweight people with too much money. Then I was going to waddle to the bar and drink until I passed out, preferably with my pants down around my ankles and excretions pouring out of me as my shivering, weakened body strove to survive. Then I'd be a blank slate, dehydrated, scraped clean, ready to start taking on someone else's water, someplace else, far away.

At the bottom of the stairs I paused and looked around. Then I headed for the door, moving quickly. I would never see the place again. It was just the home of someone I used to know. Outside, I stood on the steps, smoking cigarettes and enjoying the ozone smell of a storm coming.